HORSE

Leon Berger

grey gecko press

Published by Grey Gecko Press, Katy, Texas.

www. greygeckopress. com

Printed in the United States of America

Design by Grey Gecko Press

Library of Congress Cataloging-in-Publication Data

Berger, Leon
Horse / Leon Berger
Library of Congress Control Number: 2012943561

ISBN 978-1-9388210-1-1

10 9 8 7 6 5 4 3 2 1

First Edition

One

y dusk, the tourist trade had slowed, but the horse was still standing in harness, his head deep in the feed bucket. All around him, a gang of pigeons flapped and argued for the grain that spilled on the asphalt, a noisy whirlwind of activity which the big animal made an effort to tolerate—a generous gesture on his part because he didn't seem to tolerate much else.

He was of mixed breed, a sturdy draft with American-Belgian genes and a handsome coloration, which aficionados would describe as red sorrel with flaxen mane and tail. At well over seventeen hands in height, he was easily capable of drawing the carriage to which he was attached, a four-wheeled barouche known here on the heritage streets of Montréal as a *calèche*. The only problem was that he was beginning to show his age.

His limbs were stiffening and his coat had become slightly chafed from the constant wear of the straps. Even his character was changing. He'd always been grumpy by nature, but these days, his disposition was considerably more irritable and his temper frayed frequently. Often that's the sign of some affliction, but after exhaustive tests, the vet had said there was nothing physically wrong with him. He'd simply turned into a senior citizen.

Behind him on the driver's bench sat his owner, Jacqueline. She was the one who'd given him the name of Groucho. It was just a joke at first, a play on the word "grouchy" which she had blurted out once while in a drunken stupor, but somehow it stuck, mostly because it got an appreciative laugh from the paying passengers.

Jacqueline was a tough-looking woman, with a short crop of bleached hair, a broad physique, and a ruddy complexion from long exposure to a climate of wide extremes. Even today in the stiff fall breeze, she wore her regular outfit: an oversized cotton sports shirt in faded yellow, tucked into sagging cargo shorts.

On her feet were well-worn trainers and on her hands, a pair of leather half-gloves with studs on the knuckles. In typical fashion, she sat with her elbows on her knees, smoking her way through an evil black cheroot as she waited for her final customers of the day.

Five, ten, fifteen minutes passed. On each side of the narrow street, the lights of the gray stone offices cast their soft yellow glow. In the meantime, Groucho continued to eat, his massive head bobbing in search of the bottom-most grain. Vehicles passed by, some a little too close, and he displayed his annoyance with a single stomp of his hoof.

For a moment, it scared off some of the birds, but they were soon back. Finally, Jacqueline looked at her watch and tossed the finished butt to the ground. Her decision had been made. There would be no more business this evening. Time to pick up the feed bucket and take the ritual drive back to the stable.

Groucho was not only sullen, he could also be downright lazy on occasion, but he knew the route home well enough and as soon as traffic allowed, he broke into an eager trot. As always, he made his way along the harbor-front area where the bars and the bistros were already starting to come alive, then branched off, taking the familiar shortcut past the historic fire station on Place d' Youville.

It was never clear at which point along the journey Jacqueline's years of self-abuse finally caught up with her, but the fatal coronary must have occurred somewhere between the post-industrial streets of Griffintown and the final destination of Pointe St. Charles, a working class district on the south side of the Lachine Canal. As she took her last breath, her head slumped and her body gave out, but she remained propped up by the *calèche* bench, the lines loosely draped in her gloved hands.

The horse must have sensed something but kept going anyway, maintaining his pace, unerring in his sense of direction. When he at last reached the familiar side street, he slowed as usual, turned into the fenced compound and came to a standstill, breathing hard and glistening with a fine layer of sweat as he waited for the wooden doors to be opened. Like the district that surrounded it, the building was long past its best days. It took some time before the owner arrived, a raw-boned man in his late seventies, fit for his age, with a full thatch of iron-gray hair.

According to his birth certificate, he was Patrick Doyle O' Shaughnessy, but he'd always called himself Doyle and that's how he had come to be known. It was here in the five-horse stable that he both lived and worked, a permanent local fixture, a human landmark in a community that most people chose to leave as soon as they could afford to do so.

"What's going on?" he asked, as he got busy hauling the first door back. "Why don't you ring the bell? What d' you think it's there for?" The device to which he was referring was a rudimentary invention of his own, which a driver could sound by tugging on a knotted cord while still seated on the bench.

Without even looking up, Doyle turned his attention to the second door while continuing the kind of grievance only uttered within the familiarity of a long friendship. "Can't see through the wall, y'know. How'm I supposed to know you're here if you don't...?" That's when he realized the horse was snorting impatiently, still waiting to be unhitched.

"Jacqueline?" he called out. He came around to see what the problem might be and found the woman still on her bench, immobile, her jaw open and her eyes glassy. That's when the shock set in.

"Oh, merciful God."

Two

"My mother was . . . Well, we all know what my mother was."

So began the eulogy of the damned by Jacqueline's thirty-something daughter, Louise, speaking in her broad, street-style French.

In looks, Louise was more like her biological father, even though she'd never actually met him, with a pale complexion, lean body, and light-brown hair, which she wore collar-length. But when it came to attitude, she was more like her mother, far more than she would ever admit. She considered herself one of life's victims and didn't mind who knew it.

In this case, the stark effect of her words, especially those that went unspoken, caused discomfort within the traditional church setting, and there was some murmuring and shuffling. As for Doyle O' Shaughnessy, sitting in the third row, all he did was look down and give a slight shake of his head. Unlike some, he didn't mind the truth, no matter how blunt. It was the fact that Louise would say such a thing here, at a time like this.

Doyle knew all about the estranged situation between mother and daughter, and he'd also known Jacqueline well enough to understand why the relationship was like that. Sometimes she just liked to scream at the world for no apparent reason. It didn't occur often, not on the street in front of the tourists, for example, and never at the horse that she adored.

But when it did take place, it was a fearsome sight to behold, a terrifying release of the anger and the rage that seemed to come from out of nowhere and, at those times, it took all his perseverance just to calm her down. He wouldn't have bothered for anyone else, but Jacqueline was special in his life. Jacqueline helped him, taking the time to explain his mail and his bills, which always seemed so complicated, and giving him little tips about how to cope with this or that. And now? Now he wasn't sure what he was going to do without her.

He glanced over at the priest, an intensely serious young man, who was clearly embarrassed, both by Louise's opening line and by the silence which ensued. He was new to the diocese and very anxious to do well by everyone.

As it happened, there weren't too many at the modest church of St-Matthieu in Verdun, less than a couple dozen scattered among the worn wooden pews. It was a dark, old building in a generally poor state of repair. Today, in addition to the normal atmosphere of dust and mold, there was something else in the air; the gentle fragrance of manure that Doyle and some others in the congregation had inadvertently tracked in.

"I never loved my mother," Louise was saying, once again exhibiting a little too much honesty for the occasion. "But I guess she did give birth to me, ten hours in labor, or so she always told me. And she did somehow raise me on her own, which was no picnic, I can tell you, for her or for me. But later, when I grew older...Well, yeah, that was something else.

"By that time, she was into the booze and the pills with all her dope-head friends, the ones she picked up off the street, some of them even younger than me." She paused to glance at the young priest. "Yeah, I can see you looking at me, Father, but what can I say? I know you don't want to hear all this in your nice church, but the truth is the truth and there's no point hiding it. God sees everything, right? Isn't that what you believe?" For a moment, she gazed around at the congregation.

"Anyways," she continued, "one night when I was sixteen, I said something, you know, for the first time and she went crazy, half-killed me, then threw me out. I mean, physically threw me out, just like that. No money, no nothing. Screamed at me, called me an ungrateful little . . . Well, never mind what she called me. So after that,

I never went back, not once. Only place I ever saw her was at the bar and even then, we didn't talk much because mostly I tried to avoid her.

"Did she have any good qualities, like I'm supposed to mention here? That's a good question. I guess she did in her own way, not that I can think of too many. No, wait . . . she loved the horse, I'll say that for her. Yeah, that good-for-nothing big lump of horse flesh, with a temper just like hers. If you ask me, they were a good match, the two of them. And now she's gone, all I can say is I hope they have a horse up there, wherever she is, because if they don't, God help the angels. Thank you."

Doyle's language skills weren't good enough to catch every word of Louise's French but he knew enough from his childhood days playing shinny in the streets of the Pointe to catch the gist—and what she was saying was more than he wanted to hear. So when it was his turn to get up and offer a few words, he decided he'd better keep it short. *Just a few essentials*, he thought, just enough that people could maybe know Jacqueline's other side too.

Once he was on his feet, however, he found he could hardly speak at all. He just stared out at the expectant faces and thought of Jacqueline, and he could say little, even in English. In the end, he simply said, "She was my friend."

After that, his voice was trapped somewhere in the back of his throat and he couldn't seem to continue. After an empty few seconds, he wiped a moist eye with his finger and went back to his seat, very self-conscious about his failure. Nobody said anything though, and, following another hymn, the ordeal was over for everyone. Even the young priest seemed to be thankful as he stood at the doorway handing out his goodbyes like gifts to the few who'd attended.

"Sorry about the smell," Doyle said as he filed past. But then he couldn't resist adding, "The Lord Jesus was born in a stable, y'know." It was something his father often said. Then he nodded briefly to himself as if in confirmation and went on his way, leaving the priest to stare after him.

Outside, the morning drizzle had graduated to a squall, dampening the asphalt of Verdun and blowing around newspaper sheets from a tipped trash can. On the opposite corner, people waiting for a bus huddled under the narrow shelter, while, a block away, a couple of men pasting up a new billboard decided the worsening weather was a good excuse to go for an early lunch, leaving half a cosmetic model's face to do battle with half a family sedan.

The rain also caused Jacqueline's daughter, Louise, to quicken her pace in order to catch up to the old man, but it wasn't easy. She was wearing her best heels this morning, not because of her mother, but because the service was being held at a church and it was necessary to be respectful.

Of course, the blasphemous words she'd uttered had totally negated the effect of dressing up nicely but, in her mind, that couldn't be helped. She reached him just as he was climbing into his battered van. It had once been white in color but that was in the distant past, before the scrapes and the dents and the rust had taken their toll.

"Excuse me, Mr. Doyle," she said in English.

He looked down at her from the driver's seat, the door still open. "No, just Doyle."

She didn't really care what his name was. "Can I talk to you? I mean, I think there are some things we need to talk about."

Doyle gazed at her for a moment, then out at the rain. "Wanna lift?"

She wasn't sure. On the one hand, the van stank worse than the old man. On the other, the line was lengthening at the bus stop and there was no bus in sight. "Sure," she replied, then walked around the other side, opened up the rattling door, and hauled herself in, heels and all. For a moment, she had to hold her breath until she could get used to the obnoxious odor.

"That's the manure does that," he explained. "This is how I make my deliveries, like this, in the van. I get some of them plastic bags and put the manure in and I sell it to the gardening place, except they want me to deliver it too, so I do. But me, I don't notice the smell any more.

"Well, sixty years now, working with the horses. Sixty years, man and boy. Took over from my father. He had the stable before me. But his name was Bailey, y'know? Patrick Bailey O' Shaughnessy. Mine's Patrick Doyle O' Shaughnessy. Neither of us liked being called Paddy, so we both used our middle names. Funny, that, don't you think?"

Louise glanced at him. She was wondering how it was he could talk so much now, yet back in the church, he couldn't seem to say a word. "Yeah, it's funny," she said without smiling.

He placed the key carefully in the ignition and turned it once, then twice more before the engine coughed into life, causing the entire vehicle to tremble. Then he jabbed his left foot on the worn rubber of the clutch and crashed the lever forward into first gear. "Where d'you want to go?"

"Just over on Wellington. I need to get back to work."

"You work on Wellington? That's where your mother . . ."

"That's where she drank, I know. Same bar where I work."

If Doyle was surprised, he didn't show it. "I used to go drinking with your mother, once upon a time. Not there, though, down in LaSalle, before I swore off the stuff. Had to give it up, no choice. What happened was a doctor at the General told me it was going to kill me and that sobered me up all right. He told your mother the same thing but she didn't listen."

"So I guess he was right."

"I guess he was, at that."

They headed up Bannantyne, past the pizzerias and the car lots and the duplex apartments, until they reached Galt, where Doyle guided the van into the right-side lane, squeezing in behind an over-sized beer truck. His wipers didn't work too well and the windshield was smeared.

While the light held red, Doyle said, "What d'you wanna do with the horse?"

She looked at him, but he was intent on observing the traffic around him, frequently adjusting the chipped rear view mirror, which kept slipping out of place.

"That's what I wanted to talk to you about," she replied. This wasn't easy for her, coping with the burden of her mother's death on top of everything else going on in her life. While the old man next to her had become more talkative, she felt like she'd gone in the reverse direction, from her outspoken reaction in the church to a kind of withdrawn isolation now. She couldn't explain it, even to herself. She could see that he was waiting for her to say something else but all she managed was, "It's green." She was referring to the traffic light.

They turned the corner and drove on toward Rue Wellington, yet another of the strange French-British anachronisms that had somehow been preserved in this schizophrenic town. It took all Doyle's strength and concentration to crunch his way down the gears, so she waited again, until she couldn't hold it back any longer.

"I don't want it," she said suddenly.

"What's that?"

By this time, it was obvious he'd forgotten what they were talking about. "I don't want it," she repeated. "My mother's horse. I don't want it."

It was the last thing he expected to hear and his expression proved it. "What d'you mean, you don't want it?"

"It was hers."

"I know. I know it was hers."

"So I don't want it. I don't want anything if it was hers."

He didn't respond immediately. He needed time for it to sink in. "But that's Groucho," he said. "He's a good horse."

"No, he's not. He's a big, lazy, stubborn horse."

"No, you're wrong there."

"Sure he is. Even my mother said it."

He acknowledged her point. "Maybe, but she didn't mean it. She used to get into moods, your mother, but she loved that horse."

"Yeah . . . Yeah, I know."

"She bought him young, did you know that? What I mean to say is, they were together a long time. He's got his ways, Groucho, but she never got upset, never cursed him, not in all those years."

"He had the accident that time."

"That wasn't his fault and she knew it," said Doyle.

It happened when a taxi driver ran a stop sign while talking on a cell phone. If it hadn't been for Groucho reacting as he did, the *calèche* might have become a pile of firewood with her mother under it. As it was, the taxi swerved into a fire hydrant, and the *calèche* wound up with two wheels on the sidewalk.

But since both drivers were issued tickets by the police, the result was technically a tie. According to the law as defined by two young officers in a cruiser, both the taxi driver and the *calèche* driver were equally to blame. This was another event that had set Jacqueline off on one of her rants, this particular episode lasting almost a week.

"It doesn't matter," said Louise, dismissing all further discussion of the topic. "I just don't want it."

"Him."

"Excuse me?"

"He's a male horse, what they call a stallion. That means he's a '*him*' not an '*it*'."

Louise was becoming exasperated with the whole conversation. "Listen. Just listen, okay? I don't want him, or it, or anything to do with that animal. Is that clear enough? Pull in over there."

"Where?"

"There, right there," she said, pointing to an illegal space at the end of a row of parking meters.

Doyle did as he was told, wrestled the shift into neutral, and heaved on the hand brake. "What do you want me to do with him?"

"What do I care?"

"You want me to sell him?"

"Who's going to buy an old animal like that? Maybe the glue factory. That what you mean?"

Doyle was genuinely shocked at the suggestion. "No," he said.

"Cool it, I was just joking, okay? What I mean is, do what you want with him. Keep him, sell him, whatever you like. He's yours."

"Mine?"

"Are you deaf or something?"

"No."

"So what's the problem? Why can't you understand? I'll say it slowly. I'm . . . giving . . . him . . . to . . . you."

Doyle ignored the patronizing attitude. "What am I going to do with him?"

"I don't know. You got a stable, don't you?"

"Sure, but . . ."

"But what?"

"They pay rent, the drivers. They pay me rent. If Groucho's there, who pays me the rent?"

"Not me, that's for damn sure."

"I'll have to feed him, look after him. There's supplies, there's labor cost. And the vet once a year. And the farrier. And the space he's taking up . . . And he needs exercise. Who's going to give him exercise?"

Louise tugged on the metal door handle, which almost came off in her hand. "You got your problems, I got mine," she said as she clambered out, nearly twisting an ankle on her thin heel. She was happy to be out of there, out of that disgusting smell. "Thanks for the ride. Enjoy the horse."

And that was it, as far as she was concerned. She'd said what she wanted to say, so she simply slammed the door shut and cut through a break in the oncoming traffic, trying not to get soaked from the tire spray.

Across the street was Chez le Diable, where she worked. The Devil's Place. It billed itself as a *bar-resto*, an attempt at trendy Parisian French, but it had been a long time since the establishment was trendy. The sign above the entrance hadn't changed for as long as anyone could recall and nor had the decor inside. It was owned and operated by a middle-aged, ex-disco king called Clément Delisle who had thought it might be a suitable retirement haven but he'd miscalculated. It hardly broke even, leaving him very much soured on the whole deal.

Louise was already later than the time she said she'd be back, so she knew she'd have some fast explaining to do. The excuse of a funeral wouldn't cut much ice with Clément. Then, tonight, she had that unfinished argument with her husband waiting for her, about the living room furniture she'd bought with her own money. It was on discount, but he had no job and he had gone crazy, a real tantrum, throwing stuff around and breaking plates, reminding Louise all too easily of her deceased mother.

Her mother, her husband, her idiot boss . . . More than once, she'd wondered if maybe a hundred aspirins ground up and dissolved in a good draft beer wouldn't just solve everything.

Three

oyle drove back to the stable and parked the van in the back, next to the assorted vehicles of the other drivers, old-model pick-ups mostly, plus a few of their horse trailers.

He'd thought about holding a wake in the old Irish tradition but he couldn't figure out how to overcome all the problems. First, the drivers didn't have time, they were already missing a morning for the funeral. Then there was the cost of the booze. He could have just bought a couple of twelve-packs from the store down the street, but beer didn't seem right somehow. Ideally, he'd have had a few bottles of whiskey, good Irish whiskey, none of that cheap rotgut rye, but he was saving up for that replacement furnace he needed.

Then again, Jacqueline never drank whiskey, she drank rum, but it wasn't right to drink rum at a wake. It didn't fit. Plus, of course, the other thing was that he, himself, didn't drink anymore, so he felt it would have been stupid holding a soda while they drank themselves silly. What kind of a wake would that have been? In the end, he'd just placed the idea on a shelf in his mind and let it stay there, unused.

So now, here he was back at the stable, just as the drivers were heading out on to the street: Jean-Claude, Frank, Marie-Josée, and, always the last, Bertrand. They were an okay bunch in general, but not what anyone might call overly friendly, and conversations were mostly to do with the daily practicalities.

Within half an hour, they'd all gone off for an afternoon's work and Doyle was alone, all except for his teen helper, Mowbray, who never said much at all—and, of course, Groucho, who was dozing in his stall.

Mowbray was something of a charity case that Doyle took on as a favor to his immigrant neighbors, Elliott from Jamaica and Katrien from Holland, who'd met twenty years ago as punk drifters lining up for social insurance. The result of their union was Mowbray, whose skin tone and accent were as mixed as his parentage.

Like many kids his age, he began to get into some trouble at school, gangs and so forth, so his parents pulled him out as soon as he was old enough and gave him over to Doyle. An "apprentice-ship", they'd called it. Mowbray tried hard enough, at least when he could be bothered, cleaning out the stalls, shoveling the dung into the sacks, and loading up the van. He liked the animals, too, but his heart and mind weren't really into it.

At first, Doyle had entertained the idea of training him to take over the stable one day, a lifetime career offered as a gift, but the kid seemed sort of aimless and it was hard even to envisage the possibil-ity. Horses needed dedication. Without that, it wasn't even worth the effort. On this day, Doyle didn't have the heart for a detailed inspec-tion, so after a quick check, he climbed the bare wooden staircase to the untidy space he called his office to get on with his paperwork. It was a job he loathed.

The small, ill-fitting window gave on to the thick branches of a maple and sometimes he liked to listen to the cardinals that roost-ed there, however there were none home at the present time, so he didn't even have that as an excuse to procrastinate. He sat back and gave a sigh.

In front of him were the monthly accounts to finish, bills to pay, backlog papers to sort and file, all of it very necessary but it was the kind of daily grind he found hard. The main difficulty was that he was a slow reader, had been since school. He was bad enough with English, mouthing each word as he came to it, but French was an agony.

With so many letters in each word that shouldn't be pronounced, the printed page seemed to bear no relation to the sounds he heard and understood from people in the neighborhood. And as for writ-ing, that was a whole other issue in either language. At best, he could form words out of ungainly block capitals, and most of those were misspelled.

It was in this area that Jacqueline had helped him the most, making sense of statements from the bank, invoices from the utilities, information from various city departments, and performing a host of other duties. She'd even taught him how a calculator could help with adding and subtracting and working out sales tax percentages.

After some practice, he was not too bad at that, so he didn't feel completely useless, and she'd promised him that one day she'd borrow a computer from her daughter so he could try it, but that wouldn't happen now. All of that was past and he had to come to terms with it. He picked up an envelope that had just arrived from the telephone company, no doubt another bill, but he couldn't bring himself to tear it open and just tossed it back down. Around him, everything was familiar. A chaotic heap of papers littered the scratched wooden table. On the wall was the small clock with the broken glass that still kept good time and the obsolete calendar that he still kept for its pictures of prize-winning draft horses.

Finally, pride of place in the center, was the framed photograph of him and his Dad, taken here in the stable on his twentieth birthday, with their own horses in the background. The horses in the photograph made him think about his other problem, the one that had just been dumped on him. He got up and ambled back downstairs to the stalls. Mowbray was nowhere around, probably in the back, either eating his sandwich or smoking a joint, so it was just the two of them, Doyle and Groucho, face-to-face.

The horse lifted his great head over the stall gate and nuzzled up to the man, sniffing him and touching him gently with his nose. Doyle was still wearing the gray jacket he'd taken out for church and there was nothing in the pockets but wool fluff, so he went out to the tiny ground floor kitchen where he made his coffee. A minute later he came back with a handful of sugar cubes and offered them to the horse, who accepted the treats greedily, snatching them from Doyle's upturned palm.

"There you go, how about that? Am I good to you, or what?" Doyle asked softly.

He always spoke to the horses in that tone, and while their first loyalty was naturally to their owners with whom they spent each and every day, it was obvious they recognized and welcomed the attentions of the old man, like a family's favorite uncle who always had a present tucked away.

"So what are we gonna do with you, eh? She doesn't seem to want you, that Louise, but I can't keep you, so what's gonna happen? Maybe somebody will buy you, another driver maybe, let you stay here and take you out on the streets. Whaddya think? That'd be good, wouldn't it?"

But even as he said it, he knew that wasn't likely to happen. Few people had any inclination to be *calèche* drivers anymore and those already in the trade would never want a horse that age, never mind one that was known to be moody. Who in the world would ever put up with him like Jacqueline did for all those years? "Do you miss her?" he asked the horse. "Sure, me too. But the fact is she's not coming back and that's the truth of it. She's gone and that's that."

Firm words but that's when he let go all the discipline, all the stalwart courage he'd tried to maintain since the day she'd died, the day Groucho had brought her back slumped over on the bench. In front of him, the animal blinked his soft black eyes and nosed his way forward for more sugar, but Doyle could hardly see anything because his own eyes were full, emotions that were unwanted but unstoppable.

Now there'd be nobody to chat with in the mornings, nobody to read the paper, nobody to touch his chin and tell him he needed a shave, and nobody to pacify, either, when she felt the urge to destroy everything around her. She'd destroyed herself instead, and now there was a gaping hole in Doyle's life—a hole as big as the horse.

The same afternoon, Doyle did something unusual. The van was stacked with bags of manure, all ready for delivery, but he didn't drive to the gardening center down in Lasalle. Instead, he drove over to Wellington, to the place where he'd dropped off Louise, at the bar called Chez le Diable.

For as long as he'd had the gardening supply contract, he'd only missed a trip once before when the van broke down but, this time, he was doing it of his own volition. He told himself it was to try to talk Louise into taking the horse but, underneath, he knew the real reason was to be where he could still feel Jacqueline's presence, somewhere apart from the stable with all its memories. He just needed somewhere to sit and dwell, somewhere without office work or manure sacks or anything else to interrupt his reverie.

When he got there, he hesitated on the sidewalk for a moment and almost walked away. It had been years since he was in a bar, any bar, and he wasn't sure if he trusted himself. It would be all too easy in his current frame of mind to get back into the drinking life he thought he'd quit for good. Yet he wanted to go in, he desperately wanted to go in. For him, it was almost like a pilgrimage, so he put his hand on the door and tentatively pushed it open.

The place was dark and almost empty, a neutral period between the lunchtime customers who wanted a quick bistro menu, and the five-to-seven crowd who dropped by for nachos and salsa after work, before going off to a show or a sports event or just somewhere nicer for dinner. There'd been an attempt at one time to continue business into the evening with the owner's discotheque expertise. He set up a booth with turntables and a disc jockey and strobe lights, but that idea soon faded, as did the karaoke concept that followed.

Nothing seemed to work anymore because the location was just too far from anything. There was little passing trade and the people who'd once made it a destination had moved on to their mid-level careers and their ranch-style homes in suburbia. All that were left now were a few hard drinkers, some of them the people Jacqueline had hung out with, and Doyle was afraid of them, afraid of the temptation—which was why he'd decided to come here in the afternoon instead of waiting until evening. He wanted to feel her presence, not meet her friends.

Due to its state of misfortune, the establishment looked dated and tacky and smelled vaguely of stale beer. Down the length of one side was the bar with its beer pumps and racks of glasses. Overhead were track lights with blue and orange bulbs, while behind the bar were mirrored shelves with their rows of bottles, including Jacqueline's preference, Caribbean dark rum, which she drank with ice and cola when she was chipper, or threw back neat when she was irate.

On the other side of the central space, opposite the bar, was a line of booths, the seats covered with red vinyl to go with the devilish theme, and in between were circular wooden tables with paper place mats, courtesy of a local brewery. It was at one of these tables, near the window, that Doyle sat himself down, apprehensive about venturing any further.

The owner, Clément Delisle, was a man in his late fifties, with thin strands of black-dyed hair combed over a large, bumpy bald patch. He stood behind the bar, his usual spot, wearing a white shirt with sleeves rolled back to the forearms and black pants with a silver belt-clasp that held up a sizeable paunch.

He nodded at Doyle, then looked over his shoulder in order to call someone from the back room. A couple of minutes later, a woman appeared, who turned out to be Jacqueline's daughter, Louise, still working her shift.

"Oh, it's you," she said flatly to Doyle. "I thought you gave up drinking."

"I did."

"Doesn't look like it."

"That's not why I'm here."

"So?"

Doyle looked at her, unsure what she was asking him.

"So?" she repeated. "What do you want?"

"I want to talk to you."

"No, I mean what do you want to drink? You can't just sit here with nothing. It's against the law."

Doyle knew better. "No, it's not."

"Well, you just can't, that's all."

"If I order something, will you talk to me?"

She looked around again. "I don't know if . . ." For a moment, she glanced around at her boss behind the bar.

"Please."

"I'll have to ask. All right, listen, let me bring you something, all right? How about a club soda? You want a club soda?"

"If you like."

"But it's not free, you have to pay."

"Then you'll sit down?"

"Yeah, if I can. If he'll let me. Just for a couple of minutes."

Doyle attempted a smile, which she didn't return, before she turned on the black heels she was still wearing and went back over to the bar. Doyle looked over at the only two other customers in the place, a pair of young men in one of the booths at the back. They wore jackets and open shirts.

It looked like an intense conversation and since Doyle preferred to mind his own business, his glance didn't last long. All he wanted, anyway, was to absorb the atmosphere, and he wondered briefly if Jacqueline had ever sat at this very table. She wouldn't have been alone like he was, of course. She'd have probably been with her friends laughing, arguing, flirting, perhaps snorting up in the back. As Louise said in the eulogy, her mother always liked them younger.

As for Doyle, he wasn't naive in these matters, he knew perfectly well what went on in Jacqueline's life, but he was a little out of touch as to how far things had progressed in recent years: for example, how much was allowed in places like this. He was gazing out at the passing traffic, thinking about Jacqueline, when Louise returned to place a tumbler of fizzy, colorless liquid on a coaster in front of him and give him a small bowl of peanuts. The glass also contained ice cubes up to the halfway mark and there was a slice of lime perched on the rim.

"You can sit down?" he asked her.

She pulled out the chair opposite and reluctantly lowered herself into it. "Not for long," she replied. "You want to talk about my mother? Is that why you're here?"

Doyle didn't really want the soda but he removed the lime and took a sip, just to show willing. "I'm not sure why I'm here," he said.

The honesty threw her a little. "I'm not taking the horse, I told you."

"I was hoping you would."

"Well, I won't, get it through your head." It was a sharp response and she looked immediately guilty. "Sorry," she said quietly. "Didn't mean to snap. I just wanted to make it clear."

"He needs exercise. If he doesn't get exercise, he'll get sick. Azoturia, they call it, when horses don't get enough exercise."

"Yeah? So take him out."

"On the *calèche*? That's yours."

She shrugged. "Nah, you can have that too, what do I care?"

Doyle looked at her, a little stunned by her generous offer. "Are you sure?"

"Yeah, what the hell."

He considered the notion, trying to imagine himself up there on the bench with the lines in his hand. He'd passed the official institute test to operate a *calèche* when he was younger, but it had been years since he'd practiced.

In the meantime, the industry had become strictly regulated by City Hall, with rules for everything from strict demarcation zones, to suitable weather conditions for working horses, to a law requiring a special poop-pouch which acted like a kind of diaper for the animal. Plus there was another problem as far as Doyle was concerned. "I don't have insurance," he said. "You need insurance to drive a *calèche*."

Louise was dismissive. She couldn't be bothered with such details. "So, ride him then."

"He's not trained to be ridden."

"All right, walk him. Lead him by the nose. You can do that, can't you?"

"It's not the same."

She looked at him, as exasperated as she'd been earlier. Then she shook herself out of it and held up her fingers, inspecting the tangerine-colored nail varnish she'd applied specially for the funeral that morning. "I think I'm a bit overdressed," she said.

Doyle's reply was a brief smile, not because it was amusing but because it was the first chatty thing she'd said to him.

"Were you ever married?" she asked from out of nowhere.

"Me? No."

"Why not? Handsome feller like you ..."

Now Doyle's smile was one of shyness. "I had a girlfriend once. What I mean is, someone who lived with me, y'know?"

"That's romantic. What happened to her?"

"Nothing. Nothing happened. She just left, that's all."

"Just like that?"

"I don't think she liked the horses. Not like I did."

"Yeah ... bummer. I guess you never thought of giving "em up, eh?"

"No."

"No, right, 'course not."

"Why did she come here?" asked Doyle.

The sudden change of subject threw Louise for a second. "Who? My mother?"

Doyle nodded. "Was it to be with you?"

He was here at the bar today in order to be close to Jacqueline, so it made sense to him that Jacqueline might have come here just to be close to her only child.

Louise didn't answer right away. She sat back and thought about it for a while.

"Yeah, maybe." Then she shook her head, as if dismissing the notion. "I don't know."

"Did you talk to her when she came in?"

"Yeah, sometimes. Well, not much really. Nothing heavy. It was like a rule we had. Nothing heavy."

"She didn't get ..."

"What? Upset? Annoyed? Violent? Is that what you're trying to say? Why don't you say it? You won't hurt her feelings, you know." She saw Doyle turn his head toward the window and she was about to apologize but then changed her mind.

Doyle looked back at her. "You're not sorry, are you? Not sorry she's dead."

"Nothing I can do about it."

"But you're not sorry."

"Look, I'm not sorry, I'm not pleased, I'm not nothing, all right? Okay? Okay?"

"Okay."

"You think I'm like her, don't you? I can see it on your face."

"No, I don't."

"You don't?"

"You're not a bit like her."

Louise wasn't sure how to respond to that, so she changed the subject completely. Her face brightened and she said, "You know, I had an idea for you. Wanna hear it?"

"Sure."

"When I came back to the bar, it just came into my head, just like that. I don't know why, it just did." She stopped, unable to explain how it happened.

"What's your idea?"

"Yeah, well, I was thinking. That old truck of yours ..."

"My van?"

"Yeah. Pretty broken down, right? Needs a lot of repairs and stuff."

"I dunno how long it's going to last."

"Right, right. So what I was thinking is, why don't you just sell it?"

"Sell it? No, I can't afford a new one."

"No, see, you don't have to. You got the horse."

"The horse?"

"Why don't you use him for your deliveries? He's big, he's strong, right? He could do it, couldn't he? That way he'd get some exercise and earn his keep and everything."

She seemed genuinely enthused by the idea but it was something that Doyle was going to have to digest.

"So what do you think?" she was urging. "Solves all your problems, all in one go. Sell the van, use the horse. It's perfect. Hey, like one horsepower. Get it? One horse ... One horsepower."

Doyle smiled at that. "That's a good one," he said but there was something else, something hesitant in his voice.

"You don't sound too sure," she said.

"It'd take me longer ... I mean, to make my deliveries."

"Better than nothing, if your van breaks down."

Doyle was forced to recognize the point. "That's true," he said. It had happened before, on Charlevoix near the canal bridge, with traffic lined up behind him. He'd had to wait for the tow truck which, added to the repairs, had cost him a small fortune.

"I mean, why wait for the thing to break down? You'll get nothing for it then. Not even for scrap. Nobody wants old vans like that. What you should do is sell it now, while you can still make some money."

"How do I carry the manure?"

"Use the *calèche*."

He laughed out loud at that. To him the concept was outrageous. "I can't carry manure in a *calèche.*"

"Why not? Take out the seats, get some insurance, how much can it cost?"

"I just can't, that's all."

"Okay, so sell it. Use the money to buy a trailer."

"A trailer?"

"Sure, like they used to have in the old days." She saw him looking blank, so she said, "You know, like you see in the old pictures, before they had vans."

"You mean a wagon?"

"A trailer, a wagon . . . Whatever they're called." She waited, but he still didn't seem to get it and she sat back in frustration. "Like I said, it was just an idea, take it or leave it."

Doyle said nothing but, in fact, he did get it. Not only that, he was even beginning to warm up to it. In one way at least, she was right. The horse was big and strong and could probably do a good job of pulling a wagon. It would take half a day to get to the gardening center and back but it might work out, he was thinking, because it was mostly a downhill slope from the Pointe to Lasalle, which was when the load would be full, and uphill on the way back when it would be empty. That would work to the horse's advantage.

"Might be good advertising too," said Louise, interrupting his thoughts. "You know . . . You driving a horse while delivering horse manure. That's good advertising. Like you're using your own product, know what I'm saying?"

Doyle didn't exactly follow that line of reasoning, so he just gave her a half-smile and sipped some more of his soda. By this time, she was already looking at her watch and glancing around nervously to see if the boss was keeping tabs on her. "I gotta go," she said, as she stood up. "Why don't you think about it?"

"I will, definitely."

"Come back, let me know, all right?"

"Mind if I stay? I mean, to finish this?" He indicated his glass.

"You got a drink, you can stay as long as you want. Eat the peanuts, too, if you like. I'll have to come back and take the money though, all right? Later. Don't worry about it now."

With that, she was gone, hurrying past the bar and into the back room to continue whatever it was she was doing before. But as she left, Doyle couldn't help noticing that the sharply dressed young men in the back had stopped talking for the time being and one of them was watching her as she left. It was nothing, just a small gesture, but he noticed it because he'd been in bars before and that was how things were, how they'd always be.

He tried to forget about that and focus on Jacqueline, which was why he came here in the first place.

His gaze wandered back to the street, just beyond the window pane, and he tried to imagine her out there right now, sitting on the bench of the *calèche*, her elbow on her knee, smoking her cheroot as she waited for people to come along. Somehow, though, the image of horse seemed to intrude on the vision, Groucho with his nose in the feed bucket, and he couldn't prevent his thoughts returning to the idea that Louise had suggested.

It was strange, but he felt kind of guilty about his mind wandering like that. He should be preserving Jacqueline's memory, locking it in so he'd never forget, but all he could think about was Groucho and how to make it work.

Then something else struck him, a whole other notion. Maybe this was how it should be, he thought. Maybe this was how it was meant to be. Jacqueline loved that animal, so figuring out a way to take care of him was maybe the best way to remember her, after all. She would have liked that, he was certain of it. What better legacy could there be?

The problem arose a day later.

Four

L ouise's idea of using Groucho for deliveries seemed laudable when she had mentioned it to Doyle in the bar. As she'd said, it solved all his problems in one go. Unfortunately, it had one major drawback. In order for it to work, it was pretty much essential to have the horse's cooperation.

Doyle began the morning with enthusiasm. He washed and brushed the animal, making sure to do a good job on the mane, which he knew the horse liked. Then he pulled on the halter and led him gently out of the stall, talking to him all the time, encouraging him.

"That's it, there's a good boy, just a little walk, whaddya say?"

The weather had cleared a little, with some bright rays breaking through, and the horse was willing enough to exit the stable. But when they reached the gates of the compound, he point-blank refused to go any further. He wouldn't step foot out onto the street. It wasn't that he was afraid or nervy, he just plain stopped with his hooves foursquare. He wouldn't move, wouldn't even budge.

"Come on now, Groucho, none of your games. We're just going for a walk, nothing to worry about, all right? Nothing at all."

But Groucho didn't want to go for a walk, or do anything else for that matter, and when a horse that size decides to remain stationary, there's not much anyone can do.

By this time, Mowbray had wandered over to see what was going on. "What's wrong wi' him?" he asked, with that strange mix of accent. It was part Jamaican like his father, part European like his mother, and part black rap like his favorite music.

"He doesn't wanna go out."

"He sick?"

"Don't think so. Ate this morning, as usual, enjoyed his bath. Now look at him."

"So what's wrong?"

"You tell me."

But Mowbray couldn't answer. He didn't say much at the best of times, but if Doyle didn't know, then Mowbray certainly wasn't going to venture an opinion, so he just stood there like the horse, doing nothing.

"All right, you know what?" said Doyle. "Why don't you go back inside, clean out his stall and I'll try to back him up, ready for when you're done."

Mowbray did as he was told, but he'd have much preferred to stay and watch. This situation was far more interesting than shoveling.

Doyle rubbed his palm over the horse's muzzle and spoke to him as softly as he could. "Okay, you don't wanna go out right now? That's fine, we'll try a bit later when you feel more like it. No problem at all. So what we'll do, we'll just back you up a little and take you back inside 'til you're ready, okay? We'll just take it nice and easy ..."

Doyle tried to ease backward on the halter, not too much pressure on the sensitive mouth area but just enough for the horse to know what he wanted. But Groucho still wouldn't budge. He didn't want to go forward, and he didn't want to go back. He just wanted to stand there calmly and watch the universe unfold around him.

Horses have the largest eyes of all land mammals, with near three-sixty degree vision. According to people who know about these things, their ability to focus is sometimes suspect, and they can't distinguish too well within the mid-tone spectrum of greens, browns, or grays.

Nevertheless, eyesight, along with sound and smell, was still a principal means of defensive surveillance. What that meant was that even if a horse like Groucho appeared to be motionless in every respect, didn't even turn his head, he was using some combination of these three senses to remain keenly aware of his surroundings within a considerable radius.

Doyle stood back a couple of paces and thought about what to do. If the horse continued to stand there, nothing would be able to get in or out, not his van and not the *calèches* when they came back later. Fortunately, the situation wasn't urgent and he could afford to wait the hour or two it might take, so he pulled the lines over and tied them to the metal fence, his notion being to leave the animal there while he went back inside and got on with some work.

However, as soon as he began to walk away, Groucho got upset, stomping his foot and shaking his big head, causing the fence to rattle loudly, which in turn caused Mowbray to peer out, to see what the commotion was all about. Doyle signaled for the young man to stay where he was, not to interfere, then returned to the horse's side. As soon as he did, Groucho calmed down.

"Oh, I see. You don't want me to leave, is that it?" Doyle stroked the horse's face and neck, then gave him a couple of sugar cubes that he dug out of the pocket of his overalls. Some owners refuse to carry a treat in their pockets, saying it can be distracting for an animal or even dangerous should he make a grab for it, but like Jacqueline, Doyle had his own way of doing things and no rule book was ever going to tell him how to do his job.

"It's not enough you wanna stand here, you want me to stand next to you, right? The both of us, like a pair of idiots. Is that what you want? Is it? Okay, okay, I'll stand here but only for a while, mind, I don't have all day. I'm not like you, y'know. Me, I got stuff to do. Unless you feel like helping me. You wanna pay the bills, eh? That'd be a help. Or maybe do the filing, how about that? Any papers you don't know where they go, you could just eat."

In response, Groucho simply blinked his black eyes at him, content now that Doyle was offering him some attention. It was more than evident that the horse was feeling the loss, that a vast presence was missing in his life and he didn't know how to cope with it. Jacqueline had been absent before, sometimes taking long weekends with her girlfriends down in Ogunquit, but this time it was as if the horse were able to sense the difference.

Or perhaps it was a lot simpler than that. Perhaps he was just feeling the sadness around him, most of that coming from Doyle himself. Groucho was big and irritable, but he was also intelligent and perceptive enough to pick up every vibration in the atmosphere around him. If that was the case, then each day that passed would represent an increasing awareness that something enormous had happened, that his existence had totally changed.

After several minutes of just standing there, Doyle decided to try an experiment. He unfastened the lines from the gate and let them fall to the ground. Then he slowly took a few steps back across the compound, while making sure Groucho stayed focused on his voice. There was a risk involved, because if something startled the animal, he'd be free and loose to react any way he chose, even to bolt. It was unlikely but, given his eccentric nature, anything was possible.

"All right now, I'm just going to step over here. You watching this? I'm not going far. See? Just over here."

Doyle waited a few seconds. Then a few more. He had no idea what would happen but, eventually, sure enough, Groucho turned and sauntered over to where Doyle was now standing.

"Attaboy, you just want some company, don't you? That's okay. Not much to ask, a bit of company." He gave the horse another two pieces of sugar and watched the giant foam-laden lips draw them in.

"There you go. All we gotta do is take one step at a time, right? You gotta get used to me. Well, I can understand that, 'cause me, I gotta get used to you too. Jacqueline knew you inside out, but not me. I was just there in the stable. I was just your landlord but that's all changed now. You and me, we got to get to know each other, all our silly ways, right? Come to think of it, we're both about the same age if you add it up right. Means we're both getting a tad cranky, so we just gotta get used to each other. All right now, tell you what I'm gonna do. I'm gonna take another few steps over that way, okay? Not far, just another few steps."

Doyle angled back again, this time toward the stable doorway and once again, after a brief delay, Groucho followed him, receiving the same tasty reward for his effort.

A couple more moves like that and Groucho was safely back in his stall. But instead of just shutting the gate and leaving to get on with his work, Doyle pulled up an old chair and stayed, maintaining a long and rambling monologue about anything that came into his head: about Jacqueline, about Louise, even about Louise's idea for making deliveries.

"How'd you like to deliver your own dung?" he asked at one stage. "That's funny, don't you think? No? Well, you know what your problem is? You got no sense of humor. Maybe we'll have to see what we can do about that, 'cause if you're gonna be around me from now on, you're gonna need a sense of humor, that's for sure. I can be a pain in the rear end sometimes too, y'know. You're not the only one. I guess you'll find that out soon enough. Maybe it'll end up you giving me some sugar for a change, just to sweeten me up. What d'you say?"

And so it went on, hour after hour, the only break coming when Doyle went to make himself coffee and a meat sandwich. Even then, he brought it back to eat in the stall, while Groucho munched his way through half a bucket of grain, his preferred mix of oats and corn with a little molasses poured over it.

"Dinner for two," Doyle said to him.

Eventually dusk fell, the drivers came back from the street and Doyle had to get busy with Mowbray, bedding down the other horses.

Days at the stable were always long but this one had been unusual, and before long, Doyle was ready to collapse onto his cot, exhausted from the sheer amount of energy it took to talk for so long. He couldn't recall when he'd last been so sick of his own voice. Yet a new relationship had been born, not firm yet, not by any means, but it had gotten underway. That, at least, was cause for some satisfaction.

The following morning, Bertrand Thibodeau was the last to depart the stable, as he always was. But this time, just before he left, he wandered over to talk to Doyle, who was busy trying to fix a wooden storage cupboard, with a spirit level in one hand, a pencil in the other, and some screws in his mouth. When Bertrand approached, Doyle stood up a little stiffly and spat the metal out into his hand.

Bertrand was the oldest of the drivers, within ten years of Doyle himself. He was short and balding, with a major belly on him. To hide his paunch, he wore a loose, poncho-style shirt in green plaid over his jeans, and to protect his head from the sun, he had a straw cowboy hat with a wide brim and a black feather. He liked to claim his heritage was part Mohawk but nobody really knew whether that was true or not.

"Hear you're trying to train ol' Groucho," he said casually, hands in his pockets.

Doyle smiled. "Who told you that? Mowbray?"

"That's a stubborn animal. Think you can do it?"

"Don't know yet."

"Had a passenger not long ago, from Chicago I think, somewheres like that. Brought his family here on vacation. Interesting guy, liked to talk. Said he was an animal trainer, got a lot of work in movies, TV ads, things like that. Dogs, mostly, but also horses. Said sometimes the film people wanted older animals, so he had to train 'em to do different things. Said he only knew one sure way to do it, same way for all of 'em."

Doyle waited for the answer but it wasn't immediately forthcoming. "What way was that?" he was obliged to ask.

Bertrand took his time answering, because he always took his time with everything. "What he said was, he just didn't feed 'em for a while. Sometimes for a day, sometimes more. Then, he said, when they're good and hungry, they're ready to do anything he wants just to get the food."

Doyle thought about it. He'd heard of that method before, knew they used it in circuses, places like that, so the fact they employed the same technique to make movies didn't surprise him at all. He just nodded slowly. "Would you do that?" he asked Bertrand.

"Me, I never had to. Got my horse when she was young." Bertrand had a white-gray mare, a nice animal he called Ange, French for Angel. She wasn't big, nowhere near as big as Groucho, but she was docile and eager to please, with a lot of heart. Each morning, Bertrand would say the same thing, *"Allons-y, mon Ange!"* Let's go, my Angel! And with just the slightest flick of the lines, she'd be away, happy to be on the move.

Doyle thought it was worth pursuing the discussion, so he said, "But if you had to do it that way, would you?"

"You mean, if I was you? With Groucho there? Why? You don't think you can?"

Doyle shrugged. He wasn't sure he'd be capable of starving an animal in order to train it. He knew it would work all right. He just didn't think he could do it, that's all.

"Up to you," said Bertrand, then turned and strolled out with that strange, bow-legged walk of his. It was almost as if his natural place was on the bench of a *calèche*. On the ground, he was as ungainly as a walrus on a beach.

Doyle still hadn't received a reply but he didn't insist because he realized it didn't matter much anyway. What Bertrand or some professional trainer might do was irrelevant. It was what he, himself, would be willing to try that was important and if he didn't feel good about it, then he wouldn't do it, simple as that. But there was something else came into Doyle's mind and he dashed out as fast as his old legs would carry him, just in time to catch Bertrand heading out of the compound. "Hey, Bertrand, wait up . . ."

"Whoa, mon Ange, whoa là!"

"Meant to ask you," said Doyle, a little out of breath. "Know anyone wants to buy the *calèche*?"

"You mean Jacqueline's?" Bertrand spent a few moments thinking about it. "Don't know of anybody right now."

"Could you ask around?"

"Might not be easy. They're talking about cutting back the number of permits up at City Hall, so I don't know who'll be willing to shell out money for a new buggy-ride."

"There's another thing too. I need a wagon."

Bertrand gazed down at him, trying to figure it out. "What kinda wagon?"

"Four wheels. Something solid to carry the manure."

It took a moment for Bertrand put it all together in his head but once he did, he couldn't help a slight smile. "You wanna hitch him to a manure wagon?"

"Just an idea."

Bertrand opened up to a broad grin, not enough to be an outright laugh, but close. "Good luck with that," he said, but he didn't mean it. He was being cynical, as if he just couldn't see it happening.

"So you'll ask around? About the *calèche*?"

"Do what I can." With that, Bertrand touched at the lines and Ange moved obediently ahead as far as the road, pausing on her own to check for any traffic before making the slow right-angled turn.

On returning to the stable, Doyle gave Mowbray his routine checklist for the day. He then spent another half-hour finishing up work on the cupboard, but once again left his office chores undone so he could be with Groucho, who'd already had his breakfast along with all the other horses.

"How we doing this morning?" asked Doyle, rubbing the animal's muzzle down near his nostrils so he could let him get the scent. Vision, voice, and smell, in that order were all important to a horse and each one of those senses was far superior to any human ability.

"So, you in the mood to try again, eh? What d'you say? You going to give me a hard time again, or you going to be a good boy today, go for a nice walk? Can't just hang around in here, y'know, livin' the life o' Riley." As he spoke, Doyle took down the halter and fastened it delicately over the horse's head, slow and easy.

"Y'know, Bertrand doesn't think you can do it but we'll see about that, right? Let's see if we can't prove him wrong, you and me." When he thought the horse was ready, he let Groucho smell his hand again before taking hold of the strap just above the jaw line. Then, with a bare minimum of pressure, and making sure Groucho could both see and hear him, he led the horse out of the stall, out of the stable, and directly out of the compound before Groucho had a chance to refuse. This was farther than they got yesterday and their progress was starting to look pretty good.

It wasn't raining or windy this morning, it was kind of neutral, with an average temperature for the time of year and a pale eggshell sky. Doyle led the way, walking as briskly as he could, with the horse walking gently alongside, seemingly content to follow him around the streets and alleyways of Pointe St-Charles.

They walked past tiny red-brick row houses, a holdover from another era, boarded up warehouses and electricity substations, thrift stores and discount supermarkets and auto body shops, as well as the ubiquitous *dépanneurs*. These corner variety stores had three main sources of revenue: smokes, beer and lottery tickets, usually in that order. In some adjoining neighborhoods, enormous swathes had been carved out and replaced by acres of condominiums and lofts, starter accommodations for urban professionals, but not here at the Pointe. Not yet.

Doyle neither liked nor disliked this area in which he'd lived all his life. For him it was just a place he happened to be. He had no nostalgia for the old ways, because he was of an age to remember just how harsh it really was. Nor did he have any special camaraderie with the people who stayed, because they were just an ordinary assortment like anywhere else. Some were reasonably honest, some less so and some had their heads full of poison.

Doyle knew who they were in each case but treated them all the same way—with suspicion. And they returned the favor. He had neighbors, but no real friends, because that was just his nature and, as he went on his way, walking in step with the horse, he looked at it all with familiar but unsentimental eyes.

"So, what do you think?" he asked. "This was where I grew up, y'know that? Not too pretty, I'm afraid. Not too many fields and trees. Wish I could let you canter a bit but this is the best I can do for now. Gets you out of the stable though, right? That's something, I guess. Don't want you turning lazy in your old age. At least no lazier than you are already."

So far, Groucho's behavior had been exemplary, much better than Doyle could have hoped, and it continued that way until they came to the intersection at Grand Trunk. Here they had no choice but to wait as one of the city's monster street-sweepers rumbled across and its passing provoked a minor reaction in Groucho. The movement was subtle, just a sniff of the nostrils and a twitch of the ears, but it was there and Doyle noticed it.

"Okay, now, no need to worry," said Doyle softly. "You've seen one of these things before, I'm sure. Just stay calm, it's gonna go right by us."

Too late, he realized that the machine was designed to emit a spray of cold water to dampen down the dust and prepare the way for the revolving brush mechanism. As it passed, a little caught Groucho on the cannon part of his front legs, just above the fetlock, and he was taken by surprise. He whinnied and lifted the affected front legs into the air and Doyle had to move fast to avoid one of those broad metal shoes coming down and accidentally crippling him.

Human limbs can be crushed under that kind of force. Yet somehow, he had the presence of mind not to let go the lines. Instead, he let them slide through his hands so he could step backward out of the way without totally releasing control.

"Okay, Groucho," he said, breathing hard at the exertion, "that's enough now, let's not be silly. It's just some water, it's not gonna hurt you." By this time, the horse was back on the ground, still snorting and stomping in anger, but Doyle's voice was having a calming effect. "C'mon now, take it easy, just relax. No big deal, you just got your feet wet, that's all. What's all the fuss?"

For a long time after the sweeper had departed, they just stood there at the junction, man and horse: the one still talking, the other still listening. There were other cars and trucks but these were minimal distractions by comparison, and eventually, Groucho was able to cool off, reassured by the close presence of the only human he now trusted.

In time, they were able to continue with their walk, but Doyle stayed alert for any possible disruption: people shouting, car doors slamming, horns honking; anything at all that might affect the animal's re-established equilibrium.

When they got back, they were both still in one piece, and Doyle was able to give out a momentary sigh of relief. But even then, he didn't leave the horse alone. He stayed with him most of the afternoon—and then followed the same pattern the next day, and the day after that. He was prepared to do it as long as it took because, despite everything, he found himself getting very attached to this eccentric animal.

Each day when he got up, he looked forward to spending time with Groucho and enjoyed measuring the progress, such as it was. He knew the horse would never be like the mare, Ange, for example, but that didn't matter. Progress was being made. The bond was forming and in Jacqueline's absence, each of them was something of a comfort to the other.

ne morning, a Friday, Bertrand came into Doyle's kitchen, not the one upstairs in his spartan apartment, but the minuscule one on the stable floor. Here was a kettle for coffee, a scratched single-ring electric hotplate on which to boil up soup or macaroni & cheese, plus a tiny, ancient fridge where he stored perishables such as a quart of milk, a little cheese, sliced corned beef, or anything else he needed to keep him going through the day.

"You want coffee?" he asked Bertrand, and immediately, memories of times with Jacqueline came flooding back. Steam was billowing out of the kettle, and Doyle poured the bubbling water over the instant brown powder.

"No, just wanna talk to you for a minute." Bertrand was still standing in the doorway, his short, broad frame just about filling the gap. "You got a minute?"

"Sure."

"We got what you might call a proposal, me and the other guys."

"The other drivers."

"Yeah, it was actually Frank's idea but, you know, they said for me to talk to you about it, so I said okay, I don't mind."

"What kind of proposal?"

"Yeah, well, it's about the *calèche*. The one you asked me about."

"Jacqueline's?"

"Yeah, Jacqueline's."

"What about it?"

"Well, not much, except we were wondering if we could buy it. I mean, if you wanna sell it."

"Sure, I wanna sell it."

"No, 'cause what I'm saying is it might be useful, you know?"

Doyle was lost, so he just shrugged, shook his head, and drank some of his coffee, in that order.

Bertrand looked at him, wondering how to explain. "Remember when Marie-Josée needed those new spokes?"

"Sure."

A truck had backed up too far and the fender banged up her rear wheel. She just about made it back to the stable, but then the *calèche* was out of service for nearly a week by the time they fixed it.

In fact, it wasn't unusual for accidents like that to happen. Such contraptions were deceptive, much bigger than they appeared. They took up a lot of space in the street and they would often get damaged, sometimes just a paint scrape or sometimes far worse.

"Well, anyways," Bertrand went on, "we were thinking, that's the other guys and me, that if we had a spare, we wouldn't lose no downtime."

"A spare? You mean a spare *calèche*?"

"We were thinking we could all chip in a bit, so they said I should talk to you, see how much you want for it."

Doyle was beginning to get the picture. "So you'd keep it here, just in case?"

"We keep it here and whoever's got a problem, that's who takes it out."

"You all buy it together?"

"Depends. How much you want?"

"I dunno. I haven't thought about it. How much you got?"

"Dunno."

"Tell you what, why don't you see how much you got, y'know, how much each of you can afford, then add it all up."

"You wanna do it that way?"

"May be easier."

Bertrand took a moment, but he could see no objection. "Maybe."

"Okay, so you guys talk about it, see what you got."

"But the only thing is ..."

"What's that?"

"Well, there's another thing."

"Okay."

"Yeah, well, see ... the other thing is, they want me to tell you, you know, make sure you understand."

"Understand what?"

"Well, if we keep it here, we don't wanna pay no rent for it."

"Rent?"

"For keeping it here."

"Oh, that. Okay, so let's see."

"See what?"

Doyle took another swig of his coffee. "Let's see how we go." He wasn't so good at negotiating stuff, not like Jacqueline. She was far better at this kind of thing. She'd have had it all wrapped up in two minutes.

"Okay," said Bertrand, for want of something better to say. Then he nodded a little hesitantly, shifted his cowboy hat on his head, and left the kitchen area to go get ready for his route. In fact, the more Doyle thought about it, the more pleased he was with that sort of arrangement. It made sense for the drivers and it solved a problem for him too. It was true he had no idea what to charge for a used *calèche*, but he figured that, within reason, whatever they could come up with, he'd be willing to accept.

And no, he thought, *he wouldn't charge them rent to keep it here.* He wasn't a mean person and he had the space anyway, so it was a service he'd be prepared to offer, like an extra little bonus, like a way of saying thank you.

"Oh, about that other thing ..." This was Bertrand, back again. "The wagon. Marie-Josée says the best place is online."

With Jacqueline gone, Marie-Josée was the only female driver left at the stable.

"Online?" asked Doyle.

"You know, the internet . . . the computer. She says that's the best place to find one."

"I never used a computer."

"Anyways, that's what she says."

With that, Bertrand turned and left for real.

Since Marie-Josée seemed to know about computers, Doyle assumed she must have one at home but he would never ask her for a favor. It's not that he didn't like her or that they didn't get on, it's just that Doyle wasn't the sociable sort. Throughout his life, he'd always found it hard to get to along with anyone. Even back at school, he often played around the yard on his own, amusing himself with small games he invented in his head. He would pick up a pebble, for example, and see how many times he could hit a certain brick in a wall. Or he'd stare at the clouds, picking out shapes.

Or sometimes, when he could afford it, he'd buy a licorice roll-up from the *dépanneur* and see how many pieces he could break off, eventually eating twenty or more, one after the other, in happy little gulps. He wasn't especially unpopular. Nobody made fun of him, not as a rule, like they did with some kids, nor did they gang up on him.

He was just there, preferring his own company and living in a world of his own making. Even the teachers didn't care much. As long as he wasn't a nuisance in class, which he wasn't, and as long as he scored the bare minimum in tests, which he tried his best to do, they left him to his own devices.

Although many things about him had changed when he became an adult, that aspect of his personality didn't. It may possibly have been why he didn't get many dates, and it may also have been why he couldn't keep the one real relationship he'd ever managed to form.

He told himself she didn't like the horses, but it was deeper than that. In truth, she just found it too much hard work to penetrate the shell he'd developed over the years—and by that time, it was so impermeable, he didn't know how to break it down himself.

That's essentially why he finally managed to develop a friendship with Jacqueline. She just plowed right through his barriers with the force of her character and never let it bother her. For all intents and purposes, she didn't even notice his introvert nature, she was so full of her own entanglements. For her, Doyle was a patient ear, a ready audience who put up with her alternating moods when so many others wouldn't, and she returned the favor by assisting him with his day-to-day difficulties.

That's also why, when it came to the notion of using a computer, his immediate thought was to approach her daughter, Louise. He found he liked her, if only from their brief talk after the funeral. Of course, she was totally different from her mother, but she'd taken the trouble to sit down and talk to him, and she'd even bothered to think up an idea to help him. Her mother was the only other person who'd ever done that. It was the one family connection that meant something—at least for Doyle, if not for Louise.

"Oh, yeah, hi, come on in."

Louise stepped back from her front door to let him in but he took the time to wipe his feet before entering. It was the ground floor apartment of a typical duplex near Crawford Park, a quiet area off the Boulevard Lasalle. It was as working class as the rest of Verdun but a little off the beaten track, which made it more tranquil. Just as Doyle stepped into the hallway, a male voice called down in English from upstairs.

"Who the hell's that so early in the goddam morning?"

"Doyle," she yelled back.

"Who?"

"I told you he was coming."

An unshaven face with uncombed hair appeared at the top of the banister. "Who?" he asked again.

She looked up. "My mother's friend, Doyle. I told you. He wants to use the computer."

"Yeah? Well, not too long. Where's my shirt?"

"Which shirt?"

"The blue one, goddammit. I got that stupid interview today."

"In the laundry."

"What?"

"I put it in the laundry."

"What the hell you go and do that for? Jesus Christ ..."

"You wannit, it's in the basket," Louise told him. Then to Doyle, she said, "Don't mind him. Come on through." He knew all about Louise's husband, Roscoe. Jacqueline had never stopped complaining about how much she loathed him and, from his absence at the funeral, the feeling was mutual.

"I don't want to disturb you," Doyle said to Louise, trying to be respectful.

"Nah, don't worry about it, he's such a jerk sometimes. Through here."

Doyle followed her through to a small, square living room that looked on to the street. It was overcrowded and messy with a little too much of everything. She led him past worn furniture, unfolded newspapers, used breakfast dishes on the dining table, and a wide-screen TV, much bigger and fancier than Doyle's own set in his apartment above the stable. The computer, an old desktop model, was set up on its own metal table against the opposite wall, and she went to sit down directly in front of it.

"Pull up a chair," she said, indicating the four melamine chairs by the table.

Doyle did as he was told. He'd taken the time to scrub carefully for the visit this morning and had put on some clean clothes but felt he still wasn't completely free of the smell. It was something he just couldn't help, but either she didn't notice or she didn't mind; or she minded but was too polite to say anything, he wasn't certain which.

"So," she began, "how much do you know about computers?" She looked at him expectantly.

"Nothing."

"*Nothing*, nothing?"

"I never used one. Your mother once said she'd show me but ..." He came to a stop.

"Yeah, all right. So you want me to show you a bit or just get right to it? Which do you want?"

"You have the time?"

"Yeah, afternoon shift. I got a couple hours."

"Will it take that long?"

"Christ, I hope not. Guess that's the first thing to know about computers, they make everything quick. Like you wanna do research, no need to go to the library. You just look it up, you get all the answers."

"Is that what people do? Look for answers?"

She glanced at him again, not really knowing whether to get into all the possibilities, from building spreadsheets to downloading porn, which her husband did a lot. "Come to think of it, let's just focus on what you want, all right?"

"Sure."

"Know anything about the internet?"

"I heard of it," replied Doyle.

"Yeah, well, okay . . . So the internet is like the connection between all the computers in the world. That's why it's called the World Wide Web . . . Y'know, when you see *www* everywhere? That's what it stands for."

"I've seen that," he said, trying to show enthusiasm. "They have it on the ads, at the end. I knew it was something to do with computers."

"Right, right, that's good. Now, something else you need to know is that all the places you want to go on the internet, they call them websites, by the way, they all start with *www* but each one's got different letters and numbers after it. They call it the address but it's not like a street address, it's more like, I guess, a telephone number, you follow me?"

Doyle nodded, trying to get all this into his head, anxious to prove he could be as up-to-date as the next person. He watched her touch something her hand was resting on. "What's that thing, there?"

"That? That's called a mouse. Funny name, right, 'cause that's what it looks like . . . a mouse. You click this with your finger and it makes everything work on the screen. See that little pointy thing? I can make it move with the mouse. See?" Doyle nodded, genuinely pleased that he was learning something.

"Right, now we have to get on to the internet. So I just move the mouse, put the pointer on this, then we wait a minute . . . sometimes it takes a bit longer, depends how many people wanna use it . . . Yeah, there we go. Voilà, the internet! What we got here is the first thing you see, which gives you the news. You can get the weather, all kinds of things. You like hockey, you got the hockey scores. Cool, eh? Me, I like the horoscope every day. Okay, so that's just, like the first thing you come to.

"Next, we have to go to this little box here. See, the problem is that there's so many websites, you can't find what you want. I mean, millions and millions, all over the world. So what they did, they invented this thing where you just type in what you want, you know, in real words, and it finds all the websites for you. Easy. Look, I'll show you. Now I just type in the word . . . *trailer*. Then we click like this and see what we get. Hell, no, that's not it. See the list? That's all different kinds of trailers for trucks and stuff. So let's change it to *horse trailer* . . . like this . . ."

Doyle was peering at the screen, but he couldn't read too quickly, even at the best of times, so he was glad just to follow her lead. He actually hadn't realized the computer would involve so much reading. He knew there was a screen, so he thought it would be more like TV.

"That's better," said Louise, as the new list came to life. "Horse trailers, loads of 'em. So let's just get in to this one, right here. This is what you call a website. All I have to do is click on it and . . ."

Doyle gazed with fascination at the images that suddenly appeared, one after the other. But that's when they were interrupted by Roscoe. He looked livid, barging into the room, his collar and sleeves unfastened and flapping, his face slightly flushed.

"Look at it!" he screamed at her.

"Look at what?"

"The shirt! The damn shirt! How can I go to a damn interview with a shirt like this?"

She seemed uninterested. "Your fault, you should have given it to me to wash."

"My fault? My fault? You never do no laundry."

"Hey, I work, you know. Not like some."

"And what's that supposed to mean?"

"You'll figure it out."

"Lazy bitch."

This last comment was said under his breath but it was too much for Louise, who began to yell back. "You watch your filthy mouth."

He came closer, more threatening, looming over her, and began to raise his hand. Instinctively, Louise put her arm out to defend herself, memories of her mother flashing through her brain, but it was Doyle who stood up, as if ready to face the challenge. For a moment, Roscoe stared at the thin old man. "Ah, Christ," he said, as if it wasn't worth his time, then stormed out the room.

For a minute, maybe more, Louise just sat there, unable to move and Doyle didn't know what he could say or do to help. So he just sat down again next to her. Then they both heard the sound of the front door slamming and saw Roscoe disappear down the street, still mad, still pulling on his jacket, obviously late for his appointment.

"Shall I come back?" asked Doyle quietly. "Y'know, another time?"

"No, no," she replied. "It's all right." But it was clear she was still a little shaken up. "Let's just ..." She tried to focus once again on the screen in front of her. "Let's go on," she said at last.

Doyle looked at her and felt bad but maybe, he thought, getting on with it would be best. Get her mind on to something else. "That's not right," he said, indicating the screen.

She still wasn't totally into it. "What's not right?"

"Trailers. You asked for trailers. Trailers are for carrying the horses. You put them behind a truck to carry the horses. What I'm looking for is a wagon ... Try writing *wagon*."

Louise was still a little shaky and took a long breath in order to pull herself together. Then she typed the words *horse wagon* and clicked the mouse. A new list of sites appeared and she selected one at random. "Horse wagons, new and used," she said, almost to herself.

When the images came up on the screen, it was Doyle who said, "There, right there, that's good." It was a photo of a flatbed wagon with slatted sides, very pretty in bright green with a yellow floral design and mounted on four wheels with rubber tires. Up front was a bench for a driver and guides for the horse. He nodded and gave her a smile. It was remarkably close to the kind of thing he'd envisaged.

"You like that one?" she said. "Okay, let's see here ..." She clicked on the image and it suddenly enlarged, complete with full sales information underneath. "General delivery wagon, thirty years old, retread tires, restored as new ... Oh ..."

"What's that?"

She looked at him. "They want sixty-five hundred for it."

His expression changed. "Sixty-five?"

"Yeah . . . too much, eh?"

Doyle didn't like to admit he couldn't afford it, even when it was totally obvious, so he just said nothing. "Okay," she said, trying to cheer him up, "maybe they got something else."

It took a half-hour, scanning over a dozen sites, but the best they could find was an old beer wagon that needed some minor work, for which they were asking twelve hundred and twenty-five. The best part was that the seller was in Ontario, so no problem with customs and such.

"I can fix that up, no problem," said Doyle.

"You think?"

"Sure, just needs a little paint. No problem at all. What do we do now?"

"Well, I guess the next thing is to contact them."

"How do we do that?"

"By e-mail. You know what that is? It's like a note you can send from one person to another. You want me to do it?"

"What do we say?"

"I don't know. I guess we ask them if we can come look at it."

"We have to go to Ontario?"

"Well, how else you gonna look at it?"

It was something else he hadn't thought about. The whole idea had seemed so simple the way she described it back in the bar but it was proving to be fairly complicated, what with the *calèche* and the wagon, and he hadn't even considered yet how he was going to sell the van. It was a little discouraging—all this, just to take care of a horse.

Louise looked at her watch. "It's getting late," she said. "I gotta get ready for work. What do you want me to do? You want me to tell them you're interested, ask them when to go see it?"

"What do you think?" he asked her.

"Yeah, I'd say that's okay. That doesn't commit you to nothing, know what I mean? It's just so they don't sell it to someone else before you get a chance."

He thought about it for several seconds but couldn't see any harm in that. This was like the old days, being with Jacqueline. "Okay," he said simply and watched her get busy.

When she was done, she quit the internet and shut down the machine. "It might take 'em a day or two to answer. I'll let you know, all right?"

"Sure. Thanks."

"Yeah," she replied, getting to her feet.

As they got to the front door, he said: "This is like it was, y'know, with your mother."

He meant it as a compliment, a way of showing his gratitude but she didn't see it that way and she just turned on him, a look of instant fury on her face.

"Don't say that," she yelled. "Don't you ever say that! You don't compare me to her, not in any way, you got that?"

Doyle reeled a little from the onslaught. "I didn't mean ..."

"You didn't mean," she repeated with contempt in her voice. "You didn't mean, you didn't mean. Look, I don't mind helping out and all, but we leave her out of it, okay? Okay?"

"Okay."

"You don't mention her again. I mean, ever." She opened the front door to let him out. "Okay, that's it for today, go back to your horses. I got enough to worry about."

Once he stepped outside, she closed the door on him and he was left standing there. He didn't even know if she'd get back to him about the wagon, not after that, and he couldn't bring himself to knock on the door again, so he just turned and ambled away.

He hadn't meant to hurt her.

Six

It was well after midnight when Doyle was woken by a noise that sounded familiar. It was jangling, and it was insistent, so he sat up on his elbow to try to work it out. Then he realized he was being dumb. It was his own bell, the one on the long rope that the drivers used. He reached over and switched on the small lamp he'd installed next to his bedside, then rubbed his face.

Downstairs, the horses grew restless in their stalls. They weren't used to being disturbed either. One was stomping and snorting a little, no doubt Groucho, yet again living up to his name. Wearily, Doyle got to his feet and hauled on his ancient blue bathrobe over his undershirt and shorts. It was frayed, but it was still serviceable, not worth buying a new one. "Okay, okay," he said to the bell, as he made his way across the room, almost tripping over the shoes he'd left in the middle of the floor.

His apartment was what might today be called a loft area. It had a fairly wide central space, with rafters exposed, some good windows, and three-quarter height sub-dividers that marked off the various spaces. This was the living area, with his sofa, TV, and radio. The kitchen was a little larger than the one he had downstairs in the stable, with a real stove and a big square ceramic sink, old and stained but functional.

There was a bathroom with a toilet and a shower-stall supplied with gas-powered hot water, and a bedroom, containing his single sized cot. He tried to keep everything clean, but he wasn't scrupulously tidy and found it hard to force himself to be. It wasn't a mess but nor was it pristine. He looked around as he made his way over to the stairs, just in case he had to invite anyone up—not that he could imagine who it might be at this hour. One of the drivers, perhaps? Or a neighbor to complain about something?

"All right, I'm coming, I'm coming," he called out.

He didn't haul open the big doors, like he would for a *calèche*, but the small, personal door at the side, and he found Louise standing there. She looked terrible. Her cheek was badly bruised from the temple down to the jawline and her eyes were smudged and runny. Over her shoulder was a large bag, like a soft-sided grip.

"Doyle . . ." she said to him.

"Louise? What happened? What're you doing here? Come in, come in."

She didn't answer, but she accepted the invitation, gratefully unloading the bag as soon as she stepped inside. Slowly she looked around. It was her first time here. The stable was dark, except for the single light at the base of the staircase. Upstairs it was brighter. "That's where you live?" she asked him. Her voice was small, lonely.

"I live up there, the horses live down here."

"Can I see him? My mother's horse."

Doyle looked at her. He was not sure how he could help her, but this seemed like a reasonable enough request. "Sure." He led her over to the stalls where it was even more dimly lit. "He's a bit put out," said Doyle. "Doesn't like to be disturbed at night."

"My mother said he doesn't like much of anything."

Doyle offered a smile. "That's true enough. Likes his feed though. Likes his sleep, too, but horses don't sleep all night, not as a rule."

"They don't?"

"Sometimes they sleep, sometimes they doze, sometimes they just stand there."

"Do they ever lie down?"

"Every few days, depends on the horse. That's why you got to give 'em enough space. They can't dream if they don't lie down."

"Really? How do you know that?"

"The vet told me. Don't know what they dream about though."

"Maybe breakfast."

Doyle laughed. "Maybe." He was deliberately trying not to comment about her face, figuring that when she was good and ready, she'd tell him—or not, depending on how she felt. That was okay by him. "So this one here's Groucho. Seems to be awake." Doyle unhooked the stall gate, opening it very slowly, encouraging Louise to step inside. "Come on in, say hello. Gently now. Horses spook easier at night."

Doyle approached first, letting Groucho see, hear, and smell him before he rubbed the horse's neck. Then he indicated for Louise to come closer. "Give me your hand," he told her. Then he raised it, palm upwards, so the animal could sniff Louise too.

"That's a good boy," he said, still very softly. "That's our friend, Louise. That's Jacqueline's kid. You gonna let her rub your nose? Sure you are." Groucho seemed docile enough so, very delicately, Doyle placed Louise's hand in the center of the horse's white face, half way between the nostrils and the eyes, where the horse could see exactly what she was doing.

"Hi, Groucho," she said as she stroked him. "Hi, there. We never really met before. You're a nice boy." Then to Doyle, "He's beautiful."

Doyle nodded.

"I'm sorry about this morning," said Louise, "about what happened."

"No problem."

"I wasn't nice."

"That's okay."

She turned to look at him, her hand still resting on the horse. "You're a good man, Doyle. I can see why . . ." She didn't finish the sentence. Instead, she lowered her arm, backed away, and then went over to wait outside the stall.

"Coffee?" Doyle asked her as he joined her, closing the gate firmly.

"You have tea?"

"Sure. Coffee, tea, whatever you want."

"Thanks for letting me meet Groucho."

"You never saw him, all those years?" It was hard for Doyle to believe.

"I saw him on the street sometimes but, well, you know . . ." Again, she didn't conclude her thought. "Oh, by the way . . ." This, a little brighter. "They replied."

"Who's that?"

"The people selling the wagon. They replied."

"Is that right? That was quick."

"They must be interested in selling. It's a good sign."

"Think so? Why don't you come on up, you can tell me."

Louise wasn't sure, then seemed to make a decision and followed him up the stairs.

"Take care," said Doyle over his shoulder. "They're a bit steep. Hold on to the side."

"I'm not a child," she replied, but she instantly knew she'd responded too quickly. She stopped half-way up for a moment to close her eyes and take a breath. "I'm sorry," she said again. "You must be getting sick of me."

"No, I'm not. I like you."

"You do?"

"Sure, I do."

On the narrow landing, they walked past Doyle's tiny office and into the apartment. He stepped back to let her in but, as she passed him, she did an unexpected thing. After a brief hesitation, she reached out to pull him down toward her and gave him a brief kiss on his cheek. It was gentle and caring, and it was surprising because it was something her mother would never have done.

While he went to the kitchen to boil a kettle, Louise found a place to sit on the old sofa. But by the time, he returned with two steaming mugs, she was stretched out, already asleep with her head on a large cushion embroidered with crude cotton horses, brown and black, that he'd bought one time at a flea market in Lachine. Her auburn hair was greasy and unwashed, and the bruised side of her face was upturned.

He didn't have the heart to wake her, so he just put the tea down and went to find a blanket to pull over her. She was the first overnight guest he'd had there in many a year, and he wasn't sure what else he should do. He was no fool, and it had already occurred to him that the most likely cause of her injuries was a fight with her husband, Roscoe. Or perhaps it wasn't a fight at all. Perhaps it was just the man's temper.

Whatever had happened, he certainly didn't want to interfere by calling the police or even an ambulance, so in the end he decided to leave her alone and went back to his own bed. In the morning, she could decide for herself what to do. As she'd said, she wasn't a child.

Before closing his own eyes, he touched the place on his cheek where she'd kissed him and wasn't sure what to think. In the course of just one day, she'd been welcoming, she'd yelled at him, she'd found her way here in the middle of the night, she'd made friends with the horse, she'd snapped at him again, she'd given him a daughterly kiss, and then she'd fallen asleep on his sofa. It was true that he liked her, liked her a great deal, but that didn't change the fact that she was pretty screwed up.

She claimed not to be hungry, but she ate a full slice of toast when he put it in front of her and also drank the entire mug of tea. It was nine and Doyle had already been up for several hours.

"Wanna talk about it?" he asked her.

She shook her head. "Not really."

"Wanna go get it looked at?"

She touched her face. The color was a little worse, some of it had turned from red to shades of yellow and purple, but the swelling had gone down. She shook her head again.

"What're you gonna do?" he asked her.

"I'm not going back there, that's for damn sure."

"You have a place to go?"

"Yeah. Kind of."

He gazed at her, but she didn't say any more and he was reluctant to pry. "You said they replied."

For a second or two, she had no clue what he was talking about. Then she caught on and seemed to appreciate that he was deliberately changing the subject. "Yeah, I wrote it all down. Where you have to go and so on. They're open most days ten through five, but you should call first anyways."

"How far is it, d'you know?"

"I'd say it's about a three hour drive."

"That'll mean four or five in my van. You wanna go with me?"

"Me?"

"I thought maybe we can go together."

"Why? You want me to do it all for you?"

"No, no, it's not that. I can do it. It's just . . . I thought maybe you could use a day out. A little trip. 'A change is as good as a rest'." He said the last part like a quote, as if he'd heard it before and was just repeating it.

She looked at him and her expression softened. "That's nice of you."

"So you will?"

"I don't know."

"You'll let me know?"

"Yeah."

"I think he liked you. Groucho, I mean. I think he really liked you."

She gave a cynical smile. "Yeah, right. What do you think, he could smell my mother? Some kind of family resemblance?"

Doyle took the notion seriously. "Maybe."

She was quiet for a moment. Then a new thought came to her. "You got the money?" she asked him. "For the wagon. How you gonna pay for it?"

"I sold the *calèche*."

"You did?"

"Sure. Well, almost."

"Who'd buy that thing?"

"The drivers. The guys here. They kind of got together, said they needed it for a spare, as long as I let 'em keep it here. I said sure, so they said they'd pay me three hundred each. What I mean is, they didn't pay me yet, but that's what we agreed."

"How many you got here? Drivers."

"Four . . . four now."

"So you're getting what? Twelve hundred? It's worth more than that."

He sensed her disapproval. "You think?"

She didn't answer.

"It's only worth more if somebody'll pay it," he said.

She looked over at him, a little surprised at such wisdom. "Yeah, well I suppose that's true enough. Look, don't mind me. You did all right, finding buyers like that."

He nodded, pleased now that she understood. "But I'm still down twenty-five," he said. He was talking about the difference between the price he got for the *calèche* and the cost of the wagon in Ontario.

"Yeah, well maybe we can negotiate that. Plus you'll have the sale of the van. On the other side, you got expenses, like the gas to get there and the paint and so on, but I figure you'll just about break even."

"I'm not sure about selling the van," he replied.

"No?"

"I don't know if it's gonna work out so good with Groucho."

"No? Why not?"

"I don't know. I walk him every day, I spend a lotta time with him, but I don't know. He's still a bit nervous, y'know? Irritable."

"He was always like that."

"I know . . . but this is different. What I was thinking, if I fix up the wagon and it doesn't work out, if he doesn't like it, then I've still got the van, and I can sell the wagon through the computer, just like I bought it. What d'you think?"

"Yeah, that's a good way to look at it. 'Course, you understand I don't have the computer now. It's back at the duplex, and I'm not going back there."

"I think Marie-Josée has a computer."

"Who's she?"

"One of the drivers."

"Well, one thing at a time. Soon as the guys pay you, we can go."

"You'll come with me?"

"Yeah, why not? I'll tell the boss I'm sick."

"He won't mind?"

"Nah, I've done it before. He thinks I got a woman's problem. Jerk."

Doyle didn't know much about that, so he didn't comment. Nevertheless, he was delighted she'd agreed to travel down with him, and for a while, they both just sat there, saying nothing. The sun was trying to penetrate the east-facing window but it only succeeded in showing up some of the dust that hung in the atmosphere.

Doyle tried to keep the windows open as much as possible to let the place air out and he also had a large industrial fan that he often used for the same purpose, but Louise didn't seem to mind the smell too much. At least, Doyle thought, she hadn't said anything.

"Well, anyways, I gotta get back to work," he told her eventually.

"Me too," she replied. "Hey, thanks for letting me stay."

"Where will you go? Tonight, I mean." He'd already decided not to ask her that but he changed his mind. He was concerned.

"I got a friend'll put me up."

"Really?"

"Why? You think I got no friends?"

"No, it's not that."

She shook her head, slowly this time, as if in apology for her own sharp mouth. "You're better off without me around."

"That's not true. You can come over any time."

"Yeah, you say that but you don't mean it."

"Yes, I do."

She smiled at him, a pleasant, genuine smile, all trace of cynicism having disappeared. "Yeah, maybe you do," she replied. Then the smile turned into a gentle laugh. "You're a strange man, Doyle, you know that?"

He wasn't sure about the word "strange" but he left it alone and went downstairs to continue with his day. The drivers had all gone out, but her big grip was still by the door where she'd left it last night. He wondered if they'd noticed it there. Maybe they thought he had a girlfriend. It was a humorous idea, and he chuckled secretly to himself.

A half-hour later she came down, having taken a shower. Her hair was still wet and unkempt, but her eyes were brighter and she was in a better mood.

Both Doyle and Mowbray watched her come down the staircase until Doyle said to him, "What're you looking at? You got no work to do?"

Mowbray just grinned, a knowing male look on discovering that a woman had slept over, then went about his business.

"I'll let you know about the trip," he said to her, as she picked up her bag and hauled it over her shoulder.

"Yeah, all right. Listen, thanks again. I mean it."

"No problem."

"Can I ask you another favor? Call a taxi?"

"Sure." He assumed that was how she'd gotten there last night. He never took taxis himself, except one time he'd cut his thumb and it wouldn't stop bleeding. He couldn't have driven like that, so he had called one to run him up to the General to get it stitched up. Since that time, he'd left the taxi number taped to the wall phone, just in case of an emergency. He'd already taken the receiver from its hook, when the belated thought occurred to him and he turned back to face her. "You want a lift somewhere?"

"Nah, don't worry about it, you got stuff to do. A taxi's fine."

Ten minutes later, he stood at the compound fence and watched her go, wiggling his fingers at the car before he realized he might look a bit silly doing that on the street and lowered his hand self-consciously.

Briefly, he wondered who she might be going to stay with but it wasn't any of his affair, so he tried to wipe it from his mind. He had the trip to look forward to, but before that, he somehow had to persuade the drivers to pay up for the *calèche* like they'd agreed.

As far as he was concerned, the sooner the better. He didn't want the people in Ontario to sell the wagon to someone else.

Seven

I t seemed to Doyle that Groucho was slowly starting to get over the loss of his former owner. The horse's behavior was generally better. He was less edgy, and he even seemed to be developing some enthusiasm for his daily walks.

They always followed the same route, rain or shine, and there hadn't been any panicky episodes since that road sweeper on the first day, even when a kid on a bike swerved and fell in the gutter one time, right in front of them. Doyle had spoken softly to Groucho, calming him, and the horse had listened with a slight flick of the ears to show he was paying attention.

Each time they came back, Doyle was able to provide a little extra treatment, which he couldn't do during the evening rush when all the drivers came back in together. He gave the horse a good hose-down and thorough brushing to cool him off and only then was Groucho allowed drinking water from the spigot in his stall.

After that came half a bucket of feed, a fresh supply of legume-hay, plus apples for dessert. By the time the other horses came in, Groucho was placid, settled, and quite content with his place in the great scheme of things. It was a pleasant, easy routine for the horse, but for Doyle, it wasn't really sustainable.

For a start, it was becoming expensive. Not only was he missing one-fifth his normal income by providing a stall and labor with no recompense, he also had to assume the regular drivers' expenses in terms of horse care, like feed supplements, health checks, vaccinations, farrier fees, and countless other outlays, both small and large. Horses may look robust, but their constitution is delicate and they don't adapt easily. They have to be watched meticulously for signs of discomfort or disease, which can quickly develop into major problems.

Another factor was that the walks weren't really providing Groucho with enough exercise. Like all his species, he wasn't designed for life in a small, inner city stable. His real place was out in the wilds, seeking the horizons, galloping at full-stretch with the wind raking his mane. All he'd known throughout his life was the *calèche* but even that option was no longer available. Since he wasn't trained to be ridden, the only option was the wagon but Doyle still had a nagging doubt about that. What if he went to all the trouble of buying it and restoring it, only to have Groucho just plain refuse to pull it?

For the umpteenth time, Doyle considered just getting rid of the animal. It was close to nightfall and he was just driving back from making his deliveries in Lasalle, going over everything in his head yet again, but he kept coming to the same conclusion. He couldn't do it. It hurt him even to think about it. So failing that, he thought, what was the alternative to going ahead with his plan? There was none he could think of, none at all.

It was eight in the evening, and Louise was just finishing her shift at the bar.

Louise handled the lunch-through-afternoon crowd, while the other girl, Sylvie, came in as an overlap to team up for two hours and then continue on through midnight. This was how her boss, Clément, had organized it but the plain fact was that the business really didn't justify that level of staffing.

It was only because he preferred to avoid any of the drudge work, having always seen himself as more of the good host type, the classic neighborhood barman, pouring drinks and swapping anecdotes with the regulars.

Such a vision was, of course, totally divorced from all sense of reality but he couldn't bring himself to dismiss the fantasy, since that had been the whole purpose of buying the bar in the first place. This evening, for example, when Louise was ready to leave, there were only five customers in the whole place and one of them was only there to wait for her.

His name was Marc-André, and he was the same guy in the black shirt who'd been eyeing her the day Doyle had come in. He was also the special friend with whom she'd taken up refuge after leaving her husband. Tonight he was taking her to a rock concert and Louise had been looking forward to it for a week.

Somehow with Marc-André, life was fun again. She even found herself laughing and that was something she hadn't done in a long while. Before leaving, she took a quick time-out in the washroom to change her blouse and freshen up her makeup. That's when she heard a knock on the door. It was Clément.

"Phone," he yelled out.

She looked at herself in the mirror one last time, running a finger over her lip gloss and touching up her hair, before dashing out to take the call. Her first thought was that it might be her husband and she mentally prepared herself to cut him off the moment he became abusive—but when she picked up the receiver, she heard not her husband's voice, but Doyle's.

"Oh, hi, yeah, how's it going?" she said. She was ashamed to admit to herself that she'd almost forgotten about him.

"Hi, Louise. I hope I'm not disturbing you there."

"No . . . no, that's okay. I'm just on my way out."

"Glad I caught you, then."

"Yeah, yeah right."

"I just wanted to tell you I'm ready now."

"Ready?"

"To go."

She paused, trying to figure out what he was saying. "Go?"

"To buy it. The wagon. The one we found on the computer."

"Oh, yeah. Cool."

"I got the money. I mean, the drivers all paid me, you know, for the *calèche*."

"So you got the money, eh? That's great. Good for you."

"I was wondering, when's good for you?"

"When's good? Sorry, Doyle, what're we talking about here?"

"Like I said, to go. Don't you remember? You said to tell you when I got the money and then we'd go together, to buy the wagon."

All at once, it came back to her and she had to shrug to her friend, Marc-André, who was gesticulating, pointing to his watch on the other side of the bar. They were already late.

"Yeah, well, listen, Doyle, about that. I don't think I'll be able to make it, all right? What I'm saying is that things are a bit tight, you know how it is. Busy, busy, running around. But you know what? I just know you can handle it. You just go there and you get yourself a real good deal, okay?"

"You can't go?"

Louise looked across at Marc-André and offered an expression of apology for taking so long. "No, Doyle, that's what I'm trying to tell you. But you don't need me. Like I said, I got full confidence you're gonna go down there and do great. Better you do it, anyways, don't you think?"

"Well, I was kind of hoping . . ."

"Yeah, I know. I'm sorry, all right? It's just not convenient. Look, I gotta go. I'm running a bit late. But you let me know, all right? You call and let me know how you did."

"Okay, sure."

"Well . . . see you then, Doyle. Good luck with that, eh?"

She waited, but there was no answer, so she put the phone back in its cradle. She hesitated a moment, feeling just a little guilty. He was there for her the night she left her husband, and she appreciated that, but on the other hand, she'd helped him that same morning with the internet search. Plus, she'd given him both the horse and the *calèche* for free, so in her mind things were all square—or at least, that's how she chose to rationalize it.

At any rate, she didn't have any more time to think because Marc-André was calling out to her, anxious to get going. She flashed him a smile to say she was ready, then picked up her purse and dashed around the bar to grab his arm.

At the stable, Doyle sat with Groucho. Night was falling, the stall was darkening and neither of them moved. For Doyle, there was nothing to say or do, and he just squatted there on the old chair, gazing into space. Mowbray had gone, the other horses were all bedded down and, by now, Doyle should have been upstairs in his apartment, taking care of his own chores, yet he didn't want to go upstairs. It was empty up there. He wanted to be down here with his friend, Groucho.

Eight

The westbound highway left the island of Montréal at Ste-Anne-de-Bellevue and took a long, majestic leap across the Lake of Two Mountains, before swooping down on the northern shores of the river.

There the road split left toward Toronto, right to Ottawa, and for a few palpitating seconds, Doyle was confused. Although his van was moving at sluggish speed, he still didn't have time to search for the dog-eared map that was buried somewhere in the door pocket, and even if could have reached it, he would never have taken his eyes off the road. As a driver, he was far too cautious to try a stunt like that. But the junction was nearly upon him and he had to decide left or right, Toronto or Ottawa. He took a last minute guess and hoped he'd chosen correctly. If not, it would be a long way before he could turn back around.

His destination was a farm property on the outskirts of Brockville. They'd given him directions, which he claimed to have understood perfectly, but a hastily sketched map was no substitute for a good travel companion who could also serve as navigator.

He still didn't know the reason for Louise's decline and wondered if it was something he'd said or did, whether he'd offended her in some way, or whether it was just because she just couldn't bear to spend several hours cooped up in a van that smelled of manure.

It bothered him that he didn't know and he couldn't prevent himself thinking about it as he drove. Whatever the reason, she did at least say that she had confidence in him and he was determined to prove that such faith wasn't misplaced. It was a long, difficult drive, more than he'd foreseen, so he was relieved when he finally spotted the turnoff number up on the green sign. This much, at least, he'd managed to memorize from their telephoned instructions. Forty minutes more and he seemed to have found the right address. It wasn't a true farm like was expecting.

There were no tractors or plows, no grain silo, no free-range animals, just an old-style brick cottage and a vast wooden barn with its doors wide open. Beyond were some other small buildings, equipment sheds and so on, and beyond that several acres of gently rolling meadow, crossed by a string of electricity pylons.

The wires seemed like spider webs, glinting in the pale sunlight. He climbed out of the cab, glad to be able stretch his legs, just as a woman appeared at the door. She wasn't as old as Doyle, but her hair was gray and her face was more lined than his. She offered him a careful smile, which made the furrows appear even deeper.

"Can I help you?" she called over.

"It's about the wagon."

"Ah, yes. You must be Mr. Shaughnessy."

"O'Shaughnessy," he stressed.. "Doyle O'Shaughnessy, pleased to meet you."

"Sheila Kendall."

They reached out to shake hands, but first she removed the dirty yellow plastic gloves she was wearing, peeling them off one at a time. They looked incongruous against her thick, checkered work shirt and mud-stained blue-jeans. On her feet were black rubber boots that, because she wasn't so tall, almost came up to her knees.

"Was it you I spoke to?" he asked her. "You know, on the phone?"

"No, that would've been my sister. She helps out sometimes. Well, I expect you'd like to see it—the wagon."

"Sure."

She seemed to be friendly enough and he followed her across an open stretch of damp, springy turf toward the barn. This was nothing like the stable. The only smell in here was dust and old wood, emanating from a wide assortment of old-fashioned implements in various states of restoration.

Doyle recognized a loom, a creamer, and several ice boxes, as well as many small kitchen items scattered around a work table, such as washboards, soap buckets, cake shapers, and rolling pins. And there, to one side near the back was the wagon. The woman, Sheila Kendall, pulled a string, which clicked on a nearby light bulb. "There she is. Like I told you, she could use a bit of work on her, but she's in fair shape. I'd say road-worthy, even as she stands right now."

Doyle stood looking for a moment. "What was it used for?" He didn't know why some people got things so mixed up. In his mind, animals were "he" and "she". Things that weren't alive were always "it".

"Don't know," she replied, "could have been anything."

"Beer?"

"Might have been beer. But these wagons were used for all sorts of deliveries . . . farms, factories . . . general purpose, really. That's why they called 'em trail wagons. Easy to use and built to last. Well, you can see that for yourself. See, you got a brake system, too, good for hills. A hydraulic brake, they call it. They don't all have that."

Doyle nodded, accepting the sales talk for what it was, then went over to inspect the wagon in detail for himself. It was more or less the same as he saw in the photo on Louise's computer but a bit rougher now that he was up close. It had a bench-and-box arrangement up front, a tailgate at the back and hinged slatted sides, which made it convenient for loading.

The wheel and axle mechanisms were mounted on a painted metal frame and looked solid enough, well-greased with no rust showing through. The rubber tires, too, were in reasonable shape, but some of the wood on the sides and corner supports was chipped and splintering. Doyle ran his hands over the affected areas.

"All that takes is a bit of sanding," she said. "Should come up good as new."

Doyle wasn't fooled. He knew there'd be considerable work involved in bringing the wagon back "good as new" but he wasn't bothered by that. His main concern was that it was mechanically sound, that it would hold up on the road. If there were a real problem, he knew he could always call in Paget, whose workshop was in Lachine and who they usually used for *calèche* repair, but Doyle didn't want to have to go to that kind of expense—not just yet, anyway.

"What kinda horse you got?" asked the woman.

Doyle smiled at the thought of Groucho. "Oh, he's a bit o' this, bit o' that. Big feller, should have no problem."

"Used to hauling, is he?"

"Sure. Not a wagon like this, though. A carriage, what they call a *calèche*. His owner died. She was a friend of mine, a good friend."

"And she left the horse to you? That's nice."

"Well, she kind of left him to her daughter, but her daughter didn't want him, so she gave him to me."

"So you got saddled with a horse . . . so to speak." At this, the woman rang out a mighty peal of laughter, high pitched and unlikely, which seemed to reverberate all around the upper reaches of the barn. "Saddled with a horse," she repeated, unable to control herself. She was almost in convulsions, tears running down her face. "Get it?" She could hardly speak, hardly even stand up, she was laughing so much. "Saddled . . . with a horse."

Doyle just stood there, smiling gently to be polite. He got the joke, all right, but it just didn't seem all that funny to him.

"I'm sorry," she said, her hand tapping her chest as she tried to recover. "My God, that's a good one. Haven't laughed like that in, well, I don't know how long. I'll have to remember that one all right."

Doyle waited for her to pull herself together. "You said the price was twelve twenty-five?"

"Yep."

"You give a guarantee?" This was something he'd rehearsed in his head on the way here. He knew he was poor at negotiating, so he'd tried to go over all the major points like, for example, a guarantee.

"A guarantee for what?" she asked him.

This was not the response he was expecting. "For the wagon," he replied.

She looked at him now, the laughter having vanished. "Sorry, we're an antique store, Mr. Shaughnessy. We're not a car dealer." She got his name wrong again.

"You buy it how you see it, that's our policy," she went on. "You want to return it, you got twenty-eight days from the day you bought it, but you got to bring it back here in exactly the same condition. We decide. And if we take it back, we give you a store credit, no refund. I always like to make that perfectly clear so there's no mistake, no comeback later."

Doyle was looking a bit lost. "So, no guarantee?" he asked.

"What did I just say? You got twenty-eight days from the day you buy, understand?"

Doyle thought about it and came to the conclusion it was better than nothing. If they were trying to cheat him about the wagon's condition, they wouldn't even offer that, so he was mildly satisfied. "Yes, I understand," he told her.

"Good, 'cause honesty's the best policy, that's what I always say. Open and upfront, that way no misunderstandings, nobody gets upset, right?"

Doyle could see how this woman could be tough. She didn't really look tough, not like Jacqueline, but the strength was there nonetheless. And he didn't mind the terms, as long as they were clear like she said. He had no issue with things being clear.

"I have twelve hundred, cash," he told her.

She shifted her head a little to one side, as if trying to size him up, and thought for several seconds before answering. "Cash, you say?"

"Yes."

"Is that real cash or a check made to cash?"

"Real cash."

"You got the money with you? Here and now?"

It was obvious to Doyle that many people must have gone there and tried to play games when it came to payment. He could imagine that happening very easily. "Here and now," he replied.

She thought about it some more. Then she said:, "Tell you what, you give me cash on the table and you take it with you now . . . it's yours for twelve." But she couldn't help adding, "Same terms and conditions."

Doyle nodded. "Long as you can help me hitch it to the van."

"You got some chains?"

"Sure."

"Okay, I'll give my son a call, he'll fix you up. Come on over to the house."

Sixty minutes and a final handshake later, Doyle was back in the van, negotiating his way very carefully back onto the road, with the wagon in tow. However slowly he drove getting here, he'd have to drive at half the speed on the way back.

The only problem he encountered was when he pulled in just before the highway to check everything was still in place, and an Ontario police cruiser stopped by to ask a few questions and check his permit. It was a little nerve-wracking, but the officer was re-laxed, a man just doing his job. Said he didn't want to be called to any accidents concerning a spilled wagon. Doyle nodded his thanks and gave the officer a thumbs-up before resuming his journey.

All in all, it had been a good day. Louise had told him she had confidence in his abilities and Doyle felt he'd proved his worth on that score. He'd bought the wagon at the price he wanted, the same amount he'd gotten for the *calèche,* so he figured he was all square on that score, and he didn't even need to sell the van if he didn't want to. He could keep it as a convenience, to run errands and what-have-you, or even for deliveries on extreme weather days when the horse wasn't allowed to go out.

It took over five hours to get home from Ontario that evening, fol-lowing his headlights into the darkening eastern sky. He was tired and hungry, but in general, he was well satisfied with the state of affairs—until he got back to the stable.

Some of the lights were on, and he recognized the vet's car parked outside. He jumped down out of the van gripped with sudden anxi-ety. His first thought was Groucho.

Nine

oyle parked the van with the trailer still attached and half-ran inside, fearing what he might see. First thing, he went right over to Groucho's stall, but the big horse was just standing there placidly, eyes half closed. Slightly out of breath, Doyle put his hands on his knees and gave out with a sigh.

In fact, the activity was all over on the other side. There, Bertrand, Mowbray, and the vet were grouped around the gray mare, Ange, in the isolated box stall that Doyle kept for sick animals. The vet was crouching down next to her head while Bertrand was leaning over, hands on his knees. Mowbray was just standing at the back, looking helpless.

"What happened?" asked Doyle as he hurried over.

All three looked up, but it was Mowbray who bothered to answer.

"She got bit by a dog."

"Where?"

"Dunno. In the street somewhere."

"No, I mean where'd the dog bite her? Which part?"

"Oh yeah, on the back leg, see? Right there.

Doyle walked up beside Bertrand and looked down at the animal. Her eyes were open, but her head was down and she appeared to be in some difficulty. A sheen of sweat glistened on her body and neck. "How bad is it?" Doyle asked.

Bertrand's eyes didn't stray from his horse. "Bite's not too bad. Some blood, but nothing serious. I put some Javex, first thing I did, just in case the dog might have had some infection."

"How'd it happen?"

"Couldn't avoid it. Was over on William Street—damn thing came out of nowhere, like he was crazy or something, barking and growling. Chased us halfway down the street, before he got himself caught under her legs. Got kicked bad."

"Dead?"

"Cried a lot. Didn't see him after that. Must have run off somewheres." Bertrand looked down at the horse. "Was more concerned about her."

"She got back all right, though."

"Didn't think it was too bad. She even took food and water, but then she just lay down. That's when I called Sauvé. Hasn't moved much since."

"She'll be okay. She's strong."

Bertrand didn't answer, he just pushed his straw cowboy hat farther to the back of his head. The vet stood up stiffly. He was a heavy-set, middle-aged man with spectacles and a pock-marked face.

"I gave her antibiotics," he said to Bertrand in French. His voice was as rough as his complexion. "No adverse reaction. We'll see what's happening in a few hours." Then he added: "For the time being, there's nothing to do. Keep the dressing on, don't let her chew it. You may need to tie her head . . . just a halter rope, nothing else." He stretched a little, then packed up his bag, preparing to leave.

"You'll come back in the morning?"

"If necessary."

"How about an emergency?"

The vet took off his spectacles, put them into his top pocket, and glanced at Bertrand with the expression of a man who suffers neither fools, nor overly anxious animal owners. "D'you know how a phone works?" he asked with some scorn. With that, he left, making his way out with his arthritic limp.

Bertrand turned to Doyle, who just shrugged. Both of them knew Sauvé of old. The man was a good vet but he had his ways.

They walked back over to the stall. "Where's her blanket?" asked Doyle.

It was as if Bertrand was still in shock about all this, as if he wasn't really thinking straight. "Blanket's a good idea," he said and set about fetching the one he kept in the *calèche*.

"Can I go now?" This was Mowbray.

Doyle nodded. "Appreciate you staying," he replied.

After another look at Ange, he went over to see Groucho, who lowered his head as Doyle approached. Doyle stroked his nose. "Got a present for you," he said very softly. "Well, I guess it's really more for both of us. I'll show you in the morning, all right? Hope you like it."

Doyle waited until Bertrand returned with the blanket, then went to get something to eat. He would have liked to turn in—he was wiped—but he didn't have the heart to leave Bertrand alone in the stall, so he brought toasted cheese sandwiches back for both of them, plus two mugs of coffee, balancing it all on a square piece of wood that served as a tray.

Bertrand accepted the kindness gratefully but didn't say anything and for the rest of the night, they both sat there next to Ange without speaking very much at all. The horses were quiet, too, and even Groucho remained tranquil, despite the late night fuss, an instinctive sensibility for the sick mare.

At one point, a mouse emerged from the straw, scurried across the floor, and disappeared into the darkness, but neither of the men moved. They just watched it with no expression. Although Doyle did his best to control the rodent population, setting his traps with their favorite peanut butter, he could never totally get rid of them.

In a working stable, it just wasn't possible. The real solution was a cat and he'd actually had one for a while, a tomcat he called Ginger because of the color, rescued him from death row at the animal society, but the cat wandered off one night and failed to return. Doyle had never bothered with another.

The night passed slowly, hour by hour, with little other disturbance. It was like sitting at the bedside of a sick relative when the clinic staff had gone off duty and all that remained was the darkness and the worry. They were watching for a sign, any sign, that the fever had broken, that Sauvé's drugs were doing their work.

As he waited, Doyle thought about Jacqueline, about the times he'd spent with her, and about Louise, too. Why didn't she come with him when she'd said she would? He wasn't upset with her, he just wanted to understand. He briefly considered asking Bertrand's opinion but he knew before he even opened his mouth that it wouldn't work. The man wasn't exactly easy to talk to at the best of times, and this certainly wasn't the moment to see if they could break the ice in such a manner. As a result, Doyle kept his thoughts to himself and the long silence was maintained.

Finally, it was close to dawn when Ange took them both by surprise. She raised her head as far as her neck would allow in an effort to pull herself up. The two men also stirred themselves.

"I think we should get her some water," said Doyle, rubbing his eyes with his knuckles. "Maybe that's what she wants."

It was Bertrand who got up to fill a bucket from the hose. When he returned, he placed it in its usual position in the stall, in the center of an old tire so it wouldn't spill. Then he stood back and watched. It was clear that Ange had scented it. Once, twice, she tried to get to her feet, and the third time she almost made it before lying back down, out of energy.

They thought she'd given up but a few seconds later she proved them wrong. This time, she managed enough momentum to get her hooves under her and although she was a bit wobbly, she shook her head, threw off the blanket and managed to take the few necessary paces over to the bucket.

Bertrand was excited as all hell, elbowing Doyle as Ange dunked her nose and began to drink. He took a cloth and began wiping down her neck and withers, her back and sides, finally her haunches.

"Told you she was strong," said Doyle. "Lotta heart, that horse."

Doyle managed to sleep for an hour or so, but anyone who keeps animals knows the morning necessities can't wait, so he was up at an early hour as usual, preparing the horses for the new workday.

It was a little easier today because there were only three heading out: Marie-Josée's cream-gray, Boréal; Frank's young chestnut, Marengo, which was the name of Napoleon's horse and therefore a nice story for the customers; and Jean-Claude's bay mare, Roxy Baby.

The two that stayed were Groucho, already used to his altered routine, and Ange, who was given the time to get back to full health. Bertrand knew it might take a couple of days for that to happen but he was ready to wait as long as needed. He said he had some people to go visit on the nearby Mohawk reserve at Kahnawake, people he hadn't seen in a long time, so he thought he may as well use the opportunity. A quick handshake and a slight tip of the hat was the only thanks he gave Doyle before he sped off, a cloud of exhaust emanating from his patched-up truck.

Once everyone had gone and Mowbray had been given his tasks for the morning, Doyle was left alone, wondering what to do. It wasn't that he didn't have anything on his agenda, it was that he had too much. The envelopes were beginning to stack up on his desk, important bills and notices mixed in with all the junk mail, but without Jacqueline, going through them would be a major chore and he couldn't face it, not yet. Mostly what he wanted to do was flop down for a little extra shuteye, but sleeping during daylight hours just wasn't his way. Besides, he had a newly purchased wagon outside and he was kind of interested to see how Groucho would react to it.

Of course, there was no reaction, none whatsoever. Groucho was far too eager to go out for his walk. "I drive all that way to buy us a nice gift and you turn your nose up. What kind of attitude is that? I think you're spoiled, that's what I think."

But later, after the walk and after Doyle had made his delivery to Lasalle in the van, he stopped off at the new hardware center, the large American place they'd just opened on St-Jacques. He had an idea. Since he had to sand, paint, and varnish the wagon anyway, he thought, why not do it up in the same white and gold colors as Jacqueline's *calèche*? That way it would look familiar to the horse and wouldn't feel that strange.

The store was far larger than Doyle expected, the size of several aircraft hangars, and full of a million things which interested him immensely. They had all kinds of gizmos for home renovation and gardening and camping and barbeques and so many other activities he'd never personally enjoyed but had seen often enough on TV ads.

They had a whole section just for outdoor children's equipment, too, and it made him stand and wonder for a minute what he might have missed in life by not having kids, or even a wife for that matter. He could have been married to Vivian by now, or Viv as he'd called her, but he wouldn't give up the horses: wouldn't or couldn't, one or the other. Even now, he wasn't sure. He allowed himself the gentlest of sighs, no more than an exhale of breath, but he'd made his choice and it was too late for regrets.

All such thoughts were banished when he managed to catch the attention of a female assistant in an orange apron that bore the store's name, a young woman with a moon-shaped face and a helpful disposition. Yes, she said, she'd be more than happy to assist him if he could describe the project he was about to undertake.

The following day, after completing his main morning chores, he got started. To be more accurate, he got himself ready to start, which meant first deciding on a place to do the actual work.

He just about had the space to do it inside in the stable but if he did that, the horses might not appreciate the toxic smell of paint and varnish. However, if he went outside, the weather might interrupt and spoil the various applications. In the end, he chose an exterior spot just behind the building and fashioned a large plastic tarpaulin above it like a canopy, with two of the corners nailed into wooden window frames and the other two tied by rope to trees.

It was a rough solution, but it would be sufficient to protect the work from a direct shower. The only problem would be a combination of high wind and driving rain that blew in from the sides but he'd just have to take that chance. With good conditions, he estimated a week of work. After a couple of hours setting up, it was time for Groucho's walk, but Doyle had yet another idea. Not only would he paint the wagon the same colors as the *calèche*, he would also let Groucho watch him do it. His notion was to let the horse get used to the new conveyance by witnessing the work first hand.

Once they returned to the stable, Doyle first let Groucho eat his fill while he had his own lunch. Then, instead of leaving him to snooze in the stall, he led Groucho back outside and tied him loosely to a drain pipe in full view of the set-up. This concept was good for another reason too. It meant that Doyle would have another creature to talk to while he labored and Groucho could continue to have the companionship he still craved.

"Okay, so we gotta start by sanding it all down, make everything smooth. After that I'm gonna fill in the cracks with wood filler, let that dry. Then we got undercoat, we got one, maybe two main coats, then the fancy work, then the varnish. And you're gonna watch, see that I do it right, okay? You can be the foreman. Now, what I'm gonna start with is this little sanding machine here I just bought. It's a bit noisy but you'll get used to that . . . I hope. You ready now? Okay, boss? So here we go."

Doyle was half-afraid that Groucho might object to the sound when he switched it on, but although the animal's ears twitched back and forth a few times, he remained calm. There wasn't even so much as a stomp of his hoof, which made Doyle feel a certain optimism about what he was doing. He even began to sing to himself as he worked, something he hadn't done in a while.

As a teen, he'd learned to render a version of "Irish Eyes" that could make some of his father's old boyo pals well up, especially after they'd sunk a few dark beers, but he didn't sing that now. He wasn't too fond of all that Irish heritage nonsense, leprechaun stuff he called it, far too sentimental for his taste, so he just hummed some melody he'd heard recently on the radio. He didn't know where it was from or who the singer was but for some reason, it had stuck in his head. Toward the end of the afternoon, Bertrand Thibodeau reappeared and after checking on his mare, came out to gaze at Doyle's handiwork.

"What you wanna do is rebuild it," he said with his hands in his pockets. "You'll never get that cart back the way it was, you don't rebuild it."

Doyle wasn't too bothered by the criticism. He just kept on working. "You think?" he asked.

"Wouldn't take long, not if you know what you're doing."

Doyle just nodded. He didn't want a debate or even a discussion. He just wanted to get on with it. In his mind, he wasn't restoring an antique *calèche*, he was merely fixing up a trail wagon in order to haul manure. "Will you be taking Ange out tomorrow?" he asked. Back to practicalities.

Bertrand shrugged. "We'll see how she is in the morning."

"You want me to get her ready?"

Bertrand couldn't seem to decide, so he just walked back over to his truck with Doyle still waiting for an answer.

"You hear me?" Doyle called after him.

Bertrand climbed in and rested his elbow on the wound down window. "We'll see how she is," he repeated.

It answered nothing but that was the problem dealing with Bertrand. The man was basically okay, cared for his horse and paid his rent, but it was like he lived in a bubble of his own. Why the other drivers had chosen him to negotiate for the *calèche* was a complete mystery but they had and somehow, inexplicably, it had worked out fine.

Sometimes, for Doyle, it was a lot easier to understand horses than humans.

Ten

A week later came the moment of truth for Doyle, for Groucho, and for all the others who used the stable. All had noted the steady progress with the wagon and all had their opinions as to whether Doyle's method was going to work: painting it up in the colors of Jacqueline's *calèche* and allowing the horse to watch so he could get used to it.

"You won't fool him." This had been the comment of Jean-Claude.

"Might work, if you bribe him." This was Marie-Josée.

"Maybe, maybe not." This was Frank's contribution.

"I doubt it." This was Bertrand, for whom no horse could ever be as good or as smart as his Ange.

Whatever their various predictions, the drivers all gathered around on the day of the try-out, waiting to witness the outcome. It was a pleasant morning, with an early sun filtering through the leaves, most of which had graduated from a brief stint as bright orange to their present state of rusty brown.

Eventually, they would all carpet the compound. The last to join the group was Mowbray, who just stood there in the back, leaning on his shovel, watching the proceedings passively as if it were some reality show put on for his amusement.

Doyle had already been out at dawn to remove the tarpaulin and now he was ready to lead Groucho out in front of the audience, a proud moment. It was Jean-Claude who began the applause, taken up by Frank and Marie-Josée. Bertrand kept his hands in his pockets, still hedging his bets but well prepared to enjoy the spectacle.

The wagon was shining with its fresh coat of bright white paint, with small touches of gold trim just like on the *calèche*. Doyle had applied more grease to the axle mechanism and had even washed the tires. It was a thorough job and he was pleased with his efforts, despite Bertrand's original criticism of how he should go about it. He knew well enough that to make it perfect, he should have done more carpentry but, at school, wood shop had never been a strong suit of his. He was okay to fix things up, like shelves, cupboards, and even old wagons, but he was no fine craftsman and he knew it. At that particular moment, though, it didn't matter. All he cared about was how well Groucho would take to it.

The first step was to lead the horse gently into the right position so he could haul on the brichen harness: first Groucho's massive collar, then the hame which sat over it. After that he fastened up the array of straps—hame, belly, pole, quarter, and breast, always in that order. Then he put on the bridle and bit, and flicked out the mane so it hung free and smooth. Last, he strung through the driving lines. After that, he hitched the horse up to the wagon by fitting the shafts into the loops, hooking the tug into the whippletree and attaching the holdback strap. So far, so good. No problems at all. Groucho was cooperating and Doyle fed him a handful of sugar cubes as a reward, which the horse snatched up greedily.

"Ever try carrots?" asked Marie-Josée.

"He likes sugar," replied Doyle. "That's what Jacqueline gave him."

"Not good for his teeth."

Doyle knew he was being tested. As it happened, he shared the same feeling about the sugar and had already replaced some of Groucho's supply by adding more apples to compensate. But he was reluctant to continue the argument, simply because it involved Jacqueline's way of doing things and was therefore none of Marie-Josée's business.

"His teeth are fine," Doyle replied dryly, as if to say that was the end of it.

He finished adjusting all the straps, offered more sugar, and then stood back to inspect. Groucho was now hitched to the wagon and standing patiently as he sucked on his treat.

"You gonna take him out now?" Frank asked him. His name was short for François but nobody had called him that in living memory.

"Sure," said Doyle.

"Got a permit?" Jean-Claude asked him.

"Don't need it for a wagon. No passengers."

"You need insurance though. You gotta have insurance."

"I know," replied Doyle, as he climbed up on to the wagon's bench. Yesterday he'd taken the trouble to call up the company that insured his van, explained what he needed, and they'd given him a contract extension to cover it right there on the phone. When he was settled, he gave a quick look around at the faces watching him. Then he took up the lines, gave them a brief shake the way he'd seen Jacqueline do it and repeated her phrase with exactly the same inflexion. *"Allons-y!"* Let's go!

The horse didn't move.

Doyle did the same thing again. *"Allons-y*, Groucho!" He got the same result. He heard some comment from the spectators, so he tried a third time. Nothing. Just like on that very first day after the funeral.

By now there was some quiet snickering and Doyle was beginning to feel embarrassed, so he climbed down and said as casually as he could, "I'll try a bit later."

"Good luck with that," said Jean-Claude and the rest of them laughed before slowly dispersing toward the stable. They had their own horses to hitch up. Mowbray, too, went back to work, leaving Doyle alone with Groucho.

"Thanks a lot," said Doyle harshly, before he realized he was being both stupid and unreasonable. None of this was the horse's fault. He went up front and stroked the animal's nose but kept the sugar in his pocket. Punishment by omission. Maybe Groucho would figure it out.

Then Doyle thought of something. "You know what? We should just take a walk first, get you used to it, what d'you say to that, eh? Would that be a better plan? Just a little walk."

He took hold of the face strap, just the same as he did every day and urged the animal forward. Sure enough, the horse moved forward as usual, only this time, he hauled the wagon behind him.

Doyle led him around the building, through the compound and out on to the street. No problem at all. Doyle could hardly believe it and kind of wished the drivers were around to see it.

"Now we're talking," he said softly. "That's not so bad, is it? Don't know what all that fuss was about before. Did you have to do that in front of everybody? Showed yourself up as well as me, y'know. What gets into your head, eh? You silly horse."

They took about half their usual walk, just enough for Groucho to get used to the wagon and its relative weight, which Doyle figured was about on a par with the *calèche*. It wasn't as long or as wide, but it had a sturdier construction. Yet it somehow seemed easier for the horse because the rubber tires made the ride smoother across the cracks and the potholes than those large wooden-spoked wheels.

One person they met along the way was Mowbray's father, Elliott, the Jamaican, who was just getting into his car, an eight-foot wide rust heap that had once been the pride of Detroit.

"Hey, man, nice wheels," said Elliott in that lilting accent of his. He was a tall, gangly individual who always wore rings on his fingers and another in his ear. His hair, which had once upon a time sported Rasta beads, was now close-cropped and graying a little at the temples.

"Thanks," said Doyle.

"Why don't you get on it?"

"Trying to get the horse used to it first."

"Lotta effort. What you goin' to carry?"

"Manure, I hope."

"Makes sense. Horse carryin' its own manure."

At this, Elliott laughed, showing those long white teeth, but Doyle just nodded. He recalled that Louise had said something similar.

"How's our boy doin'?" asked Elliott. "Stayin' outa trouble?" He was talking about his son, Mowbray.

"Sure. Doing fine."

"Workin' hard?"

"He tries."

"Not smokin' the weed too much?"

"I don't know." Doyle didn't want to get Mowbray into any trouble.

"Well, if you see him doin' that, you just give 'im a clip around the ear. Say it's from me, all right? No, say it's from his mother. I swear that boy's more scared of her than he ever was of me." Another big laugh.

Before Doyle could respond, Elliott was sliding into his car. When he started up the engine, it blew out exhaust and made a tinny, rattling noise before pulling away, reminding Doyle of his own van and making him wonder yet again if he was doing the right thing with the horse and wagon.

At certain points along the route, Doyle had thought about getting up on the bench while Groucho seemed to be in the mood but each time he decided against it. He just didn't want to overdo it on the first day.

Besides, he wanted the outing to be remembered by the horse as a positive experience. If he tried to drive the wagon and failed, it might only serve to intensify the rejection and neither he nor Groucho would feel good about that. He therefore returned to the stable exactly as he had left: on foot.

When he arrived, Mowbray helped him unhitch the wagon and unfasten the harness before leading the horse back inside to be groomed. Let him get settled today, thought Doyle, try again tomorrow.

Doyle's habit was to wake before dawn. He liked the early hours, liked to be up and about, but the previous day, he went out too early and made a fool of himself. He didn't want to make the same mistake today. Instead he waited until all the drivers had left, even Bertrand, before leading Groucho out to where the wagon was parked.

"You gonna try again?" Mowbray asked him.

"Might as well."

"Think it'll work?"

"Nothing to lose," said Doyle. "Get that other side, will you?"

Together, they attached Groucho to the wagon but before Doyle climbed up, he had a quiet word with the horse. "Now, you gonna be okay today? Remember the walk we had yesterday? Well, this is no different, except I'll be up back of you, all right? We won't canter, nothing like that. Just a walk."

With that, he rubbed the horse's muzzle, patted his neck and his flanks, then got up on the bench. A quick flick of the lines, an encouraging word . . . and nothing. The horse wouldn't move. He just stood there like before, his hooves planted firmly on the ground.

"What's going on now?" Doyle asked him. "We walked yesterday all right, didn't we? Why not today? What the devil gets into you? Come on, let's go, let's go! *Allons-y!*"

There was no response, just a twitch of the ears, which suggested that Groucho was hearing him all right. He just didn't want to budge. For Doyle, it was frustrating in the extreme and he leaned on his knees with a major sigh. He looked at Mowbray and shook his head.

He had no idea what else to do, except maybe give up the whole idea. Maybe he'd call Louise, advertise the wagon on the computer, same way he'd bought it. Maybe he could get his money back somehow. He clambered down from the bench and decided he'd go make himself coffee. After that, he'd try one last time before calling it quits.

Twenty minutes later, he was back outside, a look of deep determination on his face. "Okay, Groucho, this is it, all right? Put up or shut up." It was an expression his father had used. He strode over to the wagon but before he could mount up, he heard Mowbray's voice behind him.

"It's the blinders."

Doyle paused, then turned to look at him. "What's the blinders?"

"You need to take 'em off."

Doyle just shook his head. He had no idea what the kid was talking about, much less make any sense of it. He couldn't remember Mowbray ever having uttered a word of advice in the past—or saying much of anything, for that matter.

"No, I mean it, man," said Mowbray. "I been watchin'."

"Okay, so you been watching, so what?"

"He wanna see you. He can't see you wi' the blinders."

Now it began to dawn on Doyle and he took a step back from the wagon. First he eyed Groucho, then looked back at Mowbray. "You think?"

"That horse loves you, man. He just wanna see you is all."

"But he's always worn blinders. All the horses wear blinders."

Mowbray had nothing more to add and just shrugged his slim shoulders. He'd said his piece, so it was up to Doyle to decide what to do.

But Doyle was locked in deep thought. It was a strange suggestion but he chose to consider it because he didn't know what else to try. Putting blinders on a horse was an accepted practice because it made sense and it worked. When a big animal is out in traffic, with distractions on all sides, he needs to stay focused on the road ahead. Unusual sights and sounds can surprise a horse and then anything can happen. And with passengers on board, it could even be perilous. But that was the difference, Doyle realized, right there. On the wagon there'd be no passengers, so less of a risk.

"Let's give it a go," he said eventually.

With Mowbray assisting, Doyle unfastened the bridle, prized off the blinders and then reattached the equipment.

"You think this'll work, eh?"

Mowbray's expression suggested he had no idea if it would work or not. He'd spotted something and had given it voice, that's all. It was a rare enough occurrence. It certainly didn't mean he was about to become talkative.

"Okay," said Doyle, "let's see, shall we?" He turned to the horse: "Now, I'm standing right here, can you see me? Yeah? You sure? Take a good look. Mowbray thinks you need to see me, so here I am, large as life and twice as ugly, you got that? You with me? All right, so now I'm gonna walk very slowly over here, like this ..."

He took a few slow, careful steps toward the wagon. "Now I'm gonna mount up. You watching, Groucho? This is me. It's nobody else. And I'm just gonna keep talking, so you're sure it's me. See, I'm getting up ..." Doyle heaved himself on to the bench. "So now I'm here, I'm just gonna pick up the lines like this. A quick flick and ..."

The horse put one foot forward, then another. Doyle couldn't believe it, and he beamed over at Mowbray, giving him a huge thumbs up. A slight adjustment in direction and Groucho was on his way around the building, walking cautiously but very much underway.

Mowbray followed on foot around to the other side of the building but there were no worries. Once Groucho saw the compound gates, he wanted to go, to get out on the street, and even though he was attached to a conveyance for the first time in a while, it was like he'd been given his freedom. He wanted to break into a trot, even in the small stretch of roadway outside the stable building.

"Whoa, now," said Doyle, easing back on the lines just a tad. "Plenty of time for that. Let's just take it nice and slow for now. We'll get up some speed a little later, all right?"

He was still concerned about a big horse like Groucho out on the street without blinders but he tried to put that to one side in the general joy of being out there, of being up on the bench and moving at last. And it had all been a result of Mowbray's insight. The kid was learning, thought Doyle, and that was worth a bonus of anyone's money.

Eleven

The first wagon delivery was set for Sunday morning, when there would be less traffic about. Normally, with the van, Doyle delivered in the afternoons but he felt that the horse would be fresher and more enthusiastic if the trip coincided with the time for his daily exercise.

To figure out the payload, he sat down purposefully at his desk and used the calculator just the way Jacqueline had showed him. He felt he had something of a flair for math, certainly compared to most other office chores, and he tackled the problem with gusto, determined not to get up and make supper until he'd solved it, his own form of self-discipline.

First he tore a blank sheet of lined paper from a school exercise book and turned it sideways. On it he drew in pencil, a line drawing of a *calèche* and next to it, another of the wagon. When he'd done, he looked at it and decided not bad. No work of art, but not bad. Then he put an equals sign between them, which was his way of showing that the weight of the *calèche* and the wagon were, by his estimate, roughly the same.

Although the wagon was smaller in size, its metal chassis added some weight. After that, he worked out the kind of payload Groucho would normally be used to hauling on the *calèche*: five people, including Jacqueline at, say, a hundred and fifty pounds each, which according to the calculator totaled seven-fifty. Obviously, some people were far heavier, but there were often children on board, so the amount pretty much worked out on average.

He carefully wrote down the number 750 under the *calèche*, then under the wagon. If Groucho could carry the weight on one, he could carry it on the other. Then came the hard part. He had to estimate how much each bag of manure weighed, which he guessed at fifteen pounds, judging by how hard it was to lift. This, too, he wrote down, but only under the wagon. He stared at this for a while, just like he used to stare at the exam papers in school. It wasn't a feeling he enjoyed.

At such time his brain often used to freeze, so this time he had to force himself to concentrate. It took a few minutes of hard thought but he refused to give up. He had no intention of asking anyone for help. Then, all of a sudden, something flashed in his brain and he realized it was easy. It was like a revelation. All he had to do was divide seven hundred fifty pounds by fifteen pounds and that would give him the number of bags that Groucho would be able to haul on each trip.

Excitedly, he pushed the buttons on the calculator with his stubby, working man's fingertip: 750÷15= . . . It came up with a number that surprised him: 50. He stared at it. Fifty bags! It was hard to believe. He did the calculation again, just to make sure he hadn't made an error. No, it was fifty bags and he wrote that down triumphantly under the wagon, drawing a big circle around it. It meant that Groucho would easily be able to haul up to fifty bags on any given trip, which in fact was far more than he'd ever be required to do. The stable just didn't produce that much manure.

Doyle sat back in his chair and looked at the piece of paper, well pleased. He could now enjoy his supper, and he cooked up half a dozen beef sausages on a stack of fried bread, one of his favorite meals, just to celebrate.

Next item on the agenda was to plan a route that would make it as easy as possible for the animal, one with no major hills or busy junctions, and no place where there might be too much congestion. As he ate, he gazed at his old, creased map of the area that was spread out by the side of his plate, supported at the back by the ketchup bottle. After studying the possibilities for several minutes, he decided that the simplest, most direct route would be the best.

From the Pointe, he'd go west along Wellington, directly past the bar where Jacqueline once drank—and also where Louise still worked, although he knew she wouldn't be there in the mornings—

then under the elevated highway to Verdun, near where they'd held Jacqueline's funeral service, all the way down to Boulevard Lasalle on the river front. From there, it was just another mile or so to the gardening center. A route like that would make each journey full of memories, almost poetic in a way, and he wondered if the horse would feel it too.

But before setting out, Doyle felt he had something to prove. As shy as he was, he couldn't let the moment pass without informing the drivers that this was his first trip, a kind of maiden voyage. As a result, they duly assembled in front of the building and this time there was no jeering. This time, everything went according to plan. Groucho was in the mood to go and Doyle was able to drive out to the sound of their applause and Frank's two-fingered whistle.

After all that effort, it was a proud moment, and he couldn't resist a regal wave goodbye over his shoulder, just like the Queen of England leaving Buckingham Palace.

"It's all right, it's just a couple of bikes. Just a bit noisy, that's all. They're not gonna hurt you." Doyle glanced at the Hell's Angels riders who were drawn up next to him at the lights and the one with the heavy beard glanced back. Their machines glistened with silvered chrome, and their engines rose to a throaty roar each time they revved. Groucho had already begun to stomp his foot, a bad sign. It was up to Doyle now to keep talking to the horse, even with all the noise, not only to reassure him but also to let him know that he, Doyle, was still there, a voice of calm amidst the rumbling menace.

"Come on now, Groucho, keep your hair on, they'll be gone soon."

In fact, this incident was exactly why conveyance drivers liked their horses to wear blinders: in order to prevent the inevitable information overload that would present itself. But so far, Doyle was glad to see that Groucho was keeping his renowned temper under control. He knew perfectly well how much courage it took for the horse to subdue his natural instinct to panic. Then, in an instant, the light had changed, the bikes disappeared into the distance and both horse and driver were able to complete the journey down to Lasalle in a suitably sedate manner.

When they reached the boulevard, Doyle reined in a little and Groucho obediently came to a standstill near the sidewalk. Here, just beyond a road-side park, was the broad St. Lawrence and beyond that, in the far distance, was the ship canal that took the big lakers upriver past the Lachine Rapids. By squinting, Doyle could just about make out a red and white funnel passing through, but he hadn't stopped there for the view. He descended from the bench and walked up to Groucho, speaking to him gently all the time.

"Well, now, that wasn't so bad, was it?" He rubbed the horse's nose and gave him a handful of sugar, a reward for having come this far. "Maybe we'll use this as a regular place to give you a break, how about that? It's not far from here, so you can trot the rest of the way if you like. You up to it? Sure you are. Long time since you did exercise like this, right? How's it feel? Good, or a bit stiff? Y'know, some mornings I feel the same way, believe me. We're both getting on, you and me, almost ready for the scrap heap, some would say. But not just yet, eh? Not just yet. We still got a ways to go, am I right? What d'you say?"

Once they were underway again, Doyle loosened the lines a little and urged the horse forward. It didn't take much before Groucho launched into a racy trot, with the juice from the sugar still oozing from his mouth and the breeze from the river flicking at his blond mane. As for Doyle, up on the bench, a big grin had spread across his face. He couldn't help it. This was the happiest he'd been in a while.

Being Sunday, the Clifford H. Sullivan Gardening Center was gearing up for one of their biggest days of the early fall season. The annual clear-out had just started and although it was still only mid-morning, the crowds had begun to gather and the car park was already half-full when Doyle and Groucho arrived.

Immediately, heads turned, children's hands pointed and smiles broadened. Everybody, it seemed, loved a big old horse and Doyle had to pull up for a few moments because of the attention. People began to crowd around but, far from getting upset or angry, Groucho actually seemed to enjoy the experience, a natural ham, nodding his head and graciously allowing parents to hold their offspring aloft and pet him.

Eventually, Doyle was obligated to dismount and lead the horse inside the center by hand. As he did so, he did his best to answer the many questions that came at him. What's his name? Is he yours?

How old is he? Where does he live? What does he eat? What's on the wagon? Then somebody who hadn't heard the first reply asked again, What's his name?

Doyle took it all in his stride, coping with it like a Hollywood celebrity arriving at a press conference to announce a new movie. He had his deliveries to make, however, and he couldn't bask in it for too long. He had a job to do.

The center was really nothing more than a vast display of plants and trees anchored by a haphazard wooden structure that housed all manner of tools and accessories, as well as checkout counters and staff facilities. But what people really came for was the exterior show: the countless varieties on offer and their resplendent colors.

Among the current seasonal buys were chrysanthemums in yellow and ochre, begonias in brilliant crimson and gold, and an impressive display of large-diameter hydrangeas in subtle shades of pink and mauve.

For the advanced planners, there were also spring bulbs: a rainbow selection of tulips and jonquils and crocus and lilium, with bright photographs to illustrate what they'd look like next May. Behind the flowers were the shrubs, a dense thicket of spirea, brunerra, hosta, and so many more, spanning the entire green and green-blue spectrum from a pale icy hue all the way to the darkest shades of spruce.

Doyle always enjoyed coming here just for the experience, just to see a little nature and inhale the scents, even though the contribution he carried was a different kind of fragrance. Today he'd brought twenty sacks and, after savoring the glorious panorama for a minute or so, became dutifully occupied in unloading them.

To one side was a broad path marked *private* and it was here that he led Groucho with the wagon. This was a unique facility, the only one like it in the city, where the manure sacks he brought were emptied out, shoveled by hand into a mound of soil, mixed with natural sphagnum as a drying agent and then repackaged in smaller five pound bags, made of stiff paper and bearing the center's name.

"Finest Quality Horse Manure," read the label in both English and French. Underneath, in smaller type, were the words: "Guaranteed 100% Organic". This was considered highly important by the center's prime clientele, defined by the management as amateur horticulturalists with high disposable income. These bags were then sealed with wire and wheeled over by small cart to the center, where they were stacked on shelves, ready for customers to carry away in their car trunks.

Doyle had been bringing his manure here for over thirty years now, an arrangement he had originally made with the current owner's father, the man who'd founded the center, Cliffy Sullivan.

If ever Doyle had an old pal in the traditional sense, it was Cliffy, whom he'd met in an amateur boxing gym just after leaving school. Doyle himself wasn't much of a fighter but he went there because he was thin as a youngster and his father felt he had to toughen up. Despite being the same age, Cliffy was at a whole other level, a promising welterweight prospect.

Back in those days, boxing was one of the tickets out of the gutter, especially for those with green blood in their veins. While the local French kids dreamed of playoff hockey, the Irish aspiration was always a championship bout with a raucous, sell-out crowd, full of businessmen and mobsters and glamorous women, all placing cash bets on the local boy.

For some reason, Cliffy Sullivan took a shine to the more modest Doyle, recognizing an alter ego of sorts, and kind of taking him under his wing in the rough world they inhabited. For his part, Doyle was able to watch Cliff sparring and give him some good pointers, because although he had neither the body strength nor the talent to compete, he was a keen observer and knew the sport well enough.

The strange thing was that Cliff actually listened to Doyle, even more than to his trainer, a slob of a man who had a whole gym full of young hopefuls to coach and didn't care too much about any one of them.

Unfortunately, Cliffy's boxing career ended with a bad mauling he took from an American, a street-tough Hispanic from Miami who was looking to build his reputation. Yet Cliffy was an entrepreneur at heart and was already making plans for the money he'd earned, even while he was still in hospital, having his ribs mended and his jaw put back together. The only reason he chose gardening was because he liked flowers, simple as that.

He'd always been a dandy dresser, especially when he went into town after his more successful bouts, and he invariably wore a bloom in his lapel, either a rose or a carnation, usually red in color. His locker-room excuse was that the ladies loved it, the idea of a tough man with a sensitive nature, but the truth was that Cliffy genuinely appreciated flowers, an unlikely quirk, and he had begun reading up on them while recuperating.

By the time Cliffy had gotten around to serious business plans, Doyle had already taken over the stable from his dad, so when the two met up again, it was natural that they would look for ways to work together. It was in a bar one evening that they came up with the idea of manure.

"Here's to the smell of manure . . . and to the smell of money!" said Cliffy in a toast, and he gave a solemn oath that he'd take as much as Doyle could deliver. "You dig it, I'll sell it," he said, as they clinked glasses.

As it turned out, the gardening business soon outgrew the manure business, but Cliffy was as good as his word—even so far as making his own son, Walter, pledge to continue the deal when he eventually took over. "Loyalty, Walter!" he used to say, like it was a pronouncement, a one word manifesto. Then he'd always repeat it. "Loyalty!"

Sadly, Cliffy Sullivan passed away at the relatively young age of fifty-eight, a victim of a cancer that had spread wildly through his still-strong body. He'd tried to fight, as he'd always fought, but once again he was outclassed. The fight was uneven. He deteriorated fast and when the end came, he had nothing left. "So, what's all this?" asked Walter, when he saw Doyle with the horse and wagon.

Walter stood taller than his father but was neither as gutsy nor as hungry, having developed a smoother, more prosperous appearance with a rounded chest and a balding crown. He had, however, inherited the same sort of business acumen and, under his guidance, the center had become a destination of note for hobbyists from all over the city. Even families who'd moved away to the off-island suburbs came back here as a matter of habit for their garden supplies.

"This is Groucho," replied Doyle. "Groucho, say hello to Mr. Sullivan."

Walter patted the horse's nose. "What happened to the van?"

"Nothing. Still back at the stable."

"Yeah? I thought maybe it finally broke down for good when I saw the horse."

"This was my friend's horse, but she died so I thought I'd make use of him."

"You bought the wagon specially?"

"I sold the *calèche* so I could buy it."

"Is that right? Well, it's picturesque, I'll give you that. Hey, you know what? I just had a thought. Maybe we can do something with this." Doyle wasn't sure what that was supposed to mean.

"Wait, don't move a muscle," said Walter, "there's somebody here should see this. Hold on, just a minute."

When he returned, he had a woman in tow, an efficient-looking career type, with dark, shiny hair and red-framed spectacles that had a matching red cord attached so she wouldn't lose them.

"Oh, this is terrific," she said as she approached, "just terrific!" She was looking at the horse and wagon but had a ready smile for Doyle. "Yes, definitely."

"This is Doyle O'Shaughnessy, an old friend of my father," said Walter, making the introductions. "Doyle, this is Ms. Travanti from CFCF. She's planning a TV ad for us . . . you know, for the end-of-sale event."

"How do you do?" said Doyle, shaking hands with her.

"Good, thanks," she replied.

She spent a moment fishing a card out of the small leather purse that was slung over her shoulder. Under her name was her job title, Producer, but Doyle didn't really know what this entailed. He'd never seen this woman on TV though, so he assumed she must be one of the people from the office, one of the people who organized everything.

"What kind of ad?" he asked her. "Everything must go?" It was a line he'd heard often.

"That's it exactly," she said, humoring him with another big smile before getting right to the point. "Listen, can you be here Tuesday?"

"Tuesday?"

"Let's say . . . ten. No, on second thought, better make that closer to eleven. Would that be good for you?"

"I don't know. I mean, I'm not sure what . . ."

"Oh, it's not much," said the woman. She had a high energy level, very animated. "We'll just ask you to drive your wagon in through the entrance, something like that, I don't know, we'll see on the day. Shall we say eleven?"

It took Doyle a moment to catch on. He turned back to Walter. He wanted to know for certain if he'd understood correctly. "You want me to be in your TV ad?"

"Absolutely. It'll be great, right, Nina? Very picturesque." He seemed to like that word.

"Right," said Nina.

"Will you do it?" asked Walter. "There's a hundred bucks in it."

Doyle felt he had little choice but it had nothing to do with the money. If he said yes, he'd be doing it not so much for Walter as for his late friend, Cliffy. It was like an obligation for everything the man had done for him over the years. "If you like," he replied.

"Great!" said Walter again, as if he'd just signed a major deal. He wasn't at all like his father.

"How long will it take?"

It was Nina who answered: "Not long. One or two takes. I'd say about a half-hour. An hour, tops."

Walter reached out to shake Doyle's hand. "So, we'll see you Tuesday, okay?" Then, without waiting for a reply, he turned and led Nina Travanti back toward the central building. They were already deep into another topic.

Doyle watched them go, then rubbed Groucho's nose. "Well, now, what do you make of that?" he said. "Looks like we're gonna be on TV, how about that? Wanna be a movie star? Do you? Sure you do. You're just a big ol' ham, anyways."

Doyle took another look around, sniffed the sweet breeze a little, then mounted the bench and urged Groucho forward, steering him carefully out of the center grounds. Just like before, customers stopped what they were doing to gaze at the sight of a big sorrel horse with fine flaxen features, pulling a freshly-painted white and gold wagon. It was a classic image, in total counterpoint to the busy car park, which was full of modern vehicles from Japan and Korea; lots of minivans, lots of SUV's.

Doyle gave everyone a cheery wave, just as he'd done with the drivers back at the stable, then he and Groucho were off again, out on to the river front boulevard and heading back home at full trot, with the empty wagon running easily on its rubber tires.

Twelve

Tuesday morning, Doyle gave Groucho an extended grooming, even taking a fresh rag to polish up his hooves. When he'd finished, the horse was glistening, with his mane and tail silky smooth and his head held high, almost as if he knew was looking especially handsome that day. Doyle also gave him a good feed with an apple for dessert, something he usually did only in the evenings, just to put him in a good frame of mind.

The only problem was that, having made a delivery just this past Sunday, there wasn't much manure left to carry, so Mowbray suggested just piling up a load of empty sacks alongside the few full ones so the wagon wouldn't look empty. This was his second-ever suggestion and, once again, it made some sense.

"That's how TV ads are done, man," he assured Doyle. "It's all special effects."

"You think?"

"'Course. Ain't nothin' what it seems."

This was no real surprise to Doyle because everything on TV was always too perfect anyway. It was just that he'd never given any thought before as to how they did it. What did surprise him, however, was this other side of Mowbray he was beginning to see. Up to this time, the kid had just been a hired hand who had to be watched and checked and who liked to go out back and smoke a joint during his break. But now, it appeared to Doyle that Mowbray was starting to have more confidence and, as he noted to himself, it was only since they'd started working with Groucho.

"Best take along a lotta sugar, keep him happy."

This was yet more advice from Mowbray and Doyle was happy to heed it, stuffing the pockets of his good jacket, the same jacket he'd worn for the funeral, and taking along a spare box of white cubes that he carried in a plastic grocery bag.

At last they were ready and Groucho was more than glad to be on his way, not lazy at all, and actually straining a little for his head.

The journey went well, even better than Sunday. The weekday traffic was heavier, but this time there were no noisy bikes growling next to them at the lights. The weather was kind too: bright, crisp sunlight with a fresh breeze off the river that made it feel like the first true day of fall.

The trouble began when they reached the gardening center.

Afterward, with hindsight, Doyle realized that he'd perhaps been over-confident, a little too ready to believe that the horse's old behavioral problems were behind him. But then, what happened wasn't really Groucho's fault, any of it. It was a confluence of things, not the least of which was a TV production team hastily thrown together at the last minute and provided by the station as a free service to any local advertiser who bought media time.

This wasn't a multi-faceted, professional unit like they have on large budget motion pictures, with specialists for every conceivable aspect of the shoot, including trained animal wranglers and representatives from the humane society. No, this was nothing more than the most basic crew, consisting of the senior contact producer, in this case Nina Travanti, plus a long-suffering cameraman and a trio of helpers to move lights, arrange props, and do any other heavy lifting that was required.

In addition, there was Walter Sullivan's relative, Hadleigh, a second cousin on his mother's side. Hadleigh was a part-time photographer, weddings and such like, whom Walter had asked to take pictures of anything and everything for future publicity. Since the place was being set up for video anyway, Walter reasoned, why not squeeze more value out of the occasion by inviting Hadleigh and his digital camera along. But it was Hadleigh who got things off to a bad start.

As it happened, he was standing near the entrance just as the horse and wagon were turning in from the car park. Seizing his chance, Hadleigh jumped out in front of the slow moving animal and snapped off a couple of shots like a true member of the paparazzi. The camera was one of the latest models and its default setting was an automatic compensation for both aperture and speed. When it sensed it had a moving target, it added the necessary flash component.

Needless to say, Groucho wasn't too eager to have a series of lightning bolts in front of his eyes and he reared up, lifting both front hooves off the ground, just like he did with the street sweeper on that first walk through the Pointe—except this time, Doyle sensed that the horse was more likely to bolt. With a wagon in tow, there was no telling the damage it could cause and a momentary panic set in as Doyle saw Groucho react in front of him.

But with a swift reaction of his own, Doyle reached for the metal lever that was down by his side. This was the brake feature that Sheila Kendall in Ontario had told him about and for which he'd had little use up to now. By yanking on it hard, he was able to secure the wheels just as Groucho came back down to the ground, just before the animal had any chance to think about charging off.

The brakes held, the wagon remained stationary and the whole contraption acted like an anchor for the horse. Feeling the resistance of both the wagon and the lines, he stomped and snorted but didn't try to challenge the restraints and finally came to an angry standstill.

"Sorry," said Hadleigh, smiling thinly as he waved an apology at Doyle.

Doyle just nodded and sat there, breathing very slowly. It had been a close call. The question now was whether he should stay and complete the session or cut his losses and leave right away before there were any more problems. The real issue was his own integrity. He believed that promises were meant to be kept and since he'd already agreed to do it, he made the decision to remain.

It wasn't necessarily a wise course of action, however, and a second mishap occurred once they began to shoot the scene. The cameraman, a bulky man whose nickname was Spike, had positioned himself for a three-quarter view of Groucho and the wagon coming toward him, with an array of blooms in between him and his subject.

"Oh, that's so pretty," said Nina Travanti, standing over Spike's shoulder. "Walter, you'll just love this one," she called to her client. Then to Spike, "Whenever you're ready ..."

"Camera rolling," said Spike.

"Okay!" Nina yelled. "Doyle, drive the wagon!"

Obligingly, Doyle flicked at the lines. *"Allons-y*, Groucho!"

As the crew, the gardening center staff and several morning customers looked on, the horse eased his way forward, walking in stately fashion, and for a few seconds it was a perfect shot. Meanwhile, in the background, one of the helpers, who was setting up the next scene, tripped over a small shopping cart that he didn't see because he was carrying a large potted shrub.

As a result, both he and the plant were propelled forward into an exotic, decorative palm that was top heavy with leaves. It didn't take much to heave this over, too, and when it came down, the tip of the plant fell across Groucho's haunches. After the incident with the flash, he was already in a sour mood and this just convinced him that he really didn't want to be there.

Startled, he immediately jumped forward and this time, Doyle wasn't quick enough with the brake lever. The left wheels of the wagon, both front and rear, plowed into the boxes of flowers that lined the alley, tipping, crushing and bouncing over the beautiful blooms. White and mauve hydrangea petals were thrown into the air like confetti. Then golden begonias followed and the cameraman, Spike, had to manhandle his equipment out of the way in a hurry, just in case the horse changed direction and chose to plunge even farther into the flowers.

For a few moments it was chaos, the way it is when a circus animal escapes, the same way it is when any creature that weighs nearly two thousand pounds is on the loose. It was fortunate that Groucho's path was finally blocked by the parked TV station truck or he might have gone on to wreak even more havoc, because Doyle had totally lost control. At that stage, he was just along for the ride, trying his best to keep his balance and not get thrown. In the end, Groucho came to a stop on his own terms but his eyes were still wild and he was exceedingly upset with the world.

Doyle kept hold of the lines as he dismounted from the wagon, then walked up alongside to try to calm his panicked friend. "Steady now, boy, it's all right, let's just cool down, shall we? Nothing to get excited about, just a few leaves touched you, that's all. What's all the fuss, eh? I think you better hope they don't make me pay for this mess, 'cause that'll be coming out of your sugar ration."

It didn't help that many people were now coming up to Doyle, to check if he was all right, to see if they could offer assistance, and it was all he could do to keep them at bay while he tried to reassure the horse. When the center's owner, Walter Sullivan, finally arrived, Doyle was quick to offer his apologies for the damage and half-expected a shouting match but Walter surprised him.

"Nah, don't worry, insurance'll cover it."

Behind Walter came the producer, Nina Travanti, who chimed in with her own positive attitude. "Hey, and Spike says we got the shot," she added.

"So no harm done," said Walter, clapping Doyle on the shoulder. "Nothing to worry about, right? Long as you're okay and the horse is okay."

Even though it was Doyle who'd apologized, it was both Walter and Nina who sounded conciliatory, mainly because their first thoughts were about possible lawsuits against them. After all, it had been her crew's clumsiness that had caused the rumpus and there were dozens of witnesses. And it had all happened on Walter's premises, so he could be deemed ultimately responsible. In response, Doyle nodded and attempted a smile but the truth was that, despite his calm demeanor, he was still fairly shaken up, just like the horse. "Maybe I'd better take him home," he told them.

"Sure, good idea," said Walter. "We're done now, anyways. Give me a call tomorrow, let me know how he is, all right?" He stretched out a hand and Doyle shook it. "Kind of exciting, eh?" Walter went on. "Nothing like a little drama to liven things up." His face opened up into a tentative grin. "Didn't know we were going to be shooting an action movie."

Next to him, Nina laughed out loud at her client's humor. "It'll make a good story, that's for sure. Something to tell your grandkids," she told Doyle. She didn't realize he had no such family. Nevertheless, her words proved to be prophetic in another way, because one of the onlookers, a rep for a garden tool company who just happened to be there that morning, had been quick-witted enough to capture the whole scene on his cell phone camera.

Thirteen

I t's not good to change an animal's routine unless absolutely necessary, so the day after the shoot, Doyle hitched Groucho to the wagon and toured the Pointe, finishing up along the main Wellington thoroughfare, the long stretch by the trees where he could break into a trot.

While the horse seemed to have forgotten all about yesterday's incident, the driver hadn't and was even more soothing with his chatter and even more cautious with his signals. Not long after they arrived back at the stable, the phone rang. It was Louise, of all people.

"Louise! What a surprise!" said Doyle.

"Hi, Doyle, how you doing?"

"Okay, thanks. And you?"

"Yeah, you know. Can't talk long. Just wanted to say hello. I saw what happened, you know, at the garden place. Pretty funny."

"You saw what happened? You were there?"

"No, silly. It's all over the web. I think it must have had a million hits by now."

Doyle was still unfamiliar with the language of the internet. He'd only ever had the one lesson. "The web?"

"The internet . . . don't you remember? The computer."

"Oh. But how . . ."

"I don't know. I guess somebody must have caught it on camera."

"Sure. They were filming it."

"No, the TV people wouldn't have done that, I don't think. Must have been somebody else, somebody watching.."

"Somebody else had a movie camera?"

Louise laughed a little, then took pity on him and tried to explain. "Doyle, you can take videos on a cell phone now. Everybody's got one, even me. Happens all the time. People take pictures and videos and stuff and then they upload 'em to, like, a special website so everybody else can see 'em too. It's easy."

"So that's where you saw it?"

"Yeah, that's what I'm trying to tell you. It was so funny."

"Wasn't funny to me."

"No, I guess not. Were you scared?"

"No . . . Well, a bit. Shaken up more than scared."

"How's the horse?"

"Groucho? Like it never happened."

"That's good."

"Louise . . ."

"Yeah?"

"I don't see you no more."

"No, well, you know."

"Are we still friends?"

"What? Sure we are. I'm calling you, aren't I?"

"It's good to hear you. I still miss your mother."

"Yeah, well . . ."

"Sorry, I know you don't want to talk about that."

"Nah, that's okay. At any rate, just wanted to call and say hi, you know? When I saw you there on the video, it kind of made me realize I should give you a call."

"Did you ever . . ." Doyle came to a stop, not sure if what he was about to say was really any of his business.

"What? Did I ever what?"

"Go back home. I mean, to your husband."

A long pause. "No, Doyle, I didn't. I . . . I met someone else."

"You did?"

"Yeah. He's great. You should meet him. You'd like him, I know you would."

This was a new Louise and Doyle was glad to hear her like this. "You sound happy about it."

"Are you kidding me? Best thing in a long while. Hell, maybe the best thing ever."

"Will you get married again?"

"Wow, now there's a question. I'm not even divorced, well, not yet anyways, not officially. Got all the papers drawn up though."

"I'm sorry to hear that."

"You are? Why?"

Doyle didn't know. He just thought it was the right thing to say, but Louise didn't wait for a reply. She was so wound up about it, she just continued, reverting all too quickly to the Louise of old.

"Damn son-of-a-bitch won't even give me what's due. What's in that duplex is mostly mine, you know? All the furniture and the plates. Does he care? No way. He's still damn well using it. But I got a lawyer on the case, don't you worry about that. And my boyfriend's a cop, so that kinda helps. Bastard can't try anything now."

"Your boyfriend's in the police?"

"Yeah, didn't I mention that?"

"No."

"Listen, Doyle, I gotta go. It's been great talking to you, I mean it. You were ..." Her voice softened. "You were there, you know? When I needed you."

"So we're still friends?" It was as if he hadn't clearly understood what she was saying and was still searching for assurance.

"'Course we are, I told you."

"You'll call again?"

"I'll call, you'll call, whatever."

"At the bar? You still work there?"

"Yeah, still there, God help me, but I think I'll start looking around. Can't stand that Clément no more. What a sleazebag. General clean-up, right?" Doyle was uncomfortable talking about such personal affairs and didn't know what to say. Meanwhile, Louise was still trying to escape the call.

"So, I'll be talking to you," she said. "Catch you later, okay?" She didn't want to hurt his feelings by being too abrupt.

"Sure."

"Good, okay. So bye for now, Doyle."

"Bye, Louise."

The phone went dead in his hand and he placed it back on its cradle on the wall. Then he went to make coffee but he did it automatically, because his head was still full, not just of Louise, but of Jacqueline too. What would *she* have thought of what happened yesterday, he thought? Would she have considered it funny or scary? He couldn't seem to decide and wondered if he was starting to forget her. Just the idea of forgetting her made him a little sad.

He took his coffee and went to sit with Groucho, just like he did on those first few days after she died. But he didn't want to talk to the horse. He just wanted to sit there quietly with him for a while. This was his best friend, even if he did cause a little trouble occasionally. In fact, despite what Louise just said, Doyle felt that Groucho might even be his only friend.

The next call came in the middle of the afternoon, another woman, but this was nobody he knew.

"Hi there, Mr. Shaughnessy?" The voice was older and had a certain husky quality. It was like she was always on the verge of a coughing spasm, as if she'd been a heavy smoker for many years.

"It's O'Shaughnessy," said Doyle. It was a common mistake and reminded him of the woman in Ontario who sold him the wagon.

"Oh, I'm sorry, I hate that, too, when people get my name wrong. I'm Prudence Carmichael with *The Gazette*. I was just calling to say I saw your video. Hilarious! Laughed out loud when I saw it. I was wondering if I could possibly come over, talk to you about that."

"You work for the paper?"

"You don't read my column?"

Doyle didn't like to admit that he didn't read much, period. "I don't know, maybe."

"Okay, not to worry, my ego's not that big. What I do mostly is human interest coverage . . . what I call Pru's P's . . . people, personalities, pets. I wouldn't take up much of your time. And of course, I'd love to meet your horse. What's his name, by the way?"

"Groucho."

"Groucho! That's perfect! So how about it? Feel up to a quick interview?"

"An interview? You mean here? At the stable?"

"Just tell me what time's convenient."

"I don't know. I guess the afternoon would be best. After lunch maybe. That would be the best time."

"Okay, after lunch tomorrow?"

Doyle didn't answer immediately. There was something bothering him about all of this. "I don't want you making fun of him," he told her.

"Who do you mean? The horse?"

"You can't make fun."

"Well . . . okay, I understand, but sometimes animals are funny, you have to admit. People love to laugh at animal stories. Did one not long ago where a goat nursed some Labrador puppies, people loved that. Another was where a cat got stuck in a bird bath, got totally soaked, looked like a little ragamuffin. Just adorable! Me, what I like is anything that cheers people up. I mean the news is always so depressing, don't you think? Crime and pollution and wars . . . I like to give people some relief from all that."

Doyle understood all of that, he really did. In fact, he pretty much shared the same point-of-view. Still, he couldn't bear the thought of the whole city making fun of Groucho. He just couldn't bear it.

"No, I'm sorry," he told her. He was adamant but she didn't want to accept that as an answer.

"Okay, tell you what, Mr. O'Shaughnessy," she replied. "I get your name right, by the way?"

"Doyle O'Shaughnessy, yes."

"So tell you what, Doyle . . . May I call you Doyle? Here's what I'll agree to, okay? You seem like a nice guy, so how about this? I'll come over, we'll talk a little about what happened, about you, about the horse, then I'll tell you the angle I'm thinking of taking. You'll be able to give me your opinion."

Doyle wasn't going to be fooled like that. "What if I don't like what you're going to write?"

"I promise you will. Like I say, I just have to find the angle. I need to raise some kind of emotion. If it's not a laugh, then it's got to be a warm smile, know what I'm saying?"

To Doyle, a warm smile was far better than a laugh. He wouldn't mind that. "Sure, okay," he said. "Long as it's only a smile."

"Terrific. Tomorrow afternoon at two?"

"Sure."

"Good. Take it easy."

Doyle returned to see Groucho but didn't sit down again. The phone call from *The Gazette* woman had lifted him out of the melancholy and he was ready to get back to work. "Now, you be nice when she comes, all right?" he said to the horse, "otherwise she's gonna make fun for sure. You got that?"

Groucho nodded his head and, for a moment, it just appeared to Doyle like the horse was agreeing. It was comic and Doyle chuckled. "You're a character and no mistake," he said.

At the end of the day, the drivers all came in and it was obvious that, thanks to the video, news of the incident had already spread. Having alternately scorned and then respected Doyle's achievements with Groucho, the balance had now tipped back again. Even if nothing was said out loud, there were some private snickers and the unanimous attitude was "told you so".

Doyle knew perfectly well that few drivers would ever put up with such an animal. The standard designation in the equestrian community was runaway, which in effect meant unreliable, dangerous, and possibly psychotic. Yet that kind of description was inherently unfair, if only because it swept all such horses into the same category. The implication was that such horses were worthless.

True, Groucho could be bad-tempered and irritable, especially when things like street sweepers and flashbulbs ventured too close, but he was essentially a gentle horse when it came to living things: friendly toward humans and other animals alike. He enjoyed children petting him and even put up with the nuisance birds that sometimes flocked around his feed bucket.

Even more importantly, there'd never been a single instance of him bullying a stable companion, not one, even with all his size and dominance. No nipping, kicking, or other unsocial behavior, as sometimes happens when horses are confined together. No matter what else the drivers whispered about him or how much they joked, they couldn't deny that basic facet of his nature, otherwise they'd have long since forced him out.

And something else occurred to Doyle too. He'd long associated Groucho's personality with that of Jacqueline, a classic case of a horse matching his owner's outbursts, but that wasn't accurate at all. If anything, he thought, Groucho was far more like his late friend Cliffy, the tough Irish boxer who liked flowers: prickly on the outside but soft and sensitive on the inside. That was Groucho, he thought, a lot like Cliffy.

Prudence Carmichael from *The Gazette* arrived forty minutes late because she was the type of person who always arrived late. Doyle thought that had to be a problem in her line of work but, of course, he was too polite to comment. When she arrived, he'd already set about other tasks but he willingly stopped what he was doing to wipe his hands and greet her because that was how he did things.

She was a big woman, not broad and strong like Jacqueline, but tall and full-figured, with bold eyes and an expressive face. Her flowing clothes were obviously expensive, and she came across as a stylish woman-about-town, the type who could always be found breakfasting at the Ritz or lunching at Le Toqué or attending a premiere at Place des Arts.

"Mr. Doyle O'Shaughnessy?" she asked, with the "O" slightly exaggerated, a reference to the fact that she'd gotten the name wrong the day before. To make the point, she touched her head with one elegant finger. "Once it's locked in, I never forget." Then she opened up into a wide smile, revealing a mouthful of perfectly crowned teeth.

"Pleased to meet you," replied Doyle, a little shyly. He stepped back to let her in. "Hope you don't mind the smell."

"Me? Not at all. Grew up in the Townships. You know that area?"

"Not much." In fact, Doyle's parents had taken him out there on a camping vacation one summer. It was good horse country but he'd never been back.

"Miss it sometimes," she said, almost to herself, "but I guess we can't always choose how we're going to end up." She stood in the center of the doorway, gazing around, examining everything without making it obvious, from the bits of straw on the floorboards to the lamps in the rafters.

"Boy, I tell you, this takes me back. Do you like what you do, Mr. O'Shaughnessy?"

Although she'd managed to remember his name, she seemed to have forgotten that she asked on the phone if she could call him Doyle. Must be from dealing with so many people, he thought, but he didn't try to correct her.

"Never done anything else," he replied.

"Ever want to?"

"No."

"Now that's what I like, a good, solid answer. A man of conviction." It was as if she were inventing a phrase to use later, making a mental note of it. A moment later she was distracted when she caught sight of Groucho over in his stall. "Oh, my, is that him?"

"That's him."

"May I?" she asked.

"Sure."

She went over, approaching with a great deal of caution. "Hello," she said softly to the horse. "And how are you doing today? My name's Pru. Are we going to be friends?" She turned back to Doyle. "Does he like people?"

"Sure. Just let him sniff the back of your hand, that's it, a bit more. Okay, now, slowly, turn your hand over and rub his muzzle. That's just above his nose. Slowly . . . That's it, not too much. Good. He likes that."

She followed his instructions and appeared delighted when Groucho moved his head a little closer, wanting more. "Oh, he's just wonderful. It's Groucho, right?"

Doyle nodded.

"Well, you're not grouchy at all, are you?" she said to the horse. It was like she was talking to a baby. "You like that, don't you, Groucho? You like to be petted."

"He likes sugar too." Doyle stepped forward and held two cubes in his hand, which the horse snaffled up.

"Aw, so cute," said Pru. "Does he often get nervous?"

Doyle knew the question was undoubtedly referring to what happened at the gardening center. "Not exactly nervous," he replied. "I wouldn't say that."

"No? What would you say? How would you describe him?"

"Jacqueline used to say he's got a mind of his own."

"A mind of his own. That's good. Who's Jacqueline?"

"His previous owner. She died not long ago."

"Does he miss her?"

"Yes, I think he does. It was Groucho brought her back. She was up on the *calèche*, had a heart attack. Too much smoking and drinking, you ask me, but that was Jacqueline . . ."

Doyle was into his reminiscing but something had caught Pru's interest and she interrupted him. "Wait a minute . . . You're telling me she had a heart attack and he what? He brought her home?"

"Sure."

"In the middle of the day?"

"No, it was almost dark."

"So . . . she had a heart attack and . . . what? She just dropped the reins?"

"Lines. They're called lines."

"Okay, she dropped the lines?"

"They were just hanging loose in her hand when she got here."

"You were the one who found her like that?"

Doyle looked down, recalling the initial shock of that moment. He didn't answer, just gave a nod. "Which means what?" she asked. "Groucho just found his way home, just like that? In all the traffic, no help from anyone?"

"He knows the way."

"Well, that's a pretty good story, right there."

"Many horses would do that."

"They would?"

"Probably."

"But not automatically."

"Every horse is different."

"But Groucho brought her home. Like a real hero."

"Don't know about that," he replied.

"Just thinking out loud."

"Was more of a hero when he saved her life."

"He saved her life? How? Tell me." She was really into this now. From her purse, she took out a small leather-bound pad plus an expensive gold pen. Then she flipped open a page and began to scribble notes in true journalist style.

"Well, not much to tell," Doyle was saying. "They were on St-Paul . . . You know where that is? It's in Old Montréal."

"Yes, yes, I know St-Paul."

"Taxi came right through a stop sign, driver was on his cell phone. He was an idiot, that's what Jacqueline called him. If Groucho hadn't moved, she'd have been dead right there."

"What happened? Groucho moved her out of the way?"

"Pulled the *calèche* right up on the sidewalk."

"Really?"

"Police said it was both their faults, you know, both sides, which it wasn't, so she got mad."

"Sounds like she was a real character."

Doyle nodded, the sadness again showing through.

"How about any other times . . . when he was a hero?"

"Any other times? Well, let's see. Not much that I can think . . . except maybe the time somebody broke in here and he kicked up a real rumpus, scared 'em right off."

"Thieves? He scared off thieves? Like a watchdog?"

"Well, don't know they were thieves. Might have been just kids, you know? Up to mischief, maybe. Might have been just kids."

"But they were intruders and Groucho scared them off. You ever tell these stories to anyone?"

"No, not really. Except Louise, that's Jacqueline's daughter." He was thinking of their conversation in the bar. "That was her idea, to hitch up Groucho to the wagon, make my deliveries that way instead of the van. She said it was like one horsepower. That was like a joke. One horsepower."

"Yes, I get it. Very clever."

"She's clever all right, that Louise. She was the one showed me the computer, how it works."

Pru Carmichael wasn't too interested in that. "So just to confirm," she said. "You've spoken to no other media." She saw him look at her, uncomprehending: "No other papers," she explained. "No other journalists or reporters."

"No."

"No TV people."

"No . . . except when we did the ad, at Walter's place. There were TV people there."

"But apart from that?'

"No."

"Good, good, I'm starting to like this. Hero horse . . . something, something. Needs a headline. Okay, go on, tell me about yesterday. What exactly happened?"

"Okay, but first I gotta say something. It wasn't Groucho's fault, nothing that happened. It maybe just looked that way when you saw it on the computer."

She knew he meant the video. "Fine," she said, "so tell me in your own words."

Doyle took a moment to cast his mind back. It was all still there, vivid, every excruciating detail. "When we arrived, there was this man with a camera stepped right out in front of us."

"The TV camera?"

"No, no, a small camera, like a regular camera, takes regular pictures. I think it was Walter's brother-in-law, set the flash off in Groucho's face."

"Walter?"

"Walter's the one owns the center now. Cliffy's son."

"Cliffy?"

"Cliff Sullivan . . . The Shamrock Welterweight. That's what they used to call him. We boxed together, you know, back in the old days. 'Course, he was much better than me. Fought for the championship.

"Didn't win though, got beat up pretty bad, so he opened up the gardening center. He always liked the flowers, Cliffy."

Pru was patient enough to let Doyle ramble for a while, knowing from experience that people sometimes utter the best stuff when they're allowed to run on freely.

"You say you boxed too?"

"Sure. Went to the same gym, so we became friends. That was before he started the gardening and before I took over my dad's stable. Then we didn't see each other so much. Too busy, I guess. But we were still friends. Always friends."

"You seem to have a lot of friends, Doyle."

He looked down. "No, not so many."

"Ever married? Kids?"

"No, nothing like that. Just me and the horses."

"Just me and the horses," she repeated, making yet another note. "All right, let's get back to that, shall we? So the flash went off in Groucho's face. Then what?"

"Sure, well, that gave him a start, y'know. He didn't like that too much but no animal would, you ask me. Horse, dog, anything."

"Was that when he ran amok?" Again, she had to explain. "When he caused the damage?"

"No, that was after. When the flash went off, I caught hold of the brake, stopped the wagon, so he couldn't do much. Well, he coulda pulled it over, I guess, he's pretty strong, but that didn't happen."

"He calmed down after that?"

"Sure he calmed down. But it kinda put him in a bad mood, y'know?"

"What happened then?"

"Well, not much. We had to wait a while, you know, until they set everything up, the TV people. Then the woman there, Nina, I don't remember her last name, the one from the TV . . . She called over to drive the wagon, so I pushed him forward, and it was okay for a while. I think they were trying to get us and the flowers at the same time, y'know, in the same picture. Then one of the others, a young feller . . ."

"One of the crew?"

"I think so. Anyways, he tripped or something. Didn't see that myself. So what happened was a tree fell on the horse's rear end, y'know? What they call the rump."

"A tree? How big a tree?"

"Not a real tree. Like one of those they have at the center, in the pots. Tall, with all the leaves, but not like a real tree in the ground."

"Like a palm tree?"

"I dunno."

"Okay, so this tree fell on the horse, on his rear end? On his rump?"

"Yes."

"Go on."

"Well, now, he wasn't too happy about that, not after the flash. It spooked him. That's what they call it with a horse, when he's frightened of something. They say he gets spooked."

"Then what? He began to run?"

"Canter, they call it."

Pru breathed a sigh. "Don't worry, I'll fix all the words when I write it. Just tell me the story."

Doyle scratched at his face, thinking he could have maybe shaved a bit better this morning, then continued,

"Well, he was spooked like I said, just didn't care where he was going. But that was a bit my fault 'cause I tried for the brake, just like with the flash, but I missed, couldn't get hold of it, 'cause I was kind of thrown, y'know, sideways, then I lost control of the lines. So it was partly my fault too. Anyways, there was some damage but Walter, that's the owner, Cliffy's son, he said not to worry 'cause the insurance would cover it. I expected a big fuss, but he said not to worry, so I didn't. But I gotta say, I was a bit shaken."

"I'll bet you were. So what you're telling me here is that neither time was it the horse's fault. Not with the flash and not with the tree."

"That's it. That's why it's not fair to make fun of him. Wasn't his fault."

"Don't worry, I won't be making fun."

"You won't?" There was relief in Doyle's voice but also some doubt, as if he wasn't sure whether to believe it.

"Why would I make fun? Groucho's a hero in my book."

"You gonna write a book?"

Pru smiled at him. "No, that's just an expression. What I mean is, the fun thing's been done already with the video, so why should I repeat all that? No news there. I'm thinking it's better to write it up the other way. People like to cheer for a hero, Doyle, always have, and that's what your Groucho is . . . a real hero. Like all those old cowboy horses, remember them?"

Doyle nodded. Sure he remembered, the cowboys and their horses. There was Roy Rogers with Trigger, Gene Autry with Champion, the Lone Ranger with Silver. Doyle could even remember the tunes they played on the different TV shows. He loved those shows. "Would you like some coffee?" he asked her. "Or some tea?" He was thinking now of Louise's preference.

"No thanks, another time maybe. Got to get back. Just need you to answer me a few more things, if you don't mind."

"Sure." Doyle was enthusiastic now he knew where all this might be going. "Long as you don't say I'm a hero too."

She laughed at his modesty. "Just a bit more background. How many horses do you have here at the stable?"

"Five, including Groucho."

"And you look after them all yourself?"

"Well, I run the stable. But the drivers do some of the work. And Mowbray does a lot of the shoveling now, I can't do that so much anymore."

"Right, right. But you do most of it. You run the place."

"Sure."

"How old are you, by the way?"

"Seventy-eight or seventy-nine . . . depending on who you believe, my father or the priest. My dad always said he was drunk, the priest, so he got the date wrong on the form." Doyle laughed at this. "Mind you, my dad also drank a bit, so it's hard to know which one to believe." He was now a good deal more relaxed. "Maybe you shouldn't put that in your paper," he added. "About the priest and the booze, I mean."

"No, maybe not. Now, you say you boxed when you were younger? Tell me about that."

"Sure, but we're talking a long time ago now. And I wasn't much good, I just trained in the gym a bit. I didn't have real bouts, not like Cliffy, so don't say I was a champ or something because that's not true."

Pru smiled but it was a little colder, a little emptier, a way of telling him to back off a little. "I think you have to trust me here, Doyle. Let me do my job, okay?"

"Sure, okay."

She looked down at the page of notes to see what she might have missed. "How long have you been running the stable?" she asked him.

"Sixty years working here, thirty years running it . . . that was when my dad died."

"Is that right? And what was his name, your dad?"

"Patrick Bailey O'Shaughnessy. See, I'm Patrick Doyle O'Shaughnessy, but we neither of us liked our first names, so he called himself Bailey, and me, I'm Doyle."

"Got it. And he ran the stable before you?"

"Owned it, more like. Me too. My building, my land. I was what they call an only child, so when he died, he passed it on to me. I just had to sign some papers."

"And your mother? What about her?"

"My mom? She died young."

"I'm sorry to hear that."

Doyle shrugged. She was never physically robust, his mother, always seemed to be sick with something. Then one winter, when Doyle was just twenty, she caught a flu virus while traveling to work on the bus. She worked in the purchase office at Morgan's department store on Sainte-Cathérine. She took time off to rest up but it had gotten worse, not better, and eventually the flu turned into pneumonia.

Back then, it happened more frequently than it does today, so Doyle never talked about it much. It was just something that happened, something accepted as part of winter, part of the cycle of life, like hard births and crippling polio and so many other illnesses and diseases that nobody thinks about any more.

"Okay ..." said Pru, looking to change the subject. "So back to the horse. How big is he?"

This was a better topic for Doyle. "Seventeen point two."

"Which means?"

"Seventeen and a half hands."

"Sorry. Hands? I just want to get it right."

"A hand is four inches." He held up his own hand, as if to demonstrate. "See? Just like a real hand."

"And where is it measured from? On the horse?"

"From the withers."

"Withers?"

"That's like the shoulders."

"I see . . . and that's big for this type of horse?"

"He's bigger than the others."

"And what breed is he? Clydesdale?" She knew that from the horses in those old beer ads.

"No, not a Clydesdale," Doyle said, smiling. "Clydesdale's too big for a *calèche*. Groucho's what they call American-Belgian. Maybe something else, too, I don't know the whole history of him."

"Well, he seems pretty big to me. I bet he eats a lot too. What do you feed him?"

"Nothing special. Grain . . . which is oats and corn mixed with a little molasses. He likes the molasses. And hay, for what they call roughage. Then you got the supplements and stuff, which he needs for his health. You gotta add that. And then you got his treats, can't forget the treats. He likes sugar, which Jacqueline always gave him, and apples, too, which I give him now.

"Some of the drivers, they give carrots, but Groucho, he likes sugar and apples the best. Sweet tooth, I guess, that's what Jacqueline always said. Thing is with feed, it's the amount that's important. You gotta judge it on the exercise he's doing. And the water too. Can't let him drink as much as he wants. That can be bad for him, 'specially when he's hot. Gives him colic."

"I didn't know that."

"Thought you were a country girl."

"I grew up in the Townships but I lived in a town." She smiled. It was a joke she'd used many times before but he didn't seem to get it, so she explained, "My sister and I, we had rabbits and guinea pigs but no horses, I'm afraid. Always wanted one, well, a pony at least, so we used to bike along to the nearby farms just to look over the fence and peek inside the barn. That's how I know the smell."

"You never got one? A pony?"

"No, afraid not," she answered briefly. She wanted to get back to the interview. "So what else can you tell me? How old is Groucho, for example?"

"He's nearly twenty now. That's old for a horse, makes him a bit stiffer than he used to be. Not as frisky, Jacqueline used to say."

"You liked your friend, Jacqueline, didn't you? Were you and she . . . ?"

Doyle waited for the end of the sentence but there was just a long silence until Pru found the words to spell it out.

"An item?" she asked, but Doyle still didn't seem to know what she meant. "You and Jacqueline. Was she your . . . your lady friend?"

"Who? Jacqueline?" Doyle was surprised at the question. "No," he said quietly, without revealing any more.

"Okay, it's just you and the horses. Got it." She squinted at her watch, more jewelry than timepiece, with a mother-of-pearl face and a tiny diamond to mark the twelve. "All right, last question. You ready?"

"Sure."

"What do you think your horse dreams about?"

"What he dreams about?" The question reminded Doyle of the conversation he had with Louise. Her suggestion was that he dreams of breakfast but he knew that was just a joke. "I never thought about it," he replied, "not seriously."

"It's a question I often ask people about their pets. Well, Groucho's not a pet exactly, I know. But animals do dream, it's a scientific fact, and I was just wondering what you think he dreams about?"

She was referring to the discovery that many animal sleep patterns included a certain amount of REM, or rapid eye movement, which indicated the type of neurological function that induced dreams in humans was present in animals. Of course, nobody really knew whether animals dreamed or not. Only they could know that, but it was a reasonable assumption.

Doyle gave the question its due consideration. "Hard to tell," he concluded.

"I know, I know it's hard to tell, but take a guess. You know him well, don't you?"

"Sure, well enough."

"So try to think like him. Put yourself in his shoes, so to speak. He eats, he works, he sleeps . . . Now, when he dreams, what does he dream about? Think carefully."

Doyle closed his own eyes for a moment, trying to imagine. It was an intriguing question for him, something he'd never considered before, not deeply, not like this. And suddenly he saw it all before him. It was right there inside his head, very clear. He opened his eyes and said, "Fields. What they call pastures, like in the church song."

"Green pastures, right. Psalm Twenty-Three. Very famous. That's what he dreams about? Pastures?"

Doyle nodded. "I'd say so."

She was scribbling it down. "Great, excellent. Very good indeed. You a religious man, Doyle?"

"No, not much. Used to like the songs though."

She'd told him that the question about dreams was her last and she was about to shut her notebook but Doyle wasn't done yet. He'd taken the trouble to think about it like she asked, so now he wanted to explain fully.

"See, he's on the road all day, what they call the asphalt and, well, that's hard for a horse, being on the asphalt. Y'know, I don't think he's been on grass since he was a colt. Maybe not even then. Maybe never."

"Yes, I understand."

"And I don't think he's ever galloped either. He's walked, he's cantered a bit, he likes that. But I don't think he's ever galloped, not like at full speed."

"Never galloped, right."

"Galloping in the pastures. I think that's what he dreams about. Well . . . that and the sugar."

Pru had been anxious to leave, but she had to smile at that, unable to help herself. "Doyle, you're a charmer. Well, okay, I'd say that about covers it. If there's anything else, I'll call you, would that be all right?"

"Sure."

She was busy putting her pen away in her purse, then took a moment to check her cell phone to see if she had any messages. Doyle waited for her until she was done. They were still standing in the middle of the stable, hadn't even bothered to sit down, which was just as well for Doyle. He wasn't keen on taking strangers up to his apartment. He'd invited Louise but that was different. She was Jacqueline's daughter, it was late at night and she had looked terrible.

"Well, thanks, Doyle, that was excellent," Pru said again and shook his hand, a single firm pump, like it was an agreement of sorts. "Now, we're going to need a picture, you and the horse. How about if our photographer stops by, let's say same time tomorrow? Shouldn't take too long."

"Okay. But no flash."

"I understand."

"When will it come out, you know, in the paper?"

"Oh, that I'm not certain. Depends on the editor. You don't take *The Gazette*?"

Another awkward question for Doyle concerning his reading abilities. "I see it sometimes."

"Have your friends watch out, that's the best thing." Another glance at her watch. "Okay, gotta run. Bye for now."

After she was gone, Doyle went back to see Groucho. It was becoming a habit, conferring with the horse like this, a way of thinking out loud without actually talking to himself. He knew what it meant to become senile or to be perceived by others as senile. It was how his father had ended up and he didn't want that.

It was partly why he, himself, had given up drinking a few years back, because he had always blamed what happened to his father on the booze, at least partly. But now he was with Groucho for most of the day, so it made it easier. He could air his thoughts and rationalize that he was talking to the horse.

"She seemed nice," he was telling Groucho. "She said she wouldn't make fun of you, but we'll see. People don't always do what they say, you know. That's the trouble with us humans. We don't always do what we say. Pretty hard to understand us, eh? Must drive you crazy. You know what? Me too, sometimes."

Fourteen

The newspaper's photographer was pleasant enough, well-briefed on the flash problem and willing to take the shot outside the stable. But after that, it was a long wait until Pru Carmichael's column appeared, over two weeks. In fact, it was Walter Sullivan, down at the gardening center, who first alerted Doyle to its publication.

Doyle was in his office when the phone rang. Right outside his small window, the sun was beaming down on the half-bare maple, the light filtering through the branches like an impressionist painting. Unfortunately, that same light also revealed that the windows needed washing and he made a mental note to do it before the winter set in.

"That was some write-up this morning," said Walter. "Great PR, thanks for that. Great timing, too, just as the TV buy's starting. Did you see it yet, the ad?"

"No," said Doyle.

"Six o' clock news, all week up to Sunday. They did a nice job, nice edit. Just hope it works, eh? All that money, hell, I don't even want to think about it. Still, cost of doing business, right?"

Doyle didn't know about any of that. "Do they show everything? On TV?" This was his only concern.

"Everything?"

"The accident, the damage?"

For a moment, Walter didn't know what Doyle was talking about. "Wait, you mean like on the video? Hell, no, are you kidding? Nothing like that. No they did a nice job, like I said. Looks great, like a million dollars. You're only on for a short time, you and the horse, maybe two or three seconds at most, but you look great. No, I mean it, really catches the eye. People have already commented."

Doyle was glad to hear about that. "What's it say in the paper?"

"The paper? That's something else. That's more about the horse."

"What's it say?" Doyle asked again.

"You don't have a copy? Wait, I got it here in the office someplace. Let me just find my specs . . . Yeah, here we go, headline says . . . let me see here . . . *Hero horse shuns spotlight.*"

Doyle wasn't entirely sure what that meant although he recognized the hero horse part.

"Okay . . ." he told Walter. "That's kind of what she said she'd write."

"Well, gotta admit you did a bang-up job with that. It's like the horse is a saint or something. Maybe I should hire you as my PR guy." A big laugh. "Listen, you want me to save it, the article?"

"Sure, thanks."

"Okay, next time you come in. Maybe I'll even frame a copy, put it up on the wall. Every little bit helps, right?"

"Thanks, Walter."

"No problem. See you next time. When, Sunday?"

"You want me to come Sunday?"

"Why not? Sunday morning, that's when we got most customers. Just before lunch. Might as well make the most of it, now you're a star."

"Me? I'm not a star."

"Absolutely, you are. You and the horse. Coupla real stars. You'll be signing autographs next." Doyle wasn't sure about that idea. He was always slow in signing his name but Walter either didn't know about that or didn't care.

"Actually, that's not such a bad idea," Walter was saying, almost thinking out loud. "Yeah, come over Sunday morning. Come every Sunday morning. That'd be great. You can talk to the customers, make it like a regular event, okay? Maybe I'll print up some fliers, tell people to bring their kids. All right with you?"

"If you like."

"No, what I mean is, for the horse. He's not going to ..."

Walter didn't even have to complete the sentence. Doyle knew exactly what he was going to say. "No, he likes children. Likes people too. Long as there's no cameras."

Walter laughed into Doyle's ear. "No cameras," he agreed. "And no falling trees, right? I guess we learned that lesson the hard way. Okay, see you Sunday."

"What if ..."

"What's that? Can you speak up?"

"What if the people have cameras?"

"You mean the kids and stuff? Yeah, maybe. That might be a problem. Didn't think of that. Okay, tell you what, we'll make a special section for you and the horse, okay? I'll get a couple of the boys to put up a rope or something, fence it off and we'll put up a big sign where people come in, No Cameras.

"No, wait, we can't do that. Kind of defeats the whole purpose, right? Parents with kids, they want a souvenir. Okay, how about this? The sign says No Flash ... how about that? Does that solve it or what?" Walter was obviously proud of himself.

"No flash. That might work," Doyle agreed.

"Okay, I'll have one of my guys at the entrance, by the rope kind of thing, you know, like a bouncer. He'll just keep telling people, 'no flash, no flash.' That suit you?"

"Sure," said Doyle.

"Good, we'll see how it goes. Nothing set in stone, we can always adapt if need be. Also, do me a favor, will you? Wear that coat you wore for the shoot. Not overalls, okay? And a hat if you got it. You got a hat?"

"No, I don't wear a hat. Got a baseball cap ... Expos." The Montréal Expos were once a summer fixture at the Olympic stadium but then they were sold and became the Washington Nationals.

Doyle wasn't much of a fan, but one day Jacqueline came back with the hat, left in her carriage by some tourists, and she'd given it to him.

"Nah, that's not picturesque," Walter replied. "Goddam Expos, bunch of losers. No, I kinda see more like a flat golfer's thing, like they used to wear. That would suit you. Something a bit classy, you know? What's the word I'm looking for? Debonair. That's it, you should be debonair. Hey, and Christmas you can be Santa Claus! Can you make your wagon into a sleigh? Put runners instead of wheels?"

"I dunno."

"Okay, okay, not to worry. All in good time, right? See you Sunday."

Doyle heard the click and he, too, hung up. He'd said "sure" to Walter but in actual fact, he wasn't sure about any of it.

He'd never been Santa Claus either, although he didn't object totally to that because his dad had once donned a costume, stuffed a pillow inside his pants and played the role at a kids' party in the Pointe.

Did it well, too, the kids had enjoyed it. So now Doyle's head was full of ideas—about hats, about pillows, about children lining up to see Groucho . . . He shook himself out of it. He had work to do.

When Sunday came, Doyle pulled on his good jacket, as requested, and tried on the flat golfer's cap that one of Walter Sullivan's guys had brought over to the stable. It made Doyle think that Walter was taking this thing seriously, so he'd better at least try to show some enthusiasm.But as he stood looking at himself in his cracked bathroom mirror, he found it hard not to laugh. He looked like a bit of an idiot, like one of those British actors in the old movies they used to show on TV, except he wasn't British, he was Irish, and he wouldn't be driving a sports car, he'd be up on a wagon delivering manure.

Maybe, he thought, he'd be better with a cowboy hat, the way that woman from the paper had suggested, but not a straw one like Bertrand's, a real one, a Stetson, like the Lone Ranger used to wear. Then he reconsidered and decided no hats of any sort and removed the golfer's cap with a swoop of his hand. To him, it just looked plain stupid.

The weather had been holding steady for the past few days, cool but bright. That was lucky for Walter Sullivan because today was his big day, final day of the sale, rock-bottom prices on everything at the center. If it had rained, his business might have been cut by sixty or seventy percent. As it was, there was already a sizeable crowd milling around even before Doyle and Groucho arrived.

Doyle steered the horse carefully through the car park, waving to adults and children alike, but it was only when he pulled into the center that he noticed the air of festivity, and he was immediately apprehensive. The place was like a fairground. There were silver balloons and a candy apple stall with music and a clown on stilts performing a juggling act. These were all attractive to customers but all potential problems for a sensitive horse, especially one without blinders, and Doyle was wondering if this was such a good idea after all. He felt responsible and for a long moment, he considered pulling out.

The saving grace was that Walter Sullivan had been as good as his word in terms of a special enclosure for the horse and wagon. The area was isolated and cordoned off by a kind of rustic wooden fencing, with one of the center's young assistants on security duty by the entrance, so while there was a lot going on, it would all be held at a safe distance from Groucho.

As for cameras, there were many, to be sure, the kind of digital point-and-shoot that all families seemed to carry, but also as promised, there was a sign that showed a crude graphic of a camera with a red bar through it, plus the words Danger—No Flash in both languages.

Doyle brought Groucho to a stop in the enclosure and hauled on the wagon's hydraulic brake. Despite all the precautions, he knew that he'd have to stay close to the horse at all times just to be safe; just to talk to him and to reassure him. It was Walter, easing through the crowd, who called up to him on the bench, "Hey, Doyle, where's the hat?"

Doyle took it out of his jacket pocket where he'd stuffed it before leaving and held it up. He wanted to show that although he didn't like it much, he hadn't forgotten.

"Put it on, put it on," urged Walter.

Obligingly, Doyle pulled it on and grinned shyly as Walter applauded. Then Doyle lifted it from his head and nodded to the people around, like a pro golfer on the eighteenth green. Some smiled appreciatively but once everybody had seen it, he took it off and didn't put it back. Walter seemed satisfied enough with the little show, so Doyle checked the wagon's brake again and then climbed down.

First thing was to attend to Groucho, patting him on the neck, rubbing his muzzle and giving him some sugar to keep him happy. "Lotta people," Doyle said to him.

Meanwhile, he was smiling and nodding as parents entered the enclosure to show their kids the big horse. All the people who entered were shown the No Flash sign by the young staffer and Doyle was glad to see they were respecting it. So far, the process was well-organized and orderly. Nearby, just beyond the fence, Doyle noticed that a kind of temporary platform had been erected, with a staircase leading up to a wooden stage. In the center was a microphone on a stand. "What's that?" he asked Walter.

"Not bad, eh? That's for the big announcement."

"What for?"

"What for?" Walter's voice was incredulous. "You didn't see the ad yesterday? I don't believe it. Cost me a fortune and you didn't even see it."

Doyle just shrugged. Yesterday was Saturday. He'd neither watched TV nor seen the paper.

Walter just shook his head in frustration. "Sometimes I wonder where you're living, Doyle, I really do."

"At the stable."

"At the stable, right, good one. Anyways, all I'm saying is you got a big surprise coming, that's for sure."

"What kind of surprise?"

"Wait and see, trust me, you're gonna love it. Just take another few minutes or so to set up, won't be long." Then just before Walter left, he said, "You okay here? I mean, you know, with the horse?" Under all the brash confidence, he too was just a little nervous. The last thing he needed was a repeat. Doyle looked up at Groucho, who was nodding his head gently as each family came to pet him and appeared to be thoroughly enjoying the attention. There was almost a smile on his face. "He's happy enough," replied Doyle.

Walter gave a brief nod of his own, then left to attend to business as Doyle got busy answering questions yet again. What's the horse's name? How big is he? What does he eat? How old will he live to be?

All the usual things that kids ask. One little girl even wondered whether Groucho was married. Doyle tried to take it all in his stride, responding in his usual modest way while managing to maintain a running commentary for Groucho at the same time. "Now, here's someone who'd like to rub your nose, you gonna let her? Sure you are. Easy now, very slowly, that's the way. He likes that, don't you Groucho, eh?"

Fortunately, nobody asked him for an autograph but if they had, Doyle had his answer all prepared. Sorry, I hurt my hand, he would say, so I can't write too well. He didn't like lying to children, or to anybody else for that matter, but his penmanship was just too slow and he simply couldn't abide people laughing at him for that reason. In the privacy of his office at the stable, he could take all the time he wanted to sign the forms and checks that Jacqueline had placed in front of him. She knew about his little secret but she was the only one. Out here in public, it was a whole other story.

After half an hour or so, Doyle heard somebody testing the microphone and looked up to see Walter's wife, Gabrielle, up on the makeshift stage. Since Walter's accent was fairly pronounced when speaking French and she was a home-grown Québécoise, she was invariably the one to take the lead with such public relations activities, be they sale events or customer relations. Today, though, he was right up there with her, beaming alongside while she made the introductions.

"Ladies and gentlemen," she began, then corrected herself. "Ladies and gentlemen . . . and children. Your kind attention please."

Many of the customers milling around stopped what they were doing and turned their heads to see what was going on, including those around Doyle, because everybody likes announcements. Walter's brother-in-law, Hadleigh, was also there, once again taking photos but this time using available light; in other words, without the flash. Doyle noticed and was appreciative.

"Today is a special occasion at the Clifford H. Sullivan Gardening Center," continued Gabrielle in her best presentation voice. "As you all know, we recently had a new addition to our professional team here. He's big and strong and he works very hard and . . . oh yes . . . he also has four legs!" She offered a big grin and there was some laughter and applause in response.

"That's right, I'm talking about our famous hero, Groucho, who's with us here today." She stretched out her arm to indicate the horse, still standing peacefully in his compound. She'd deliberately used the word "hero" from *The Gazette* article, yet she couldn't resist adding: "And I'm glad to see he's behaving himself!"

There was more laughter and it was evident that many had either seen or heard about the notorious video. She stood there smiling along with them until the reaction had died down, then like any good public speaker, smoothly changed to a more meaningful attitude.

"With him, of course, is his proud owner, an old friend of the Sullivan family . . . May I present Mr. Doyle O'Shaughnessy!"

Doyle was embarrassed when he too received a round of applause and he wasn't sure where to look, so he just raised a tentative hand and gave a brief smile.

"Now as you may know, our Groucho has recently become a big media celebrity . . . Newspapers, TV, internet, everything . . . so what we've decided to do here at the center, is make use of all that publicity. Well, that's just good business, right? So how we gonna do that? Well, we're going to name a product after him. That's right, we're gonna use the name Groucho on one of our products. Now I'm told that in all those fancy marketing companies downtown, they call that creating a brand, so that's what we're doing here today, all of us together. We're creating a brand in honor of our hero, Groucho."

At this point, she turned to Walter, who walked over to a tall easel that shared the stage with them. Perched on the easel was a tall rectangular shape covered by a large black cloth.

"And now," announced Gabrielle, "the Clifford H. Sullivan Gardening Center is proud to present . . ." She waited until Walter removed the cloth. He did so with a grand gesture, revealing a colorful poster. "Our new brand . . . Groucho!" said Gabrielle triumphantly. "Finest quality horse manure! As always, guaranteed one hundred percent organic!"

The poster that Walter displayed was of the new packaging. It showed a stylized, head-and-shoulders portrait of a sorrel horse with a blond mane and white blaze, just like Groucho, set neatly inside a horseshoe. Around it was bold text, in stark white with a black outline, like the kind they used in the old days. The general feeling was of heritage and tradition but that was deliberate, simply in order to give it an air of authenticity.

"Ladies and gentlemen," Gabrielle continued, "you can't create a brand without a brand promotion, so for today only we're offering you two bags for the price of one. Yes, that's right, two for the price of one. Use Groucho manure for your seeded lawns, for your flower

beds, for your tree and shrub areas. If you've got an orchard or veg-
etable patch, it's perfect. There's nothing more natural.

"Look on the label . . . No chemicals, no phosphates, nothing arti-
ficial at all. That's what hundred percent organic means. Just a mix
of horse manure direct from the stable, good black soil and a drying
agent called sphagnum which is a natural plant. You can't do anything better for your garden or for the environment.

"And one more thing . . . for every purchase, we'll donate a per-
centage of the revenue to the SPCA for the care of sick or injured
animals. And here today, we have with us Mr. Roger Tremblay,
deputy director of the SPCA . . ." She indicated a man down in the
crowd who lifted his hand in acknowledgment, much the same way
as Doyle had done.

"Welcome Mr. Tremblay. Your organization does outstanding
work. Ladies and gentlemen, a big hand for the SPCA!" There was a
round of applause, before she addressed the crowd once again. "So,
how can you go wrong? You help your garden, you help the environment and you help the animals. What can be better than that? So I'd
just like to say thanks from Walter and me to everyone for coming
along today. Have fun, look around, be our guests . . . and please, go
over and say a big hello to Groucho. Ladies and gentlemen, another
big hand, please, for Groucho!"

This time, Gabrielle herself began the applause. She was immediately joined by Walter and the center's young staff, and it became
infectious. Soon, the entire crowd was clapping along, the juggler
was whistling, and people were congratulating Doyle, as if he'd had
something to do with it. In fact, he was as surprised as anybody, and
he had no idea how to react, except for his newly ingrained habit of
talking to the horse.

"Well, now, what do you say to that, eh? That's your name up
there, your very own bag of manure, isn't that great? Groucho manure, that's what it says. Your name and your picture, how about
that? You like that, you big ham? Sure you do!"

Doyle returned from the gardening center show with his arms
full of souvenir gifts. In addition to the flat cap, he now possessed
a Groucho brand coffee mug, a cotton shirt like Jacqueline used to
wear but with Groucho on the pocket, a framed photocopy of the

Prudence Carmichael article in *The Gazette,* and a large paper sack of Rougemont apples for the horse.

In addition, he had a contract for the use of Groucho's name that he promised to sign and take back to Walter but that was troubling him a little, because he didn't really understand it. Walter had tried to explain it to him but what with all the festivities and the people, the circumstances weren't exactly ideal for either explaining or negotiating the fine details.

Eventually, Walter told him to take the contract home, study it at his leisure and, if there were any questions, to call back. But that was the problem, right there. Doyle could hardly read the contract, much less understand it, and he went upstairs to his small office in a quandary about what to do. He didn't have Jacqueline anymore.

The situation also served as a nagging reminder that he still had a stack of unanswered mail on his desk. Some had been there for a few days, some for weeks. He'd been able to pay the bills all right, because he was okay at math and could, without too much trouble, see from the invoice how much he was required to pay. It was the other stuff he found difficult, the long explanatory letters or the government notifications or the official forms demanding information, full of bureaucratic terms and asterisks.

In theory, he could have asked one of the drivers for assistance but he was reluctant to do that. He loathed asking them for help because he felt they'd just laugh at him, perhaps not in front of his face but behind his back, and he hated the idea. Yet he also knew that Walter was expecting an answer.

Slowly, he picked up a pen, found the place on the paper that Walter had marked with an "X" and prepared to inscribe his signature, an effort that took all his concentration. But then he paused. His father had warned him not to sign anything without understanding it first. It was right there in the will after he died, the part concerning ownership of the stable. His father had been very specific.

Doyle, he'd written in the attached note that the lawyer had read out, *don't you sign anything without understanding it.* Doyle didn't mistrust Walter. On the contrary, he really liked the idea of Groucho's name on the manure bag, liked it a great deal, and felt like it was an accomplishment of sorts, a result of his own efforts in befriending and working with the animal. It was an achievement from which he could take a great measure of gratification—but only if he could sign the contract.

Doyle felt trapped. He couldn't sign but he couldn't *not* sign. And he couldn't ask the drivers for help. He therefore did the only thing he could. He found the number of the bar and put in a call to Louise. It meant swallowing his pride and admitting his handicap to a stranger but he rationalized it by telling himself that when all was said and done, Louise was still Jacqueline's daughter. Inside, though, he knew the real truth. There was just nobody else to whom he could turn.

The plan was sound and the reasoning logical but the execution hit a snag.

He didn't get Louise on the line. Instead, he found himself talking to the bar's owner, Clément, who told him that Louise wasn't working there anymore. Apparently, she was now waitressing at a much fancier bar for a much fancier wage up in the avant-garde area of the Plateau. Clément didn't sound too happy about it, either, like he'd been personally insulted by her decision to quit, and only gave out her new number with some reluctance.

Doyle noted it down, hung up, and then took a deep breath before dialing the digits. He felt shy calling strange places, especially fancy places uptown, but he really needed to talk to Louise.

Fifteen

"Hi, how's it going?" asked Louise when she appeared in front of him at the stable door.

"Hi," said Doyle. But he was little discouraged to see that she wasn't alone.

It was Saturday morning and she'd arrived with her new boyfriend, Marc-André, the one she'd said was a cop. He didn't look much like a cop to Doyle, with his slick-backed hair and black leather jacket, but he seemed pleasant enough. And Louise sure looked better than the last time Doyle saw her.

The bruises had healed up, her hair was styled differently and she was wearing a cream-colored blazer over a pair of designer jeans, an outfit that suited her well. On top of her head was a large pair of sunglasses.

"Congratulations," Doyle said to her. "I mean, on the new job."

"Thanks," she grinned, obviously happy about it. "Can we come in?" They were still on the doorstep.

He stepped aside to let them in and Marc-André immediately went over to the only occupied stall. "Hey . . . so this is Groucho," he said over his shoulder. "Great horse."

"He's a celebrity," said Doyle, repeating the word that Walter Sullivan's wife, Gabrielle, had used.

"He sure is," agreed Marc-André. "You know, I worked with horses for a time."

"Is that right?"

"Yeah, yeah, about six months. In my younger days, up there on the mountain." He was referring to the special mounted police precinct that the city maintained on Mount Royal but the horses there were nothing like Groucho.

They weren't draft breeds, they were palomino saddle horses, expertly trained in crowd control. "Oh yeah, this guy's great," said Marc-André, patting Groucho's neck.

Louise was still standing with Doyle. "So what were you saying there on the phone?" she said to him. "Something about a contract?"

Doyle felt awkward talking about it with Marc-André present. "It's for Walter at the gardening center. He wants to use Groucho's name on a product."

"Yeah?" she said. "Sounds interesting."

Doyle was actually surprised she hadn't heard about that. It seemed to him like it was a big event. "He wants me to sign a contract, y'know, so he can use the name and all."

"Okay, so what's the problem. It's in French?"

"No ..." Doyle was still hesitant to admit his failings. "I just need an opinion," he said. It was something he'd rehearsed in his head. "Just your opinion."

"Fine, whatever. Let's go take a look." They left Marc-André with the horse and made their way up the steep flight to Doyle's office. He'd tidied up a little in advance, so it wasn't the usual mess.

"My God, what's all that?" she asked as soon as she came in. She was pointing to the pile of unopened envelopes on his desk, nearly a foot high.

"Just mail," he told her.

"Just mail?"

She looked at him with a disapproving expression, like his teachers used to do. "Doyle, are those your bills?"

"No," he answered defensively. "I paid the bills. It's just mail."

"What if it's important stuff? You can't just ignore it like that."

"Here's the contract," he said, changing the subject. He picked up the document from the desk, five legal-sized sheets held together by a paper clip, and handed it to her. "Want some coffee? No, you like tea, I forgot."

"Okay, thanks."

While Doyle went to the kitchen, Louise wandered into the apartment where she'd slept the night she'd left her husband. For a few seconds, she just stood there, looking at the sofa, remembering. Then, in an effort to dismiss it from her mind, she sat down and made a deliberate attempt to concentrate on the contract. By the time Doyle came through with his wooden tray, she'd gone through it twice and Marc-André had come upstairs to join her. Doyle unloaded the tray, taking care to show them both his new mug with the Groucho brand logo on it.

"Neat," said Marc-André.

Doyle indicated the contract in Louise's lap. "You read it?"

"Yeah." She sipped at her tea but it almost burned her mouth it was so hot and she had to put it down again. "Most of it's in legal talk, but basically I think it's pretty simple. What it says is that when you sign, you allow the Sullivan company the rights to use the name and picture of Groucho for . . . well, basically for whatever they wanna use it for. It's up to them. Now, what it also says is that you get paid in return."

"Paid? I didn't think I'd get paid."

"No? So what did you think? You'd have to pay *them*?"

She said it as a joke and Marc-André chuckled but Doyle took it seriously.

"I didn't know," he said.

"So there you go. That's nice, eh?"

"Does it say how much?"

"Yeah, well, see, that's the thing. It doesn't say. That's the part that's not too clear. What it says is that if they make a certain amount of profit per annum . . . that means in a year . . . then you get a fee."

"What fee?"

"Like I said, it's not clear." She showed the relevant paragraph to Marc-André. "Tell us what that means," she said to him.

Marc-André studied it with a slightly furrowed brow. "I think it means that if they do well, Doyle does well. The better they do, the better he does too."

To Doyle that sounded eminently fair but he needed confirmation. "What do *you* think?" he said, addressing both of them.

"Sounds okay to me," said Louise, "but, hey, it's your life."

He looked at Marc-André, who rubbed his chin and considered the question before answering. When he spoke, it was slower and more thoughtful than Louise's instant response.

"Me, I'd say you can probably hold out for more," he said. "Way I see it, they made a mistake. They went ahead and did it without your permission. Now they want you to sign, which means you can ask for better terms and they got to agree."

"You think?" asked Louise.

"Absolutely."

Doyle wasn't certain. "I don't think Walter's trying to cheat me," he said.

"No, I didn't say he was," replied Marc-André. "I just said I think you can hold out for more."

"I don't know," said Doyle. "Me and Cliffy were friends."

"Who's Cliffy?"

"Walter's dad. We were friends."

"Up to you, but that's what people do now."

It was Louise who asked, "What people?"

"Athletes, rock stars, movie actors, everybody. That's what they do when they negotiate. When they think somebody needs 'em, like, I dunno, the sports team or the movie studio, they hold out for what they want. They have agents who negotiate that stuff. That's how it's done."

"Yeah," she said, "but Doyle doesn't have an agent. Who's gonna do the negotiating?"

Marc-André shrugged. He couldn't deny the logic of that. "Just an idea," he said, as he added milk and sugar to the coffee that Doyle had made him.

They all sipped in silence for a while but Doyle had just about made up his mind that he was going to sign it. He'd only helped Walter out in the first place as a gesture to ol' Cliffy, so why would that change? And the notion of Groucho becoming a famous hero was really to stop people making fun of him.

With his name and picture on the product, that couldn't happen anymore. Even if what Marc-André said was true, Doyle was well enough satisfied with how it had turned out and didn't really want to hold out for more. As his dad used to say, money's important, but it's not everything.

Louise hadn't been well-educated but she wasn't stupid either, and she'd soon managed to figure out why Doyle had needed her help in looking at the contract. Of course, she didn't say anything out loud because that would have been embarrassing and insulting to him but she knew all right. That's why, as they passed his small office on their way out, she felt a twinge of concern about that large stack of mail on Doyle's desk.

"You wanna wait for me in the car?" she asked her boyfriend. "I'll just be a minute." When Marc-André was gone, she turned back to Doyle. "I think I'd better go through that stuff, don't you?"

Doyle looked at her face and immediately saw that she knew about his literacy problem. It was a bad moment for him, the realization that his secret was out, that his deception hadn't really worked. No words passed between them, so Louise took it as a sign of acquiescence and she stepped into the office to begin sorting through.

Briefly, she scanned each envelope to see who it was from and the likely importance, then arranged them into piles. It was the mail from the government she tore open first and there were half a dozen of those. Some were demands for information about his enterprise, others were notifications of tax changes. But it was the one from City Hall that caused the stunned look on her face, the mouth to drop open.

"Oh my God . . ."

"What is it?" asked Doyle. When she didn't answer, he became concerned. "What's the problem?"

Doyle sat in his apartment late into the evening, just clutching the letter in his hand and staring into thin air, his expression blank. He could neither believe nor fully understand what Louise had told him.

In recent weeks, he'd gotten into the habit of talking things over with Groucho but tonight he couldn't even do that. He was too overwhelmed. Nothing had ever happened like this before and he couldn't even begin to see how he was going to cope.

Louise had been sympathetic to the point that she was worried about him. First she assumed the letter was some sort of mistake but then, when she read it again and understood the implications, she'd touched him on the shoulder and told him that she and Marc-André would do everything they could. It was supposed to be some kind of reassurance but it hadn't reassured Doyle at all, and he just sat there, empty of thoughts or ideas.

He looked again at the official paper in his hands and peered for the hundredth time at the ominous words at the top of the page: Eviction Notice. According to Louise, it had been sitting on his desk since the time her mother died and the date to appeal the ruling was already overdue.

How could he now tell Groucho, and the other horses, too, that they were all going to be thrown out of their home in a matter of months? How could he tell the drivers? Where would they go, he wondered, what would they do? He couldn't figure it out. He had no answers for them and that was why he remained upstairs in his darkened apartment, alone, trying to comprehend.

He couldn't work out how such a thing could have occurred and he didn't know, either, what would happen if it ever came about. This was his whole life. He'd never known, or ever wanted to know, anything else. He'd even given up the chance of marriage and a family, just for the horses.

It was as if his neural system had failed him by simply shutting down, and he sat there perfectly still into the small hours of the morning, listening to the rain that had begun to pound on the windows but staring at nothing. He was alone. His entire world was falling apart, and he was alone.

Sixteen

The bureau that dealt with *calèche* issues wasn't located in the baroque City Hall building on Notre Dame where the mayor had his office, but up on the fifth floor of the bland district offices of the Arrondissement de Ville-Marie, the borough administration located on Boulevard de Maisonneuve.

Doyle and Louise were there first thing Monday morning, even before it opened, waiting for the ragtag assortment of counter clerks and bureaucrats to show up. Doyle, in particular, couldn't help noticing how inexperienced they seemed, or how uncaring and unconcerned they were about anything except their weekend chitchat and the lattes they each carried in from downstairs.

One young woman with an eyebrow ring was talking to an even younger man with a pony tail, evidently describing a violent argument she'd had with her husband and demanding her colleague's sympathy for her side of the story.

Doyle just sat and watched them for a while, but he wasn't entirely indifferent because he could see that, right next to him, Louise was affected by it. He could see it on her face and could appreciate how it might bring back harsh recollections of her own recently failed marriage. Despite the supposedly official opening hour of eight-thirty, it wasn't until eight forty-five that the first service booth was available and by that time, there were several others in line behind Doyle and Louise.

The clerk was still signing into her computer program: not the woman who'd been complaining, but another the same age.

"*Oui?*" she said, without even looking at them.

It was Louise who explained the situation in French: that her friend owned a *calèche* stable and that he'd received an eviction notice. She passed the letter over the counter to the clerk, who scanned it briefly.

"And what exactly it is that you want, madame?" she asked. She was still waiting for some question to be asked.

"We'd like to speak to someone about this."

"Concerning what?"

"Well, this letter."

"Yes, but concerning what?"

Louise glanced at Doyle, who understood just about enough of the language to be able to follow what was going on.

"Concerning what we can do about it," she replied.

"Do about it?"

"How we can answer it."

"Answer it? I don't understand. Please explain what you want, madame. We're very busy, and as you can see, we're short-staffed."

Louise could see nothing of the sort and was beginning to lose patience. "What we want," she said firmly, "is to talk to someone in authority about this damn eviction notice and we're not moving from here until we do."

It was a flash of the old Louise, the Louise before Marc-André, the Louise who was still stuck in the middle of an abusive relationship, a dead-end job and, a vitriolic mother.

At this, the clerk made a face like she'd just sucked on a lemon, then turned and disappeared into the back area of the office, presumably to consult with someone—or it might just have been to take her break. Since she'd said nothing, it was unclear to either Doyle or Louise where she'd gone.

"You think she's coming back?" asked Doyle.

Louise's only response was to try to contain her own dislike. "I loathe these people," she said, almost to herself, still speaking French. "Stupid morons with their stupid rules and their stupid unions."

"Thanks for coming with," Doyle told her.

She gave him a quick, empty smile, as if to say she wasn't mad at him, just at them. He was glad of that, at least. He was upset enough.

Three minutes later, the same woman came back. She was holding a small sheet of paper, which she placed on the counter in front of them. On it was a phone number, scribbled by hand. "You have to call this number," she said officiously.

Louise picked it up. "What is it?"

"You got a problem, that's the number to call."

Louise glared at her. "What I meant was *who* is it?"

"I don't know. Another department."

For a brief moment, Doyle thought Louise was going to take a swing, punch the woman's lights out, just like his old buddy Cliffy when the fight bell sounded. He didn't want any trouble, figuring that fisticuffs wouldn't help him at all, so he put a gentle restraining hand on her shoulder.

"Let's just go call the number," he said to her.

Louise was reluctant to leave and began to yell abuse at the clerk in the most coarse street language, swearing and cursing at the top of her voice. Even with his limited language skills, Doyle knew all these words from his early days at the gym, also from all those years at the stable with Louise's mother.

He was embarrassed about causing such a scene. "Let's just go call," he told Louise calmly. "We can always come back and kill her later."

The unlikely humor didn't really pacify Louise but it served its purpose, allowing him to escort her to the elevator, then out onto the sidewalk where she could use her cell phone.

The number turned out to be the office of the city ombudsman, but the only contact she could make was through a complex automated system. Refusing to play that kind of game, she dialed zero and held on while a local radio station played middle-of-the-road music for six minutes.

Eventually, a real human answered, only to tell her that no appointments were possible for the next four months. When she hung up, the fury had re-emerged and all she could do was breathe deeply several times in order to find some sense of equilibrium.

"We can't wait four months," said Doyle.

"Yeah, tell me about it."

"So what do we do now?"

"Damned if I know."

All in all, it had been a frustrating lesson in civic administration. But depressed as he was, he insisted on treating her at a coffee chain franchise a block away on Sainte-Cathérine. As it turned out, the quiet break away from the noise on the street helped her relax, and she just shook her head.

"Sorry, I guess I kinda lost it," she said. "I wasn't much help."

"That's okay."

"I guess I must have reminded you of . . ." She came to a stop, her voice trailing off without completing the thought. Doyle knew what she meant. She was referring to the obvious similarities to her mother but instead of filling in the blank, he just took a bite out of his fruit danish. Louise sighed a little, then did the same. "Fattening," she said, changing the subject as she wiped the stickiness from her mouth with a paper napkin.

"Little bit of what you fancy does you good," replied Doyle. It was something else his father used to say. For her sake, he was trying to remain positive, but inside, he was sick at the thought of not being able to do anything constructive.

When Louise told him she'd accompany him to the city offices, he'd pinned his hopes on the idea that, somehow, she'd be able to get to the bottom of the matter, maybe even find that a mistake had been made. Maybe the city had sent the notification to the wrong address, or maybe somebody had gotten things mixed up in some other way.

Anything was possible. What he hadn't considered, however, was the possibility that they just wouldn't be able to talk to anybody at all and that's what he was finding difficult to accept. Surely, he felt, there must be somebody, somewhere in the administration, to whom they could appeal.

It was Marc-André who came up with the next idea and it was a good one too, stemming from Louise's suggestion they should perhaps consult a lawyer. When Doyle was fearful of both the process and the cost, Marc-André recommended a place he knew about from his work on the force: a store front citizen's advice bureau that was staffed by volunteers, which included, but was not strictly limited to, certain aspects of legal aid.

Located in the heart of Snowdon, it was the local immigrant population who formed the majority of the project's clientele, looking for help on all kinds matters from rental difficulties to employment visas. Yet it was also open to anyone who had an administrative or procedural problem with the government, whether federal, provincial or municipal. All you had to do was show up during office hours on any given weekday and wait your turn.

Once again, it was Louise who accompanied Doyle and, once again, they had to wait to be seen. This time, however, it wasn't just a few minutes, it was several hours, to the point that Louise feared she'd be late for her afternoon shift. Around them sat an entire spectrum of faces: Moroccan, Haitian, Senegalese, Vietnamese and many others, some with elderly family members, some with small children, all chatting quietly amongst themselves in their own native tongues.

A regular Tower of Babel, thought Doyle as he gazed at them, wondering about their lives and what kind of tragedies they might have endured just to get here. In some ways, he felt like an interloper, but Louise kept telling him he had a perfect right to be there, that his grievance was as legitimate as anyone else's.

It was close to two and she was just about to leave when, at last, their number was called and they were shown through to a small cubicle, just one of many in the large back room of what was obviously a well-used building. It wasn't that the place was run-down as such, but the furniture was old and scratched and the equipment, whether phones, computers, or printers, was grubby and technologically obsolete.

Nevertheless, the volunteers who staffed the operation had the best of intentions and the bespectacled young man behind the desk received them with concern and courtesy, in total contrast to the city employee that Louise had so despised. His hair and skin were not in the best of health but his attitude made up for those shortcomings.

"Hi, my name's Irwin," he said in English, as he adjusted the small Jewish cap that was perched precariously on the back of his head. "What can I do for you today?"

Louise was immediately more responsive. "Hi . . . Yeah, I'm just here with my friend, Mr. O'Shaughnessy and, well, he's got a problem that's a bit unusual. We were wondering if you could maybe help."

"I'll do my best."

She lifted the letter from her purse, unfolded it and handed it across the cluttered desk to the young man.

"Oh, an eviction notice," he said, his expression becoming serious as he focused his attention on the contents, reading it through a couple of times, first to scan it and second to absorb the details. When he was done, he checked the top of the letter for the date. "When did you receive this?" he asked.

"Yeah, see, that's the thing," replied Louise. "It's kind of been sitting there on his desk for a while."

Doyle remained silent, his face masked with guilt.

"I see," said the young man. "The trouble is you seem to have missed the appeal date."

"I know," said Louise. "But they can't just throw him out, I mean, can they?"

Irwin put the letter down in front of him, then blinked rapidly as he pushed his glasses back on to the bridge of his nose and once again adjusted the circular, dark blue head-piece. He seemed to have many minor affectations, all totally unconscious on his part. "You're in Pointe St-Charles?" he asked Doyle.

"Yes."

"Yes, well, I know for a fact they want to gentrify a lot of that area. Seems you're one of the people in their way."

"What's that mean?" asked Louise. "We can't stop them?"

"No, I'm not saying that, not at all. At least, not yet. There's a whole bunch of things we can try but . . ."

He came to a stop and Louise was quick to pounce.

"It's not good, is that what you're telling us?"

Irwin was trying to be nice. "I don't want to lie to you," he said. "On the other hand, they seem willing to pay you compensation."

"Will he be able to afford another building in the same area?"

"No way to tell. All I can say is that the price is usually based on the municipal evaluation, not the true market value, so it's never as much as people expect . . . unfortunately."

"There's the permit too," added Doyle. "I gotta have a permit to run a stable."

"It's a stable?" asked Irwin. "Your building's a stable? With, like, animals and stuff?"

"Horses . . . *Calèche* horses."

"Really? That's a first. Don't think we ever had anyone in here with horses before. How many do you keep there?"

"Five, including mine."

"Is that right?"

It was Louise who got them back on track, looking at her watch, anxious about the time. "What are the chances?" she asked. "If he just wants to keep it, you know, without selling or anything, what are the chances?"

Irwin gave her a shrug. "These things are never easy . . . but we'll do what we can, okay? Have you spoken to anyone yet?" Briefly, Louise described their frustrating visit to the Ville-Marie offices and then the call to get an appointment with the city ombudsman, while Irwin jotted down notes on his pad in his scrawling script.

"Nobody else?" he asked.

"Not so far."

"Okay, leave it with me."

"What will you do?" Doyle asked him.

"Not sure yet. I'll try to call some people, that's the best way to start. See what gives."

"And you'll call us? You know, if you have some news?"

"Yes, yes, absolutely. We always call back, Mr . . . ."

"O'Shaughnessy."

"Sorry, yes, we always call back, that's our policy. Let me just take down your details and make a quick copy of this, all right?" Once he'd scribbled Louise's name and number on top of the letter, he stepped across to the wall and pushed a button on the clunky machine.

A minute later he was back, but he didn't sit down, he just handed Louise the original along with his card. "Well, pleased to meet you," he said, indicating their time was up. "Eviction from a stable! Nobody's gonna believe this one."

"Worse than Jesus," replied Doyle, as he got to his feet. He said it with a straight face, but the unlikely remark caused Irwin to laugh out loud.

Louise smiled along and was about to follow Doyle out, but she turned back for an instant. "He doesn't say it, but he's very worried," she confided quietly to the young man. "It's his whole life, the horses."

Irwin was already tidying up his files, preparing for the next problem to walk into his cubicle. "Like I said, I'll do my best." Louise looked at him with some uncertainty but had no alternative but to leave it at that. She was already late.

As they stood on the corner of Victoria and Van Horne, waiting to cross over to the Métro station just opposite, Doyle said, "What d'you think? Seemed like a nice young feller."

"Yeah, maybe."

"You're not sure?"

The lights changed and they stepped off the sidewalk with half a dozen others. "I dunno if nice is gonna be enough," she replied.

That afternoon, after Groucho's belated exercise, Doyle sat for a while in the stall, just for the company. The big horse was in a quiet mood and stood dozing contentedly while Doyle ruminated.

In Doyle's hand was an empty coffee mug, the one with the manure logo, and he gazed at it, lost in thought. Visions of Jacqueline appeared to him, and he wondered what she'd have to say about all this.

Probably scream and yell even more than Louise, Doyle decided, and he smiled to himself at that. He could just hear her going off on one of her tantrums, loud enough to wake the whole neighborhood.

Another thing bothering him was the fact that he still hadn't told the drivers the bad news and hadn't even informed Mowbray, uncertain how to break it to any of them. It wasn't just the possibility that he'd have to shut down the stable, although that was painful enough, but that he'd been stupid.

He'd been stupid not to open the letter; stupid, too, for not having learned to read in the first place. "That should be my name," he muttered to Groucho from out of nowhere. "It shouldn't be O'Shaughnessy at all. It should be Patrick Doyle O'Stupid, that's what they should call me . . . Patrick Doyle O'Stupid!"

At the sound of the human voice, the horse half-opened his eyes and twitched his ears but then went straight back to sleep. Just like a child, thought Doyle, just like an innocent child who might soon become an orphan without even realizing it.

For Doyle, the nights were the worst times, as the fears chased each other around his brain like squirrels around a tree, and the night he came back from the advice bureau was especially bad.

Even though the young man they'd seen had been pleasant enough, Doyle had felt Louise's general pessimism and the sense that hope was disappearing; that a great dark chasm was opening up in front of him as he tried to imagine life without the stable, without the horses . . . without Groucho. He wasn't worried about money, nor did he care where the next crust of bread might come from. What caused him to lie sleepless on his cot was the notion of facing his final years alone. Not just alone without friends, but alone without the horses. He wasn't sure he could do it, or whether it was even possible.

His dad had once been friendly with a man who later jumped off the Jacques Cartier Bridge and Doyle wondered he if he'd have the courage to do the same thing. He could see himself there on the parapet, looking down at the stone gray waters. All he'd have to do would be to close his eyes and lean over, to feel the air rushing past him as he fell, to hit the water and then submerge into its depths without any struggle at all, to let himself go all the way into oblivion.

Was there a heaven, he wondered, *like Louise had mentioned in her mother's eulogy, a heaven where there might be horses?* Doyle couldn't even begin to hazard a guess about that. When he was a kid, he'd asked his dad and had received a very simple reply. "Why spoil the surprise?" he'd been told, which had the effect of ending any further discussion.

At about three in the morning, he got up and went downstairs for no reason at all, except that he felt like it, and realized that he'd left the radio playing very softly just outside Groucho's stall. It was a tiny, cheap machine that he'd had for many years and he'd begun using it as company for the horse during the daytime hours when the animal was there on his own, without the others.

Horses like company and Doyle knew that at some stables out in the country, they even kept different species for that very purpose, sometimes a goat or a small pig, but that wasn't too practical in the city. It was one of the reasons he'd bought the cat that time, the cat he called Ginger; but Ginger wasn't interested in making friends with the horses and preferred to spend his time elsewhere. In fact, it was Bertrand who'd suggested the radio and Doyle had thought that a good idea, so he set it up and found that Groucho seemed to like it too.

When he got to the stall, he bent down and switched off the music, which left a sudden emptiness. Groucho stomped a hoof, not violently but gently, just enough to show he was displeased, so Doyle obliged him by doubling over again to turn it back on. "Spoiled," he said, "that's what you are, just plain spoiled. What you gonna do if I'm not around to spoil you, eh? What you gonna do?"

Groucho snorted quietly in reply, and Doyle rubbed the animal's muzzle, enjoying the moment, perhaps because he was finally beginning to realize that these times were precious. One way or another, he felt there might not be many more.

Seventeen

L ouise and Marc-André were still asleep at eight-thirty in the morning when the phone rang.

"Ah, hell," she said.

"Leave it," he mumbled, as he turned over. "That's why they invented answering machines."

Morning was their own time, about the only spare time they really had together and they mostly used it for some extra shuteye. Her new job required her to work evenings and weekends and he'd managed to arrange his police duties to match. It was a killer schedule but they were trying to save for a condo. Only after they'd showered and dressed did Marc-André remember to retrieve the call. "You know someone called Irwin?" he asked her.

She was beating up some scrambled eggs. "Who?"

"Irwin somebody . . . about some project. Wants you to call him back."

"Oh yeah, right." She'd almost forgotten. It had been nearly a week since she'd gone along to the citizen's advice place with Doyle.

Meanwhile, Marc-André was playing the fool. "Irwin . . . Irwin . . . Does she have a new lover?" he said, talking like a TV announcer in melodramatic style. "Is this the end of their affair? Is it all over for Super Cop?"

She pushed him aside to take the phone. "Super Jerk, more like," she replied, as she found the card she'd saved in her purse and dialed through to the number shown. Of course, the line was busy now, so she sat down opposite him to eat breakfast. Outside the window of their apartment, the traffic on St-Joseph was already thinning out, the last remnants of rush hour.

This had been Marc-André's place before, an ordinary bachelor accommodation in an older building, but after Louise left Doyle's stable that night, she'd moved in here with him on a permanent basis. It wasn't large or chic but it was convenient and with her new job, it allowed them to save, so they'd decided to stay put for the time being.

"It's the thing with old man, isn't it?" he asked, his mouth full of toast.

She didn't answer, she just pulled her bathrobe around her and ate. Objectively, she knew, she'd long since repaid her debt to Doyle for his kindness but there was more to it than that, even if she couldn't really put it into words.

Marc-André paused with a cup in his hand. "It's not your problem, you know."

"I just feel kinda bad for him."

"It's life. Shit happens," he said, utilizing the familiar English expression, even while speaking French.

"I know, I know." She was becoming impatient, with her own emotions as much as his insistence. "It's just that . . ."

"What? It's just that what?"

"I don't know."

"Hell, say it if you want to."

"Say what?"

"That he's like family, the only family you've ever known. Isn't that what it's all about?"

She looked at him, amazed that he could pin it down so easily, so casually, when she'd been having so much difficulty sorting it out. There was a long silence while she digested both the food and the kitchen table philosophy.

"I'll try calling back," she said, and this time she was lucky enough to get through. "Yeah, is that Irwin? Louise Vallières here. You called me. Yeah, about Mr. O'Shaughnessy... you know, the guy with the stable." She listened for a good few minutes as Irwin related what he'd managed to find out, only interrupting to clarify points she didn't completely understand. At the end, she thanked him on behalf of Doyle, then put the phone down with a grave sigh.

"Not good news?" Marc-André asked her.

She shook her head. "He told me he talked to City Hall, he even talked to Doyle's city councilor. Someone called Quintal, ever heard of him?"

"No."

"Well, basically, it's a done deal. Even if Doyle had appealed on time, it wouldn't have made any difference."

"Okay... so he'll just have to find another building. Might cost a bit more but ..."

"No, it's worse than that. They're not going to renew his permit."

"They're not?"

"No."

"Even if he finds somewhere else?"

"Quintal's office said nobody wants a stable around there. They said when the wind blows, the place stinks something awful, especially in the summer. People complain all the time."

"Hard to argue with that."

"They said, off the record, they've been looking for an excuse to shut it down for years."

Marc-André shrugged. "He can try another district."

"No, he can't."

"Sure he can."

"No," she insisted. "It's all zoned by the city, that's what the guy said. There's only a few stables left and they all have to be in certain districts. Doyle won't get another stable unless the municipality agrees, which means hearings, negotiations, public consultations, the whole works, and he says nobody's gonna do that. More trouble than it's worth." Louise breathed a long sigh and put her head in her hands. "Christ, how'm I gonna tell Doyle?"

"It's not your problem," said Marc-André again, but he could see she wasn't listening, so he gave up. He had to go get ready for work. He'd recently been assigned to a special investigative squad out of the West Central precinct on Rue Guy with a major corruption case pending.

"It's gonna kill him," she kept muttering, "it's just gonna kill him."

After he left, she thought about calling Doyle but she couldn't face it. Not yet. She still had a couple of hours, so she got on with some chores: the bed, the dishes, a load of laundry. She didn't mind because at least Marc-André shared the work whenever he could, unlike that bastard ex-husband of hers, Roscoe.

But even as she got busy, she couldn't prevent herself thinking about the call—and in particular about what Marc-André had said afterward, the part about Doyle being the closest thing to family she'd ever had.

For some reason, she didn't like that very much but in a way, she had to admit it was true. Yet it was weird at the same time. A semi-literate old man who smelled of horses and who she'd only known for a matter of weeks had become her . . . what?

Her thoughts came to a stop and her feet came to a standstill in the middle of the kitchen as she tried to figure out exactly what kind of connection she had to Doyle. He was too old to be a surrogate father, so what then? A grandfather? A godfather? An uncle?

None of those seemed right, but then again, neither did the simple word *friend*. What she felt was a mixed combination of human responsibility and personal attachment—but where one ended and the other began was an enigma she couldn't seem to solve.

Despite the heavy pall of worry and apprehension, Doyle still had a job to do. The horses still had to be tended and the stable cleaned out as if nothing was happening. He still had to make his deliveries, too, and be unremittingly cheerful whenever he showed up at the Clifford H. Sullivan Gardening Center, simply because he felt that it was now expected of him.

It was hard to put on such an act each and every day, extremely hard, but helping him get through it all was the simple pleasure of being with Groucho.

Ever since that festive day when they'd announced the new brand of manure, the horse had behaved impeccably—or at least as impeccably as could be expected, given his character. There were the usual minor gripes and hoof stomping whenever things weren't exactly to his liking, but overall, his progress had been remarkable, and Doyle was warmed by his deep inner conviction that Jacqueline would be proud.

Perhaps in retrospect, he should have realized it couldn't last, and it didn't.

On the same day that Louise received the bad news call from Irwin at the bureau, Doyle had to cope with his own small emergency when Groucho was accused of nearly biting off a child's hand. The way it happened was laughable, except it wasn't at all amusing for Doyle or the other people involved: either the child's mother or the bus driver who made the accusation or the officer who was duly summoned.

What caused the incident was not one thing but a large number of unconnected factors. Amongst them was the unlikely high pressure front that had brought a couple of days of unseasonably warm weather, what they used to refer to as an "Indian summer."

Then there was the engineering crew who'd been given a repair task at the intersection of Bannantyne and de l' Eglise and who had set their traffic cones just a little too wide. There was also the bus driver who was in a foul mood because, the previous evening, his son had been arrested and charged for possession of stolen goods. Finally there was Doyle himself, whose mind was understandably wandering and not paying full attention to the road.

The child in question was five years old and his mother had just taken him for a vexing medical appointment. To soothe him and keep him quiet on the journey back home, she'd bought him a large ice cream, one of those expensive, chocolate-covered vanilla bars on a stick, and it served its purpose admirably.

The boy was more than content and stood up on the seat next to her so he could stick both his head and his ice cream through the open window, a favorite position of his, whether on the school bus or on public transport. Sure enough, the events combined with an uncanny precision of timing.

Doyle hauled Groucho to a halt behind several vehicles at the junction's red light. The bus pulled up in the left lane alongside but, thanks to the cone configuration, came just a little closer than usual. There was clearly enough room, however, and although the driver might have been faulted for not giving sufficient clearance to the animal, there should really have been no danger.

The emergency only arose when the boy found himself an arm's length from Groucho's massive head and generously offered his confection, half expecting the horse to stick his tongue out and take a lick. Being a city kid, he didn't know that horses are not like dogs in that regard. Instead of being polite, Groucho turned his head and grabbed the entire treat in his teeth, wooden stick and all, yanking it suddenly from the tiny hand.

The child was naturally surprised and screamed at the top of his lungs, causing instant panic on the part of his mother who immediately thought her son had been bitten. She in turn yelled for the driver, who swiveled in his seat to see what the hell was going on in the back of his bus.

Since an outbreak of late night intimidation some years previously, all buses in the fleet had been equipped with direct emergency communication to law enforcement and the driver, lacking his usual patience, availed himself of this procedure just a little too rapidly.

The predictable result was a police cruiser intercept, a noisy and confusing articulation of witness accounts and considerable questioning for Doyle on how come he couldn't control his animal. The mother was convinced that only a miracle had saved her child from being incapacitated for life and the driver was only too willing to support her claim. The fact that the boy had actually offered the thing to Groucho and that the latter was, after all, simply being a horse seemed to have no effect whatsoever on the debate.

In the end, just to add to his other problems, Doyle received a verbal admonition and a written summons from the sweating police officer, who had more important things to do and really didn't want to hear any more about it.

"No, for the last time," said Marc-André. "I'm sorry, I just can't do it." He was emphatic but it wasn't the answer Louise wanted to hear.

"How much would it cost you?" she argued.

"That's not the point."

"What *is* the point?"

Marc-André was fastening a tie and the discussion made him flip it the wrong way, so he had to undo it and start over. This morning it was the ivory-colored silk to go with the dark red poplin shirt, the one with the pinstripes. Over it he wore a black leather vest. His dress style was a far cry from the detectives of old, with their square sports coats and polyester pants. Oftentimes, with his slick black hair, his face stubble, and his thin gold chain, he looked more like a Mafia hoodlum than a member of the squad's most professional elite.

"Louise, look, I know you're worried for him, but it's just a stupid traffic violation. It's not a bank robbery. He's not gonna go to jail. He'll pay the fine like everybody else and it'll all go away. What's the big deal?"

"The big deal is that he's an old man and he's got the whole world crashing down on his damn head."

"So who said life's fair?"

That was just a little too cavalier for Louise and she reacted with some venom, using the same words she'd used at the *calèche* bureau.

"Don't swear at me," he told her.

That's when she looked at him and suddenly realized she didn't want this relationship to go the same way as her marriage. "No . . . No, you're right, I'm sorry," she said softly. "It's just that . . . Ah, forget it."

His sleeves were still undone, but he came across the bedroom to where she was standing in the doorway and he held her, his long arms wrapping around her bare shoulders. She was still in her underwear, one of the new sets she'd bought before moving in with him: pale yellow gingham, very frilly and feminine, like a page from a Parisian glossy.

He placed one finger under her chin and lifted her head up toward him. "Even if I tried to fix this, which I can't," he said quietly, "it's not his real problem. It wouldn't solve anything."

"I know. I just feel like a piece of crap, that's all."

Last night, when she had come in, she'd found a rambling, almost incoherent message on the machine but it had been enough to give her the essence of what happened . . . Almost an accident on the street with the horse. Nobody hurt. The police were blaming it all on Doyle . . . But she knew Marc-André was right. The real problem was Doyle being thrown out of the stable. The incident on the street was just a sideshow.

"You haven't told him yet?" Marc-André asked her.

"When did I get the chance? I was kinda thinking I'd tell him today."

"On the phone?"

"I don't know, I guess so."

It was clear she wasn't looking forward to it, and he was about to repeat what he'd said yesterday, that it wasn't really her problem, but he decided the whole thing had all gone too far for that. It actually *was* her problem because she'd chosen to make it so. She'd gotten involved. As far as he could make out, she'd developed some kind of emotional commitment to the old man, for whatever personal or psychological reasons of her own, and now she just couldn't seem to back away. To make her see common sense under these circumstances would be next to impossible, so he let it go and just looked at his watch.

"I gotta move," he said.

Maybe, he thought, it would even be good for her to fight somebody else's battles for a change. She'd been fighting her own for long enough.

"Well, you had to do it, didn't you?" Doyle said to Groucho, as he led him slowly out of the stall.

"You had to take the ice cream from that kid. You just couldn't say no. Well, I hope you enjoyed it, that's all I can say. Y'know, if you'd bothered to ask me, I'd have bought you one. Might've been a lot easier. A lot cheaper, too, by the way. You're costing me a fortune, you know that, don't you? Problem with you is, you don't care, do you? Just don't give a hoot."

"Know what I think? " asked Mowbray, who was hovering at the back, waiting to get in there with his shovel. "I think he got an evil streak." It was noticeable how much Mowbray had come out of himself since the Groucho adventure had begun, making comments that he would never have made before.

On this occasion, Doyle nodded at the validity of the observation. "I think you're right about that," he agreed. "Sure knows how to get himself into trouble."

"Get *you* in, more like."

"Sure, that too."

While Mowbray started work on the stall, Doyle led Groucho by the halter over to an ancient contraption that looked like a metal framework, large enough for a horse to enter. There were leather restraints to keep him in and chains to keep him from turning or twisting. It was designed specifically for shoeing and this was the day the farrier came, one of his regular appointments every few weeks that were scheduled a season in advance.

Horse shoeing was a vital function at any stable, but particularly so for a city establishment like his, where the horses were treading the asphalt every day. And while some enthusiast country owners liked to do it themselves, Doyle would never take on the responsibility. The hooves of a horse were one of the most vulnerable areas, and many a disease or disability had begun with a minor defect that went undetected and untreated. It took an expert's eye to search for the minuscule clues and, in addition to the traditional fitting and hammering, it was this essential function that a modern farrier was trained to do.

Some horses, like Bertrand's mare, Ange, were so docile that they could be shoed in their own stalls but, knowing Groucho's moody temperament, Doyle didn't want to risk anything. It wouldn't take much of a blow to put even a grown man into long-term care, so he always took the trouble to lead the horse into the frame and secure him as much as he could. Even then, a crisp, fresh apple every time Groucho was willing to cooperate was a wise precaution, not just as a reward but also as a necessary distraction.

At Doyle's stable, the farrier they used was a part-timer, an angular man by the name of Yves Rémillard who also ran a veterinarian supply store, a business he'd inherited from his father, just like Doyle. But he was capable and experienced, and knowledgeable enough to be popular with the drivers who were the ones who paid his fees.

He'd already unpacked his gear and was just starting to get busy when the phone rang on the wall. Doyle watched for a moment as Groucho condescended to raise his left rear leg, then went over to take the call.

"Hi, Doyle. It's Louise."

"Oh, hi there, Louise. Did you get the message I left?"

"Yeah, about the accident. Sorry about that. I mentioned it to Marc-André but there's not much he can do. Whole other division."

"That's okay." In actual fact, Doyle had only called her for the want of telling someone, not because he expected any favors. At the time, he'd even forgotten that Marc-André was a police officer. He waited with the receiver in his hand but there was a long pause, followed by a hesitation.

"Yeah, Doyle, listen . . . That's not . . . Well, that's not really why I called."

"Okay."

"No . . . no, it's not okay. I don't have very good news, I'm afraid."

For a brief moment, Doyle closed his eyes, an unconscious attempt to shut out the reality that kept forcing its way, unwanted, into his life. "It's about the stable?"

"Yeah."

"That young feller in the office there. He call you back?"

"I think he tried his best, Doyle. I think he really tried hard and I thanked him for it, you know, for you. He even called your city councilor."

"I don't know who that is."

"No? Well, he found the name and the number and he called through but whoever he is, that guy, he's got it in for you."

"He does? Why?"

"Aw, come on, Doyle. You know what I'm talking about. You got a stable, you got horses. You're in the middle of the damn city. Whaddya want?"

Doyle understood perfectly well what she was talking about. "It smells," he replied simply.

"Well . . . yeah. Some people don't like it. The city says they had complaints."

Doyle nodded, even though she couldn't see it at the other end of the line. "I know there's been complaints. Nothing I can do about that. I tried perfume but they don't like it too much, the horses."

It took a moment for her to realize that he was kidding and another to appreciate that he could maintain a sense of humor at a time like this. "Perfume," she laughed, but her response was more to relieve the tension than anything else. "I'm sorry I don't have better news, Doyle. I mean, really sorry."

"No, that's all right. Thanks for helping out and everything."

"What will you do now?"

"First thing, I gotta tell the drivers."

"How do you think they'll take it?"

"Don't know. Nobody likes to change unless they have to."

Across the stable, the farrier had just about finished trimming the first hoof. They continually grew, like human nails, and if there was a lot of wear, care would have to be taken to keep them at the correct angle in order to maintain the horse's posture.

"Doyle . . ."

It sounded as though she was very upset. He could hear it. "Don't feel bad," he said to her.

"I just wanted to say we're still friends. I couldn't help you much, but I just want you to know, we're still friends, okay?"

"Okay."

"I'll call you tomorrow."

"Sure. Take care, Louise."

"You, too, Doyle."

He hung up the phone and wandered back over to the shoeing frame where Yves Rémillard was about ready to apply the metal to the hoof wall. The shoes Groucho wore were enormous, the largest size possible, with a thick pad in between the shoe and the sole to cushion the tread and keep him comfortable.

Doyle liked this particular farrier because the man took his time, never hurried the job and there'd never been any problems due to his work for as long as Doyle could remember. It was a big thing to say.

As he watched, he realized that Rémillard would also have to be told about what was happening, as would Sauvé the vet and Paget who serviced the *calèches* and the harness gear, plus all the other suppliers and contractors: the ones who delivered the feed and the hay and the ones who repaired the tools and the ones who fixed the plumbing when it was backed up.

They'd all have to be told eventually and Doyle wasn't looking forward to any of it.

Eighteen

It was dusk and they were all back, facing him, expectant, and all he could do was gaze back. It was like being in the church at Jacqueline's funeral when he was supposed to offer a eulogy and he just froze. This felt exactly the same to Doyle.

In front of him was Jean-Claude, Marie-Josée, Frank, and Bertrand, as well as young Mowbray, all in a big semi-circle with the horses in their stalls behind them, but he just couldn't seem to find his voice. The words were stuck in his throat.

Bertrand was already bored and stood there with his hat on the back of his head and his hands in his pockets. "Let's go home," he said, "come back tomorrow."

The others were more polite, but Doyle could still feel the pressure building up. There was tension, too, because they'd sensed it was important when he'd called them together—but now the time had come and he just couldn't bring himself to do it.

"Come on, Doyle" said Marie-Josée, trying to encourage him. She was an athletic type who'd kind of gone to seed, a little too much flab where there were once muscles. "Doesn't matter how you say it, just spit it out."

But still, the silence extended, longer and longer, the only sounds coming from the horses, a couple of them chomping on feed and one splashing the automatic water fountain, although it was difficult to tell from out here which one was doing what. Finally, it was Mowbray of all people, leaning on his broom, who spoke up to give them the news. "Stable's gonna close," he said very casually.

"What?" said Marie-Josée.

Mowbray shrugged. "It's gonna close. They shuttin' it down."

"Who? Who's shutting it down? What're you talking about?"

"The city. They shuttin' down the stable or somethin'." Mowbray glanced over at Doyle and felt awkward, so he added a shrug of apology: "Sorry, man, I know I ain't s'pposed to say nothin'."

Doyle looked at him, not certain how the kid even knew about it, but his questioning stare had its effect and Mowbray was compelled to offer further explanation. "It's like I kinda heard you talkin' about it, you know, wi' Groucho there."

Doyle looked a little embarrassed at the revelation. He didn't really want people to know how much he talked to the horse but it was out now and, since the content was essentially correct, all he could do was nod slowly.

The drivers took that as confirmation. "You mean it's true?" Jean-Claude asked him. "They're gonna shut you down?"

Doyle nodded again.

"Ah, shit."

"My God," said Marie-Josée.

"Nothing you can do?" This was Frank, who also didn't speak much. Sometimes he looked more like a wrestler, especially when he had his sleeves rolled up and his thick arms folded, showing off his many elaborate tattoos. "You can't talk to 'em or nothing?"

"Talk to 'em, sure," repeated Bertrand, as if he were adding something fresh to the discussion. "That's what you gotta do. You gotta talk to 'em."

"I did," said Doyle. It was the first thing he'd managed to utter.

"And?" asked Marie-Josée, still trying to get more out of him. "What happened?"

Doyle looked at each of them in turn, unsure of how to respond, unable to tell them where he'd been and who he'd contacted. "I tried," was all he could say.

"You went alone?" Jean-Claude asked him, his tone accusatory. "By yourself?"

Again, it was Mowbray who replied, perhaps emboldened by his first comment which had sparked the conversation. "Nah, he went wi' that woman," he said. "You know, Jackie's kid there, that Louise woman from the funeral. Man, that is one tough bitch."

"You watch your mouth!" said Doyle, suddenly loud and angry. This came as a shock to all of them. Nobody had ever heard him speak that way. But not only did he not like the word bitch in relation to Louise, he also objected to Mowbray referring to Jacqueline as Jackie, as if it were a sign of disrespect.

In reaction to the verbal aggression, Mowbray just blinked for a moment. He was about to say something, to defend himself, but then seemed to shrivel and shut down in surrender. As for the rest, they just put the frayed temper down to the strain of the situation. They glanced at each other but made no comment.

It was Doyle, now that he'd found his voice, who continued. "Anyways, that's the news, like he said. What I wanted to tell you. City's gonna shut the stable, take away my permit."

"When?" asked Marie-Josée. "When's it gonna happen?"

Doyle found it hard to look at her. "Few months, maybe spring. You're all gonna have to find a new place."

"How we gonna do that?" she asked. "The other stables, they're all full. How we gonna find a new place?"

"An' what about the rent?" asked Bertrand. "You got the best rent. We gonna have to pay more somewheres else."

"That's true," said Frank.

"We gotta fight this," said Jean-Claude, looking to all of them for support. Occasionally, he liked to pretend he was the leader of the small group, because he was a little younger, a little taller, but that was just his attitude, all in his own head. The others didn't really listen to him.

"How?" asked Marie-Josée cynically. "Fight how?"

"I dunno. We'll go to City Hall, talk to the mayor."

"Sure, sure, talk to the mayor." She laughed scornfully. "You think the mayor's gonna listen to *us*?"

"Okay, so we'll protest, like the unions do. That works."

"How we gonna protest?" she scoffed. "We got four *calèches* between us, what're we gonna do?"

"Five," said Doyle, correcting her for no real reason. "We got five *calèches.*" He was thinking of Jacqueline's, the one they'd all clubbed together to retain as a spare.

"Okay, five *calèches,*" she said, still in the same mocking tone. "What kinda protest we gonna make with that? You think they're like garbage trucks, we can just block the street?"

Bertrand laughed at this and Frank, too, couldn't resist a lopsided grin, but Jean-Claude took the objection seriously enough to want to justify himself. "I dunno what we'll do," he answered her. "But me, I think we gotta do something, that's for sure. We can't just give up, do nothing."

Doyle listened to all of this without adding or subtracting anything. If they wanted to protest, he thought, good luck to them, he'd be the last one to stand in their way. It didn't mean he held out much hope though. Personally, he was far more inclined to trust Louise's opinion, depressing though it may be. But at least now they knew the facts and it was like a burden lifted from his shoulders. When the stable closed, he'd be the one most affected, yet he'd been dreading the idea of telling them.

After the four drivers had gone home, Doyle was finishing off his evening chores in the stable with Mowbray, who appeared to be still sulking from the slight. "So am I fired or what?" he asked Doyle.

"No, you're not fired."

"But I gotta find a new job, that what you're saying?"

"Only in the spring."

Mowbray looked at him steadily for a long time with those dark eyes, then he, too, walked from the stable, leaving Doyle alone in the encroaching darkness. Just him and the horses. Automatically, he strolled over to Groucho's stall and went inside. The horse snorted his welcome and bobbed his head. "Nobody asked me about you," Doyle said to him softly. "Nobody asked me what I'm gonna do with you."

He rubbed the animal's muzzle and stroked his neck, wondering how he'd cope when it came to saying goodbye and couldn't help recalling his father's friend, the one who committed suicide. Yet again, the morbid thoughts came back to taunt him and overwhelm him and he couldn't seem to prevent them. He didn't know if he'd ever have the courage to go through with such a final act, but at the same time, he knew he couldn't face the pain of parting from everything he'd known. It seemed that each way he turned, he was facing an abyss.

Contrary to Doyle's expectations, Jean-Claude was as good as his word.

He and the drivers did actually try to do something, following a similar path to Doyle and Louise, albeit with some embellishments. Their initial destination was the same *calèche* permit office on Boulevard de Maisonneuve and although they were treated with more civility, they essentially achieved the same result. They were directed to call the ombudsman's office, where they obtained the same reply: a four month wait before an appointment.

The difference was they didn't stop there. The next stop was City Hall, as Jean-Claude had promised, and he marched the mini-delegation of himself, Marie-Josée, and Frank right into the lobby and demanded to be shown up to the mayor's office. Bertrand had declined to accompany them, claiming he'd just be a useless addition, and they'd agreed because he was probably right.

Needless to say, the three brave musketeers were rebuffed at the very first hurdle: the security desk. Impossible to see the mayor, they were told, and just as impossible to see anyone from his office.

The recommendation was to make an appointment and they were handed a nice pamphlet with the mayor's smiling photo about how easy it was to interact with the city and how transparent the administration's open-door policy was trying to be. Marie-Josée tore it up. She didn't have the temper of Louise, but she was naturally suspicious and highly dubious about anything official.

Finally, instead of going to the citizen's advice bureau, they went for a sandwich lunch with an articled junior at one of the city's top law firms, a woman called Belinda whom Jean-Claude had once tried to date during high school.

She'd turned him down back then but she'd accepted to meet him this time, because she'd learned in her career that networking was the way ahead, no matter who it was. So they sat in the food court of a downtown mall eating their chicken salad pita and sipping peach juice while she listened attentively enough to the list of troubles. Afterward, she promised faithfully to investigate and report back, and Jean-Claude was well satisfied, even smug that his personal contact had paid dividends, that at last they were getting things done. Even Marie-Josée was impressed, having come to believe that legal pressure with its implied threat might be the only way to get anyone to listen.

But as the days passed and Belinda failed to call, their combined optimism began to fade. When Jean-Claude eventually got hold of her, she apologized that she'd been busy: heavy workload, late nights, high stress, etcetera, which was all true, except that she didn't think she'd be able to help them anyway. Yes, she'd spoken to someone higher up who'd told her they weren't allowed to take any more pro bono cases and that, in any event, their forte was corporate law, not municipal politics.

So that was that.

The entire process had taken another eight days but at the end of it all, they were no further ahead and a general atmosphere of gloom invaded the stable as it slowly dawned on all of them that they really might have to move out. However, there was one more hurrah and it came one evening when Marie-Josée happened to spy the framed article from *The Gazette* that Walter Sullivan at the Gardening Center had presented to Doyle the day that the Groucho brand of manure was launched.

"The papers!" she declared, in what amounted to a real eureka moment. "If we can't use the law, we'll use the papers!"

Jean-Claude was just leading his bay mare, Roxy, into the stall, but to his credit, he immediately saw the possibilities. "You know anybody at the papers?" he asked her.

"No, but we can start with that first woman who was here. What was her name again? The one at *The Gazette*?"

"Pru," said Doyle from over the other side. "Her name was Pru."

"Pru what?"

Doyle couldn't remember. "It's written there in the frame."

"Okay, so let's start with her. She knows us, she wrote some nice stuff. Why not?"

Jean-Claude was about to reach for the bridle when he paused. He had another thought. "The mayor doesn't care about *The Gazette*," he said shrewdly. " What we need is *La Presse*."

Marie-Josée was forced to agree. In Québec society, the English language paper had neither the influence nor the effect of the French heavyweight media. "Know anyone there at *La Presse*?"

"No . . . but we can send 'em *The Gazette* story and offer this as a follow-up. What d'you think?"

Marie-Josée thought about it. "Not bad," she agreed. It was a rare compliment from her.

Jean-Claude smiled to himself, and even Doyle raised his eyebrows, happy to see they still hadn't given up, that they were still fighting. He was not sure anything would come of it but it made him feel a little better.

It was unclear which editor made the decision or why the story had generated some appeal but within a couple of days, someone from *La Presse* had contacted them to schedule the interview.

The call came through early at the stable when the drivers were all still around. It was Doyle who answered, but he immediately handed the receiver to Jean-Claude so the latter could communicate more effectively in rapid French. After a moment or two, Jean-Claude's face lit up.

Apparently there'd be a reporter, a photographer, and even a video cameraman for the paper's official website, *Cyberpresse*. After he hung up and relayed the news, there were self-congratulatory celebrations all round and they toasted each other with juice, milk, coffee, whatever they could find. Even Doyle wore a smile, for the first time in weeks.

Yet when the article appeared, a week and a half later, it wasn't at all what they were expecting.

It was Marie-Josée who was the first one in with the paper, striding directly into Doyle's kitchen, the small one downstairs in the stable. "*Maudits espèces de . . .*" She couldn't even complete the curse as she opened it up to the offending page. That's when she switched to English. "Son-of-a-bitch," she said, the first thing that came into her head. "Look what they wrote here, piece o' shit, piece o' garbage."

Doyle gazed at the open page and saw several color pictures of the stable and the group of drivers, including a prominent one of himself with Groucho.

It was a good shot, too, a nice portrait, and there was even a close-up of Doyle's coffee cup with the Groucho brand logo on it. But Marie-Josée wasn't complaining about the standard of photography. Her beef was with the words, which she began to read with a growing impatience.

The headline translated to *End of an Era* and the text went on to describe, in somewhat flowery prose, how the closing of a *calèche* stable was merely indicative of the changes taking place within the grand metropolis.

Within the context of what it was trying to do, it was a good article, trying to wring emotion out of the endless battle between the longing for a mythical past and progress toward a visionary future.

However, this had nothing to do with either the injustice of the specific affair or sympathy for the people affected and long before she reached the end, Marie-Josée had thrown the paper down in disgust.

It was not long after that Jean-Claude came in, followed in a few minutes by Frank and Bertrand. All had seen the paper and all had an opinion as they crowded into the tiny kitchen space. Even Mowbray poked his head around the doorpost as Doyle tried to usher them all out.

At the start, the consensus was mixed, with Marie-Josée sticking to her point that it was a disaster, while Jean-Claude intimated that it wasn't too bad, repeating the legend that any publicity is good publicity, an adage he'd heard one time. But after considerable debate along these lines, the general perspective swung completely over to Marie-Josée, with Frank just shaking his head, Bertrand walking away disgruntled, and Jean-Claude falling silent. Mowbray looked at Doyle and simply shrugged, as if to say that's the way it is, man, what more did you expect?

Once the drivers had gone out and Mowbray was about his chores, Doyle went in to see Groucho, ostensibly to haul on the harness and prepare him for manure deliveries but, in actual fact, to converse.

"Up and down, up and down," he said to the horse, "like a roller coaster. Up and down. Just be glad you're not human, that's all I can say, all this stuff we gotta put up with. All you gotta do is haul the wagon. Sure, well, I know that's not easy sometimes, 'specially in the wind and the rain out there, but still, it's an easy life compared to some. I know you maybe don't believe me, but I'm right. You don't know how lucky you are, that's your problem. Hey, want a nice apple, eh? Let's see what we got here."

Doyle handed the fruit to Groucho, who snaffled it up, relishing it as much as he ever did. Doyle had just about weaned him off the sugar and no longer carried it around with him.

As long as there were apples, Groucho didn't seem to miss the small white cubes, although he still hadn't adapted to carrots, regarding such vegetables with complete indifference. Doyle had long since accepted the animal's sweet tooth, since Jacqueline had encouraged it and there was little he could do to change it anyway.

Of course, he, too, was dismayed about the article and he prepared Groucho for his daily outing with a renewed despondency. Like the others, he'd hoped the paper would somehow take up their cause, act as a mouthpiece for their opposition to the closing, but instead, it had simply used the subject as inspiration for a feature of its own.

Yet, in the back corner of his mind, Doyle knew something else too. He knew the newspaper was actually right. This was indeed the end of an era. What was happening was, in a way, symbolic. The city was shutting down the stables and soon the horses would completely vanish from the streets. People like him were obsolete, nothing but dinosaurs left over from a different age, and there was nothing could be done about it. Not by Doyle, not by anybody.

Nineteen

That same evening, the drivers of Doyle's stable did two things they'd never done before. One was to go out for a drink together, and the other was to take Doyle with them.

It's not that they didn't drink. On the contrary, it was a favorite activity, but they preferred to do it with their own people in their own parts of the city.

For Marie-Josée, for example, it was a noisy dive in a back-end section of the Plateau, an area that hadn't yet become fashionable. In the back room they ran a card game, and when she had some spare cash, she liked to sit in.

For Jean-Claude, it was something a little more pretentious, an eclectic jazz bar where the drinks were horrifyingly expensive and where he could sit with his yuppie friends, tapping along to the rhythms and nursing the same wine cooler all evening.

Frank's preference was a hole-in-the-wall tavern in Lachine, a place where the police were often summoned, either to break up an argument or raid a drug sale or prevent urination and other rowdiness in the street outside. As for Bertrand, there was no set location, because he was acquainted with people everywhere and just tended to drift around as the mood took him: bars, apartments, parks, construction sites. It was all the same to him where he did his drinking.

The point was that none of them had ever invited Doyle along on their adventures: none except Jacqueline. So when they asked him that evening where he wanted to go, he immediately said, "Chez le Diable", which had been her favorite hang-out. He knew that Louise didn't work there anymore, she'd moved to her new job uptown, but that didn't change the memories.

When they arrived, they immediately became the largest crowd in the place. Without even asking permission from the owner, Clément, they got busy pulling up two of the tables and arranging chairs so they could all sit together. They'd even insisted Mowbray come along with them, even though he was reluctant, and even though he felt strange being among what seemed to him to be an older generation.

Why they were doing this right now was a little unclear to any of them, since there were still several months to go before the potential closing, but the idea had been suggested by Frank and they'd all just agreed. That's all there was to it. So now, here they were, ordering beer and noisily munching the free peanuts like horses chewing their snacks. They talked about this and that, about the horses, naturally, and also about their minor ailments and prices of things and the generally poor state of the streets with all the unfixed potholes.

There were some jokes, too, but these were mostly in French and Doyle didn't get them. For a long time, he just sat there quietly at one end of the table, staring at that first full glass of beer in front of him without touching it.

"Cheers, man." This was Mowbray, next to him, raising his glass.

Doyle looked at him, then did the same and they each took a long pull. It was the first time he'd tasted anything alcoholic in years and he wasn't sure he even wanted it—but he was here, they were all together for the first time and somehow it just seemed appropriate. He burped loudly with the influx of fizz and Mowbray laughed.

"Listen, man," said the youngster, "I just wanna say that what you do for them horses, that's good, man, that's good. An' I know it's gonna end an' all, which is not good, but I wanna say there's not many done what you done." He could see that Doyle wasn't following too well, so he went on: "No, see, what I'm trying to say is, all these people wi' their jobs in the banks and the stores, they ride around in their cars, but they ain't done what you done, know what I'm sayin'?"

Doyle nodded but this time, a nod wasn't enough. "I don't know what I'm gonna do," he confessed, the first time he'd ever said it out loud, at least to anyone but Groucho. This evening seemed to be a time for firsts.

"Ah, you'll find somethin'," replied Mowbray. "Man like you, million things you can do."

"Like what?"

"Like what? Well, I seen you make furniture, you can do that."

"Just a cupboard and a few shelves."

"Well, that's a start. People need cupboards, put their stuff in. An' you're healthy, I mean for your age an' all. Must be lotta other things you can do."

Doyle wasn't so sure, but he didn't pursue it. "How about you?" he asked.

"Me? Hey, don't worry about me, man."

"What will you do?"

"You know, I was thinkin' about that. Had an idea I might take a trip, you know? Was thinking I might go down to Jamaica a while."

That was an interesting idea to Doyle and his expression signified approval. "Ever been before?"

"No, that's the thing. My dad talks about it, but I ain't never been."

"What's your dad say? Does he think it's a nice place?"

"Nice?" Mowbray laughed. "Ain't nowhere nice, man. There's cool an' there's dumb, but ain't nowhere nice. I know that much. How about you? Ever been any places apart from here?"

Doyle shrugged. "Not much. Went to Ontario to buy the wagon."

"No, I mean you ever, like, take a plane some place."

"No, I never did that."

"Ever want to?"

"I can't leave the horses."

"No? Well, you can now. Won't be no more horses."

Mowbray was trying to be upbeat in his own way, trying to point out the possibilities with all the optimism that the young invariably possess, but his comment had the opposite effect and it caused Doyle to shut down the conversation like he was slamming a lid on a dumpster.

"Hey, listen, I'm sorry, man ..." said Mowbray, trying to make up for it, but it was too late, so he took another swig of his beer and sat back, dejected.

Further along the table, Frank had just come to the end of a crude joke and the laughter rang out, especially from him, but eventually that too subsided and there was a strained silence as they each paused. The more the seconds passed, the more it became like a sort of communal contemplation, only to be interrupted when Bertrand passed some gas, which made them all react, wafting their arms in exaggerated disgust.

The beer continued to arrive and, since they were such good customers, even Clément came to sit with them for a while, straddling the back of a chair as he smoked a cheroot, just like Jacqueline, and entertaining them with stories of when she used to come in there, even speaking English for Doyle's benefit.

However, it only served to darken the old man's demeanor even more, and as he listened, he had trouble fighting back the moisture that insisted on forming in the corners of his eyes. He was totally choked up to the extent that he had difficulty breathing, but was it for Jacqueline or was it for the horses this time?

Whatever the reason, he was having a hard time holding it back and the two people who noticed most were Mowbray and Marie-Josée, who happened to be sitting on either side of him. She put a hand on his forearm, but there was little she could say and didn't even try.

By nine-thirty, the last glasses had just about been drained, and the party was winding down. One by one, the drivers stretched, pushed back their chairs and got up to leave, until eventually there was only Doyle and Mowbray. And finally, at some time close to ten, even Mowbray got up.

He said he was just going to the washroom but when he returned, five minutes later, his eyes were a little glazed and he didn't sit down again. He just tapped Doyle on the shoulder, mumbled, "Stay loose, man," then sauntered out.

Clément had returned to his usual place behind the bar, straightening up, and the waitress, Sylvie, with no one left to serve, was back there helping him. It meant Doyle was now on his own, made even more apparent by the empty chairs and the tables that were still together. The only beer glass that was left was his and it was still three-quarters full, the golden liquid flat, having lost all its creamy head.

Another half-hour went by, with Doyle having almost fallen asleep in his chair. When Sylvie came over, she noticed how old and thin he looked and tried to be gentle in nudging him awake. He was the last one left, he wasn't ordering anything and Clément wanted to close up.

But that's when the door swung open, letting in a cold blast of night air. The Indian summer was a distant memory and the temperature had plummeted in recent days.

It was a man in his thirties who entered, half-drunk and swaying slightly. "Where are you?" he slurred, but neither Sylvie nor Clément had any idea what he was talking about.

Doyle's eyes were now open but he, too, had no clue what was going on.

The man was now inside, supporting himself by holding onto a thin pillar. "Where the hell are you?" he demanded again. "I know you're here, I know ..." He staggered over toward where Doyle was sitting and brought his fist down heavily on the table, knocking over the glass so that the stale beer flew all over the floor.

And in that moment, as the two of them looked at each other, there was a blurry mutual recognition. It was Roscoe, Louise's ex-husband, whom Doyle had met that one time when he went over to their house to work with Louise on the computer.

"You," said the man, pointing. "You know her, I know you do. Where is she? Where the hell is she?"

Doyle tried to tell him that she didn't work there anymore but the words wouldn't emerge. When there was no answer, Roscoe lurched closer and tried to grab Doyle by the collar, but he wasn't too steady and his movements were slow. Instinctively, Doyle scrambled out of the chair, just as he'd done when the man had threatened Louise back in their dining room.

This time, though, Doyle had his fists up in front of him, his feet moving automatically into the crouching stance of the old gym boxer, the memory ingrained. But he wasn't as nimble as he used to be and one of his soles slipped on the beer-soaked floor. He staggered backward, attempting to catch onto the table but it gave way under his weight and he toppled over, his head crashing into the side of the bar with a heavy thud. Then, slowly, he slumped down, unconscious, leaving an ugly smear of blood on the woodwork.

Sylvie was the first to emerge from behind the counter. When she saw what had happened, she came to a stop with her mouth open. She didn't make a sound, but she couldn't move either.

Clément was more concerned with the intruder and reached for the hockey stick mounted on the back wall: a dusty trophy that had been signed by the '86 Canadiens at a charity auction. Charging past Sylvie, Clément came out like a Dervish, swearing loudly and swinging the stick wildly in the air until Roscoe had no choice but to retreat, back through the front door and into the street, hands raised defensively against the threat.

Once he was gone, Clément shut the door and slammed home the bolt. He was breathing hard, almost doubled over with the exertion, as he turned to assess the damage. When he saw Doyle, he swore some more and ordered Sylvie to call 911, but she still couldn't move, so he found his way over, picked up the phone and punched the buttons himself.

Twenty

"How is he?" Louise asked the E.R. receptionist. It was late, and she'd grabbed a taxi up here to the General the moment she'd heard.

In fact, it was Clément who'd contacted her right after the ambulance left his bar, calling her at the new place she was working simply because he couldn't think who else to inform. Not only was Doyle her friend, but the fracas had been instigated by her ex-husband.

"Are you a relative?" asked the nurse. She had pale blonde hair, which looked a strange color under the fluorescent lighting, and wore steel framed spectacles.

"I'm the closest he's got." The nurse looked dubious, then appeared to make a decision in Louise's favor, tapping a keyboard to call up a screen in front of her.

"Let's see here . . . Patrick Doyle O'Shaughnessy, brought in last night at 10:56. Traumatic head injury with concussion." Then she began reading the display like it was a shopping list: "Laceration, cerebral contusion, minor skull fracture with intracranial hemorrhage, possible subdural hematoma . . ."

Louise hardly understood a word. "Can you please just tell me how he is?"

The nurse looked up at her with a certain amount of impatience. "He had an MRI, and now he's in surgery. We won't know how he is for a while."

Louise took a deep breath. "Is there any danger . . . I mean, you know . . ."

"It's a very serious injury."

"I know but . . ."

"We don't know yet." That was all the nurse was prepared to say.

"Will you tell me . . ."

"It won't be for a while," she repeated. "You may wish to go home, come back in the morning."

"No," said Louise firmly. "Thanks, I'll stay."

The nurse didn't care one way or the other and got up to attend to other duties as Louise went to find someplace to sit, out there amongst the wounded and the diseased who were still waiting to be seen, as they had been for hours. Doyle's emergency had catapulted him to the head of the line, because the Medicaire triage system was primarily geared to preventing death, which was little comfort to those who were simply in pain.

Louise found an empty chair in a row along the wall, but she couldn't sit for long, she was too anxious. So she got up again and walked along the corridor to the vending machines, just for something to do. The tea she obtained was undrinkable, so she repeated the operation with another coin and selected hot chocolate. It wasn't much better.

She glanced around in vain for Marc-André. She'd left a message for him at the precinct but didn't know if he'd taken it or, even if he had, whether he'd be free to come. She sat down again with nothing to do but warm her cold hands on the cup, stare at the somber, fatigued faces, and feel a wrenching guilt at having been partly responsible for what happened.

Logically, such blame was misdirected, she knew that well enough, but it didn't help and, as a way to mitigate her culpability, she promised herself that she'd see her miserable ex-husband burn in hell for the grief he'd caused.

It was close to one when Marc-André came to join her after his shift. After persuading her there was little she could accomplish by hanging around, he drove her home—but she was back again by eight. By that time, the news was mildly encouraging in that the operation had been successful, at least relative to the dangerous state in which he'd entered the hospital. In the doctor's words Doyle was now "resting comfortably" in the recovery ward. It was promising, but apparently, it was still too early for a definitive prognosis.

When she went in to see Doyle, it was something of a shock. His head was, of course, heavily bandaged and there were tubes for blood and insulin, as well as wires leading to electronic monitors, but it was his face that surprised her. This wasn't the energetic, rough-and-ready figure she'd come to know, the stable owner who worked tirelessly each day from dawn to midnight, but a meager old man with an ashen complexion and brittle, veined skin.

At first glance, he looked like he was on his deathbed but Louise knew she couldn't let thoughts like that invade her mind in case the negative vibes were transferred across the room and he descended even further. She resolved to be cheery and set about talking to him in much the same way he spoke to Groucho—a kind of unanswered running prater, saying nothing of any consequence but letting the sound of her voice both soothe and encourage him.

After fifteen minutes, one of the day nurses arrived to check on Doyle and asked Louise politely if she could leave. Before doing so, Louise leaned over the bed and gave Doyle a gentle kiss on the cheek, just to tell him he wasn't alone. She kind of hoped it might wake and restore him, a bit like the children's tale of the princess who kissed the frog, but he didn't move or stir. Despite her best intentions to remain positive, she left his bedside wondering if he'd ever wake up again.

By this time, three of the four drivers had already arrived and were sitting outside the recovery ward, chatting amongst themselves. Nobody knew where Bertrand was, or whether the kid, Mowbray, had even been informed. As self-styled next of kin, Louise greeted them and took it upon herself to explain Doyle's condition to them, taking care to submerge her fears and present a generally rosy view.

After this, she flipped open the new cell phone she'd bought with her increased earnings and made two calls. The first was to the stable to give Mowbray the same story and to ask him to relay the message to Bertrand when she saw him. She was also considerate enough to ask him if he could cope on his own, taking care of the horses and so forth and he replied not to worry, he was fine.

"Only one problem," he told her just before she hung up.

"What's that?"

"Groucho. What do I do with him?"

"What d'you mean?"

"What do I mean? I mean I can't take him out. Doyle would kill me."

"Yeah, well, Doyle's in no position to do anything right now."

"I know, but still. I mean, I ain't got no permit to drive no wagon and if I take him out by the halter . . . I mean, I just don't know."

Louise had no advice to give him. Although she'd heard tales of Groucho's character, she basically knew nothing at all about coping with horses, eccentric or otherwise. "I'm sure you'll manage," she told Mowbray.

"How?"

"How? How do I know how? Just do the best you can. You can't do any more than your best, right? So just do what you think is right. You got any problems, ask the other guys." She called over to where the drivers were sitting. "Hey guys, no problem if Mowbray asks your advice and stuff, you know, just while Doyle's in here?"

"Mowbray?" asked Marie-Josée. "Mowbray's gonna be running it?"

Louise cupped her hand over the receiver before answering her. "Who else is there? C'mon, he needs your support."

Marie-Josée was doubtful but gave a reluctant okay, as did Jean-Claude and Frank when faced with Louise's questioning gaze. Louise took her hand off the phone. "Yeah, Mowbray, I just spoke with them. They're all gonna be there for you, anything you need, so you don't have to worry, all right?"

"What about Doyle?"

"Don't worry about Doyle, I'll square it with him soon as he wakes up."

"You sure about this?" asked Mowbray, his voice betraying his considerable apprehension.

"Sure, I'm sure. Listen, I gotta go, but I'll be checking in with you, all right? You know, see how you're doing."

"Tell Doyle I'll try to get up there some time."

Louise wasn't sure whether she'd really gotten through to Mowbray about the true nature of Doyle's injury but she didn't want to get into it in any more detail. Why discourage the kid? "Just take care of the horses," she told him, "that's what he'd want you to do."

"I guess. Can I call someone? I mean to help out."

"Who?"

"Friend of mine."

"If you have to."

"He needs payin'."

"How much?"

"I dunno."

"Okay, okay, long as it's not too much. And long as you behave yourselves in that stable, you hear me? No noise, no dope. No girls either."

Mowbray's tone suggested he was insulted. "Who, me?"

"I mean it. I live with a cop, so don't get any ideas, okay?"

"Okay, okay, I got it."

"I hope so. I'll try to call you tomorrow, see how you're doing."

She gave him her new cell number, just in case, then hung up. She knew he was afraid of being all on his own at the stable but not as afraid as she was at the idea of leaving him there like that. In the end, though, she knew she had to trust him to take care of things, if only because she had no choice. It wasn't like a store you could just shut while the owner's away. This was a stable with horses that needed constant care and there was nobody else. It was Mowbray or nothing.

The second call she made was to Marc-André, who was still at the apartment. For this, she needed a little more privacy, so she moved away from the waiting room and out into the corridor. He was still half-asleep when she got through and yawned loudly. "How's the old man?" he asked her.

"Yeah, not bad, you know, considering. They seem pleased with how the surgery went."

"Good."

"I was thinking ..." she said slowly. "I was kinda wondering when you're going to arrest him."

"Arrest who?"

"My ex, that's who. My dear bastard ex."

"You want *me* to arrest him?"

"Why not? You're a cop, you know what happened."

"It doesn't work like that."

"Why the hell not?"

"Take it easy."

"I don't wanna take it easy, Christ."

"And don't start swearing again, okay?"

She realized she'd begun to raise her voice and glanced up and down the corridor to see who might have objected. It was all right, there was nobody within earshot, but she reduced her tone to a semi-whisper anyway. "The man nearly died," she told him.

"I know."

"So arrest the bastard."

"Look, he's not my favorite person, either, but I'm telling you I can't."

"And I'm asking you why not?"

"Well, for a start, somebody's got to file a complaint."

"A complaint? Christ, the victim's lying unconscious, what d'you want with a complaint?"

"Louise, listen to what I'm saying, okay? It's not assault. There's no crime here. The old man slipped and fell, hit his head on the bar, isn't that what you told me?"

"That's what Clément says. But it was Roscoe caused it."

"We don't know that."

"Sure we do."

"Okay, look, look . . . If Clément comes in, volunteers an official complaint, I'll see what I can do to move things along, all right?"

"Yeah, well, he'll volunteer all right, don't you worry about that."

"Louise . . ."

"What?"

"Don't do anything . . ." He didn't complete the thought.

"Don't do anything, what? Stupid? Is that what you were going to say? Thanks a lot."

"Louise . . ."

"Can't talk, battery's dying, catch you later."

It was true she had almost no power left but it was also convenient timing because she really didn't want any further discussion. If she wanted to be stupid, she felt she had a perfect right to do so, without the continual need for either warnings or supervision. That was one of the reasons she'd gotten out of her marriage.

She hung up, switched off her phone and looked at her watch. Clément should be opening up in a couple of hours or so, and she figured she'd just about have enough time to get over there before she had to be at work.

It was a strange feeling for Louise, walking through the door of Chez Le Diable, almost like she'd never left. She could easily imagine herself removing her jacket to start work as if nothing had changed.

When she got inside, however, it wasn't the same at all. It was still a mess from the previous evening, because Sylvie had been too much in shock to clean up and Clément couldn't be bothered doing it himself. Now, here they were, the two of them, just getting down to work, Sylvie with a sponge mop and Clément righting the furniture. They stopped when Louise walked in.

"*Salut,*" she said to them, but they didn't respond. They just looked at her, wondering what she was doing here. She looked around, and that's when she saw the red smear still there on the front side of the bar. "Is that where . . ." She couldn't even say the words but Sylvie's face confirmed what she was thinking.

"Did you see him?" Clément asked her. He was obviously referring to Doyle.

She continued to stare at the stain. It was as if she couldn't pull her eyes away. "What? Oh . . . yeah. He was in surgery half the night."

"And?"

"And they don't know yet."

Clément sighed. Then, as a cheap joke, he said, "Come over to give us a hand?"

Louise refused to acknowledge it. "Did the police come?" she asked.

"No. What for?"

"What for? There's blood on the bar and you ask me what for?"

"It was an accident. He fell and hit his head. I told you that last night."

"Yeah, you also said it was Roscoe came in here and caused the disturbance."

"Okay, so he caused a disturbance, so what?"

"So he should be arrested."

"Why? Because you say so?"

"No, because . . . Because he damn well should, that's why."

"A little revenge, is that it? No divorce settlement, is that why you're doing this?"

"No."

Clément just looked at her, the disbelief evident from his smirk. "Okay, you want him arrested, tell that boyfriend of yours. He's a cop, isn't he?"

"I did tell him. He said he needs you to file a complaint."

"Me?" Clément laughed. "I don't think so."

"Why not?"

"Because I'm not going to, that's all."

"What's the matter? You afraid they'll find out it's a cash business, tell the Feds?"

Clément looked at her the same way he'd looked at Roscoe the previous evening, but he didn't grab the hockey stick. He grabbed her by the arm instead and pulled her over to one side where they could talk quietly.

Furious, she pulled her arm away and glared at him. "Don't you ever touch me," she said to him.

"Or what?" he replied, trying to laugh it off. "You'll have me arrested too?"

"All right, now listen, asshole, I'll tell you this once. Either you file an official complaint against that bastard or I'll call the tax office. You think I won't? Just try me. And while I'm at it, I'll call the city inspectors, get you shut down for sanitary violation."

"What sanitary violation?"

"Are you kidding me? You got mice, you got roaches, I even saw a damn bat in the back there. Nearly flew into my face."

"You're out of your mind."

"Yeah? Okay, suit yourself."

She made as if to leave, but he got hold of her arm again. This time, she swung around with her fist and caught him on the side of his nose, forcing him to let go and hold the place where the blow had landed. A dribble of blood trickled from his nostril at the same time as a stream of profanities erupted from his mouth.

"I told you not to touch me," she said. "Now, you either file an official complaint by five o'clock today or first thing tomorrow I start calling. Up to you. Me, I don't care. I'll either get him or I'll get you. One sleazebag or another, your choice."

"You're sick, you know that? You should be put away."

She put her fist in front of his face and saw him pull back. "Five o'clock today," she said again.

"Go screw yourself."

"Five o'clock or I start calling."

Then she strode out past the newly frozen Sylvie, who'd now witnessed two displays of bloody violence within a twelve hour period.

Mowbray Groves, son of Doyle's neighbors, Elliott and Katrien, called his parents to say he wouldn't be sleeping at home that night, he had to stay with the horses after what happened to the old man. He felt kind of responsible, he told them, which made his father apprehensive, yet proud at the same time. The man couldn't recall when his son had last felt responsible about anything.

Later that night, once most of the chores were done and the horses had been bedded down, Mowbray came to sit with Groucho, just like the Doyle did, pulling out the same rickety chair.

"So, man, I guess it's just you an' me now. What you gotta say about that? Tomorrow I gotta call that place where you go, that garden place where you haulin' the shit. I gotta tell 'em you ain't gonna be goin' for a while. They gonna shit themselves at that."

Mowbray laughed at his own humor. "Guess I should call up Lanky, too, get his rear end over here, gimme a hand with all this. Yeah, you'll like that Lanky. He kinda tall like you, that's why we call 'im that, but not as mean as you. Don't stomp or nothin'. His feet not as big as yours neither. Don't know what I'm gonna pay 'im though. Don't know the goin' rate for an assistant to an assistant."

Mowbray paused to grin and said it again, just for fun. "Assistant to the assistant. Of the superintendent. Man, that's like a rap tune, right there. Man, I should be writin' lyrics, instead of shovelin' your shit. Get me a Grammy or somethin'. Yeah, sign autographs, ride in one of them long, stretch cars, you know, them limousines."

He practiced saying that again too. "Lim-mo-zeenes. Yeah. Hey, you know what? You good to talk to, man, 'cause you don't say nothin'. I can see why that Doyle comes in here. He got a good thing goin'. He talks and you don't give no answer. That's loose, man, I can buy that. Yeah. You an' me, we gonna get along fine. I keep talkin', you keep on not answerin', we gonna do great. You wanna apple?"

Twenty-one

lthough the hospital medical team had assured Louise that Doyle's surgery appeared to be successful, it still took longer than anyone expected before he was finally able to speak. Even then, it was just a few words of recognition.

One day, a week later, she came to see him, as usual, in the morning and found someone else had arrived ahead of her, a big woman sitting outside, making a call. The woman hung up and got to her feet.

"Prudence Carmichael," she said, handing over a card like it was confirmation of her identity. "I write for *The Gazette*."

"Louise Vallières . . . I'm a friend of Doyle's."

"Yes, I know. The young man at the stable told me."

"Mowbray?"

"I saw him yesterday, he said you wouldn't mind if I came along."

"No . . . I guess." Louise didn't have a clue what this was all about until she recalled the first article, the one Doyle had in a frame. "Oh, wait, you wrote that story, the hero horse thing."

Pru wasn't sure whether to be flattered.

"That's right, the 'hero horse' thing."

"That was nice. Doyle liked that a lot."

"Good, glad to hear it." She indicated the ward. "He seems a little better today. We already said hello. But I didn't want to tire him out."

"You were waiting for me?"

"Yes, as it happens. I'm thinking of doing a follow-up piece."

"About the stable closing?"

"Yes . . . You know, I do wish you'd have called me first instead of *La Presse*."

"That wasn't me, that was the drivers. The *calèche* drivers at the stable. That was their decision."

"I see. Well, anyway, I'm here now, so let's get on with it, shall we? I've got this great idea I'd like to talk to you about. Before we go in and see him, if you don't mind."

"I think he's expecting me."

"Won't take long. You see, here's the thing. He's up here, the stable's down there, right? But the magic is when he's in there, with the horses. What's the big one's name?"

"Groucho."

"Groucho, of course. The magic is when he's with Groucho."

"That was my mother's horse."

"Oh, really? So you're the daughter of . . ."

"Jacqueline."

"Right, right, the friend who died. I hadn't realized that was you. Good, that's good. So here's what I'm thinking. What we do is we set up a visual link between them, then shoot the old man's reaction when he sees the horse, get the idea?"

Louise looked a little lost. "I dunno . . ."

"A webcam. You know what a webcam is?"

"Sure."

"So we set up a camera down there in the stable and feed the image through here on a laptop. Easy."

Louise nodded vaguely. "You can do that?"

"Well, not me personally. Not much of a technophile to tell you the truth, don't understand how it works, but we got people who can do that, no problem. So what do you think?"

"You mean he'll be able to see Groucho?"

"Exactly. From right here. We'll put a screen right in front of him, he can say hi to his horse."

Louise was showing a little more enthusiasm now that she realized the possibilities. "That's a great idea. When can we do it?"

"I was thinking tomorrow."

"Great."

"There's just one thing."

"What's that?"

"Well, what I really want is the look on his face. You know, when he first sees the horse. So what I'd like to do is, well, kind of keep it as a surprise."

"You mean we don't tell him?"

"Not till the whole thing's set up. That all right with you?"

"Yeah, a surprise. Why not?"

"Good, I'll set it up. Oh . . . one more thing. Can you talk to the hospital, make sure it's all right?"

"I guess so."

"Not now, later. After we see him. We'll need access to a high-speed link if they've got one. I'm sure they do . . . somewhere."

"Can't you do that? I mean, I think it'll sound better coming from you. More official kind of thing."

Pru thought about that. "Maybe you're right." The technological aspect was crucial and she was having second thoughts about trusting that to anyone else. "Let me talk to someone back at the paper, see what we can do. Okay, leave that with me. You just tell them to expect a call and that you've approved the idea, all right?"

"No problem."

"So what do you say, shall we go in and see him now? Remember, not a word. Just say . . . Just say we're coming back to take a picture. That's all he needs to know for now."

Inside, they found Doyle awake but still weak. He'd just managed a couple of mouthfuls of breakfast and was trying to sip a weak, milky coffee through a special plastic cup with a lid and an attached straw.

"Let me help you with that," said Louise.

Doyle smiled when he saw her. "Hi, Louise."

"Hi, there."

"Hi, again," Pru said to him, as she followed Louise in and stood at the other side of the bed.

"Just having my coffee," said Doyle. "First time." He gave it to Louise so she could hold it for him as he drank.

"I bet that tastes good," said Pru.

"Sure does."

"How you feeling?" Louise asked him, encouraged by both his awareness and lucidity, a marked improvement, even over yesterday, and enough to assure her that there was a good chance there was no serious brain damage. Even the doctors weren't entirely certain about that.

The brain's a difficult organ to judge, they told her, very delicate and very difficult to make any predictions following a blow of that magnitude. Each person and each circumstance was different and even the slightest variation could change the whole outlook. The shape and thickness of the skull and cranial cavity, the angle and height of the fall, the age and constitution of the patient, each of these could have an effect.

"I'm feeling okay," he replied to her question. Then he managed to lift his own hand, unsteadily, but enough to hold on to hers. "How's Groucho?" This was what he really wanted to know.

"Groucho's doing fine." She smiled. She'd like to have said, "you'll be seeing him tomorrow," but she resisted the urge. "Mowbray's looking after him."

"He is?"

"Yeah. Doing a good job, too. Maybe too many apples, but the horse doesn't seem to mind."

Doyle managed a smile. "Very selfish, that horse," he said, then coughed a little. "Give him an apple and he's yours."

"Just like all men," said Louise.

Even Prudence Carmichael laughed at this.

But Doyle wasn't finished being worried. "He needs exercise."

"It's okay, relax," Louise replied. "Mowbray takes him out every day."

"He does? He can't drive ..."

"No, not driving. Just for a walk. Like you used to do, around the Pointe."

"Tell him ..."

"Tell him what?"

"Tell him, be careful of the cleaning machine. In the street. Groucho doesn't like the cleaning machine."

"I'll tell him."

"You will?"

"Yeah."

"And the feed. How about feed? He needs to order some. He's got to call up ..."

"All taken care of. Mowbray's there, the drivers are there. It's all taken care of."

"The bills ... The bills need paying."

"Well, I can do that."

"No, I got to sign."

"Okay, so I'll bring you everything here, you can sign. Don't worry about it."

"I got to pay the fine."

"What fine?"

"From the time with the ice cream. I didn't pay it yet."

"The city can wait."

"No ... I gotta pay it. They said it was my fault, so I gotta pay it."

"All right, all right, we'll fix it. You're not supposed to worry your head about this stuff. The doctor said so." It was a lie and Louise glanced at Pru to make sure she was in support. She was, but she was also getting bored with all this minutiae. She was here because she had a job to do.

"Hey, Doyle," she said, just to change the subject, "how about if we come take your picture tomorrow?"

"Like this?" He couldn't turn his head very well, it was still strapped up, and he'd been told to try to resist moving it, so he just swiveled his eyes toward her instead.

"Absolutely, like this," she replied. "What's wrong with like this? Good-looking guy like you."

This embarrassed him a little, and he looked back at Louise. "You know what she asked me the first time."

"No, what did she ask you?"

"She asked me what he dreams about. Groucho. What he dreams about."

"You remember that," said Pru, surprised.

"Sure." Then to Louise again. "You know what I told her?"

"Breakfast?" she smiled. That had been her own joke from what seemed like a long time ago now.

Doyle also tried to smile at the recollection. "No, not breakfast," he replied. "I said he dreams about fields."

"Galloping on the pasture," added Pru.

"On account of how . . . of how . . ."

He'd done very well so far, but at this stage, he couldn't seem to get any more words out, so while Louise lifted the cup back to his lips, Pru filled in the blanks.

"On account of how he's always been in the city, never on grass, right? And how he always walks, never had the chance to gallop."

"And canters," said Doyle, trying hard to rejoin the conversation. "Walks and canters."

"Right, but never gallops," said Pru. "But you never told me what *you* dream about, Doyle."

"Me?"

"Yes, you. What do you dream about? What are your secret longings?"

"I dream about Groucho," he said simply. "He's my friend. I like to be with him."

The two women just looked at each other, just a hint of caring complicity passing between them. They were nothing like each other—Pru was a well-educated woman-about-town, Louise was a waitress who'd barely finished high school—but in this respect, they were of the same mind. They both saw a harmless old man, a gentle soul who deserved better than for fate to play such filthy tricks. First his friend had died, then the eviction notice, and now this. It was cruel.

In fact, to Louise, it was worse than cruel, it was vindictive, and that was part of why she wanted her ex to pay for causing it. What justice could there be, she thought, when the person to slip on the beer was Doyle and not Roscoe? But at least the bastard had finally been charged, even if it was only for being drunk and disorderly. At least she'd managed that.

"Will you be up to a few questions?" Pru asked Doyle. "I want to talk about the closing. Think you'll be able to manage that?"

"Sure," said Doyle, but his answer was weak. He was tiring.

"Maybe I can help a little with that," said Louise. "I went with him. To the city office and to the advice place."

"Great," said Pru. "And I'll need to talk to the drivers, too, get their reaction."

"Marie-Josée," said Doyle, hardly audible.

"What's that?"

"Marie-Josée," answered Louise. "She's one of the drivers. At Doyle's stable. What about her, Doyle? What about Marie-Josée?"

"Talk to her. She's ..."

"She's what?"

"She's the best one ... to talk to ..."

"Okay," said Pru. "Marie-Josée, got it."

Doyle tried to nod in his usual fashion but wasn't able to do it. Even his hand collapsed back down onto the bed in a combination of exhaustion and frustration. Then he coughed again, and Louise pulled a tissue from the box on the bedside table to wipe a little drool from the corner of his mouth. "I feel like an idiot," he managed to say, at which the two women smiled.

"I see you haven't lost your sense of humor," said Pru.

"Gets me through," he replied.

"A real joker," Louise added. "That's our Doyle."

"A charmer, too," said Pru, which was something she'd told him before.

"Two women now," said Doyle, doing his best to tease them. He wanted to say more, to ask them where they'd been all his life, but he couldn't manage it and his eyes closed with fatigue. Instinctively, Louise reached over and touched him on the cheek, just to see if he was all right. His unshaven gray stubble felt like steel wool. When his eyes opened again, she was relieved and smiled at him. "We'll be back tomorrow, all right?"

"Sure."

"Think you'll be up to it?"

"Sure."

"Okay, so we'll let you get some rest. Are the drivers coming to see you tonight?"

"Dunno."

"Want me to call Mowbray, tell them to come?"

"Sure."

"All right, so let me see what I can do. Sleep now."

They left his ward, but as they arrived at the elevator, Pru reminded Louise of her agreement to talk to the hospital. "You think he'll be up to it?"

"I think so. We'll be an hour . . . max. I promise."

"Okay," said Louise, but her voice was hesitant. At first, she'd been enthralled at the idea of Doyle seeing Groucho but now she wasn't certain. She felt that maybe the whole thing, with cameras and questions, might just be too much for him. Then, as they rode down to the hospital lobby, she said, "No flash."

Pru was already checking her phone, see what messages she had. "Sorry?"

"For the webcam. No flash. The horse doesn't like flash."

A wry expression. "Yes, I think I got that message by now."

"You should maybe tell them anyway."

"Fine, I'll tell them."

"Will they be able to see Doyle? I mean, at the stable?"

"Why? You thinking about the horse?"

"Just wondering."

"You know what? I don't think their vision allows them to see what's on flat screens. To them it's just color. At least I think so . . . but what do I know, right? Anyway, all we really need is a one-way link. Much simpler. The whole thing is just for the surprise factor."

"Also for Doyle."

"Right, right," Pru agreed belatedly. "Also for Doyle."

The following morning, it took a lot longer than anyone expected, as these things always do. But Doyle was more alert and enough to be fascinated with everything going on. The bustle was not unwelcome after the monotony of a hospital bed.

"Lotta stuff just to take a picture," said Doyle, watching. "Lotta people, too. Like a railway station in here."

In front of him was a tripod with an expensive-looking digital camera, a couple of small lamps, not too intense, and a lot of wiring, some of which led to a slim, notebook-style personal computer. There were five people in the room: Louise and Pru, of course; the photographer, fussing with his light meter; a web technician from the paper's back office, clicking busily on the keyboard.

In the background hovered a junior nurse, with strict instructions not to let this get out of hand, except she wasn't sure how much was too much. Pru came to where Louise was sitting holding Doyle's hand and said, "Won't be much longer, I promise. Almost ready. Got to get it right."

"Wish you could get *me* right while you're at it," joked Doyle.

"You? You'll be right as rain in no time. Strong as a horse." Then she thought about that for a moment. "Now why do you bring out all the clichés in me?" she asked, but she made that comment almost to herself, because neither Louise nor Doyle knew what she was talking about.

Eventually, at Pru's direction, the photographer got ready behind the camera while the technician placed the laptop, with all its trailing wires, on to the bed table in front of Doyle, adjusting the position so the screen was at the correct angle for everyone. "What's this?" Doyle asked. "We gonna learn the computer again?"

Louise smiled. "Just watch," she told him.

The technician was now leaning over Doyle's shoulder, moving a pointer on the screen by tapping the mouse that was next to the keyboard. "Okay," he muttered to himself as he accessed the file.

"What are we watching?" Doyle asked Louise.

"You'll see, in one minute."

"Fingers crossed," said Pru, standing to one side. Then to both the technician and the photographer, she said. "Let me know soon as you're ready."

The man behind the camera took a final light reading and made a final adjustment on his equipment. "Ready," he said, gazing at his viewfinder. His thumb was on his remote release.

The technician took a little longer but eventually, he too said, "Ready."

"All right, stand by . . ." replied Pru with her right hand in the air. She looked like she was at Houston Mission Control. With her left hand, she was clutching the cell phone, pushing her hair back in a well-practiced movement so she could hold it tightly to her ear. The expensive watch she wore on that wrist glinted briefly as the diamond reflected the lights.

"Doyle, your job is to watch the screen. Just keep watching, okay? That's all you've got to do."

"Okay."

Then Pru spoke into the cell phone. "You guys ready?" She was the only one to hear the response but apparently it was affirmative. Since there was no high-speed access in the stable, they ran the cable connection all the way along to young Mowbray's house, where he still lived with his parents.

It was an elaborate set-up and had taken considerable organization, but Pru had some major clout at the paper, and she'd managed to bully the project through in remarkably short time. In great part, that was the secret of her success. When she got an idea in her head, she broke through all obstacles and made it happen by the sheer force of her personality.

"So," she said, "if we're all ready, we'll count down from three. Doyle, you just keep watching the screen. Okay, three, two, one, and . . . now!" The technician gave a final click of the mouse, Mowbray's grin appeared next to Groucho's white face on the screen, Doyle's eyes opened wide in total astonishment and the photographer got his image.

Pru was just delighted and kept saying "Great! Great!" to everyone. On screen, Mowbray was waving his fingers and the horse was bobbing his head. "Tell Mowbray to say something," Pru said into the phone, obviously to some technician at the stable who was out of sight.

Mowbray looked away as the instruction was relayed, then back at the screen. "Hey, Doyle," he yelled. "How you doin', man? I got somebody here wanna say hi." He looked at Groucho and gave him a gentle rub on the muzzle, then fed him an apple, which the horse took in his usual manner.

Louise looked at Doyle and saw the sheer, open delight on the man's face, also the slight tear forming in his eye, and she couldn't help choking up herself.

"Groucho ..." said Doyle. "That's him, that's Groucho! He's there! Hi, Groucho, hi!"

"Speak louder," Louise whispered.

"Hi, Groucho!" said Doyle again. "Hi, how you doing?"

A moment later, Mowbray responded, "He's doin' fine, Doyle. Always hungry. I take 'im for a walk, bring 'im back an' he's hungry again."

"Sure, that's Groucho," said Doyle. "But you gotta judge how much to feed him. Not too much. Depends on the exercise."

"Yeah, I know, I know," said Mowbray. "Not too much. Don't worry, man."

"You order the feed?"

"Sure, I ordered it," said Mowbray. "You think we gonna starve down here? Hey, Doyle, how's it goin' with you?"

"I'm okay," Doyle said.

"You lookin' good, man."

"I'm okay," Doyle repeated. He was trying to match the volume of Mowbray but he couldn't really do it.

"When you comin' back? All the drivers askin' me that."

"I dunno," said Doyle. "Soon."

Mowbray gave another grin and a huge thumbs-up into the lens. "I need you here, man. Ain't got nobody to boss me around." The grin widened even more.

"I hear you're doing fine," Doyle told him. "I'm proud of you."

At this, Louise was beaming so wide, she thought her face was going to break apart. Even Pru, the experienced columnist, knew she was present at a very special event.

"Anything else you want to say?" Pru asked Doyle.

"Mind the street cleaner," Doyle yelled.

"Mind the what?" Mowbray called back.

"The street cleaner. In the street. The machine that cleans the street. Groucho doesn't like it."

"I told him already," said Louise.

And as if to confirm it, Mowbray came back and said, "I know, man, I know."

Doyle nodded. "How about the other horses? How's Ange? Any more problems?"

The delay was longer this time. "No, Ange is fine. They all fine. We takin' good care."

It was at that point the screen went blank and the technician came over to see what had happened, but the malfunction was of no consequence, not to Doyle, because he'd seen what he wanted.

"Link's severed," the technician said to Pru. "Want me to try get it back?"

"If you can. If not, don't worry."

"So, Doyle," she said, "what do you think of that? Modern technology."

But Doyle was having the moisture dabbed from his eyes by Louise. In between, she was trying to cope with her own, alternately wiping and blowing. While they were waiting, the screen came back, but the technician warned, "Don't know how much longer."

"Okay, Doyle," said Pru, "we have to say goodbye now."

Doyle waved. "Bye, Groucho. Bye Mowbray. Take care."

A second or so later, another thumbs-up and then they were gone, vanished from the screen.

"Wow!" said Louise, speaking for both herself and Doyle. "That was great, amazing. We gotta thank Pru and the guys, right?"

Doyle smiled at them all and lifted his hand. "Thank you ..." he said, but he could hardly speak the words. He tried to clear his throat and repeat them but he didn't do too well the second time either.

"You're most welcome," replied Pru, helping him out. Her two colleagues were already busy packing up their stuff. It was clear that Doyle was tired now. The emotion and the bustle had worn him out.

"You know what," Louise said to him, "I think we should all leave, let you get some rest now. It's been a lot. We'll come back tomorrow. Well, at least I will. Maybe not all these people." She felt him squeeze her hand, as if to say no, don't leave yet. Not just yet. "Okay," she said, "just a bit longer."

Gradually, the three from the newspaper got themselves out, trying at the same time to leave the room as tidy as they found it. The young nurse gamely helped them.

Finally, just before leaving, Pru said to Louise, "I'll call you if I need any more, okay?"

Louise had already given her everything she knew about the stable closure but she agreed nonetheless. She didn't know if another article would achieve very much, but she was willing to be as helpful as possible, especially after what Pru had done today.

After they'd all gone, Louise remained for a while at Doyle's bedside. He was already asleep, so she just sat silently watching him, thinking how different her life might have been if he really had been her grandfather, or her uncle. She knew he was no saint, she could see that well enough. He could be as stubborn and contrary as the horse when the mood took him but she still regretted not having known him much earlier.

Twenty-two

high pressure front had moved down the St. Lawrence Valley, bringing a mixed combination of bright sunlight and chill wind, enough to cause the unmarked police car to drift slightly as it crossed the open river.

Detective-Sergeant Marc-André Héroux of the SPVM wrestled with the effect on the wheel as he tried to adjust the car's heater and change the radio station, all at the same time. He was heading out of town via the Champlain Bridge, and the rapid effect of light and shade caused by the girders was disconcerting until he cleared the superstructure above the Seaway and began the gradual descent on to Autoroute 10.

From here, the wide, curving exit ramp led to a choice of either north-east, following the river downstream to Quebec City, or due south toward the US border. The alternative was to stay on the central lanes and head directly for the region known in French as Les Cantons de l' Est, in English as the Eastern Townships—and this was the route that Marc-André took.

He was on his way to see the aging ex-chairman of the city's Executive Committee, who'd chosen to retire to his roots in Montréal's rural hinterland so he could spend all his time on his hobby farm. His name was Pierre-Paul Lafontaine and he'd once been the civic enforcer, a power broker who reigned through consecutive administrations with a combination of backslapping, arm-twisting, and head-banging. When one wouldn't work, the other would be employed, and everyone from the mayor's office to the party caucus knew to be extremely cautious in how far they tested the limits of his authority.

The property was near Bromont, a hundred or so acres of mixed pasture and forest with a rambling, century-old house, situated close to the road. On one side, where the landscape dipped, was a naturally sourced pond with a wooden dock, no doubt where the grandchildren played during the weekends.

On the other, was a random assortment of barns and out-buildings, some original and some more recent additions. Some place, thought Marc-André as he stepped out of the car—the kind he might visualize for himself one day if he could ever progress beyond a police sergeant's pay scale. The house had been freshly painted an off-white color and he took care to ring the ancient doorbell instead of knocking on the woodwork.

In response, a dog began to bark, a large breed from the sound, and he heard a woman's accented voice telling the animal to hush. When she answered, he saw a stern, elderly woman, half-bending, trying to restrain an overly friendly golden retriever by holding on to the collar. Since he knew Lafontaine had recently lost his wife, Marc-André assumed this must be the Portuguese housekeeper. He pulled the badge from his inside pocket.

"Detective-Sergeant Héroux, Montréal police," he said in the kind of no-nonsense manner many officers adopted as a way to cut through the bullshit their jobs so often entailed. "I have an appointment with M'sieur Lafontaine."

She looked at him with open suspicion. "I'll let him know," she said. "Wait here, please." She shut the door in his face while she went to get confirmation.

He didn't care. He was used to that kind of reception and was content enough just to look around and breathe the late fall air, his mind trying to calculate the market price for a spread like this and how much it might cost each month to run. Before he had any of the answers, she was back.

"Come in, please. Wipe your feet. M'sieur Lafontaine is on the phone, he'll be with you soon."

Marc-André did as he was told and found himself in a wide hallway, decorated with heirlooms and old photographs of the city boss in all his glory. Some depicted Lafontaine in his younger days with Mayor Drapeau and Premier Bourassa, others showed him at various stages of his career with department heads and uniformed police chiefs and union officials.

There were group shots with fire station personnel and school children, plus, for the sake of ego, a few with visiting celebrities, from Céline Dion on stage, to Leonard Cohen in a studio, to Guy Lafleur at center-ice.

"Memories, what good are they?" asked Pierre-Paul Lafontaine in that basso voice of his. At college, one of his great passions, apart from politics, was amateur operatics, to the point that he actually thought about applying to a professional company. It was pragmatism, he always claimed, that stopped him making a fool of himself like that.

"You're not proud of your life?" Marc-André asked him.

"Proud? I shuffled some papers, managed some budgets. So I held on to my job for a while, so what? What's to be proud of?"

"You worked with famous people."

The older man laughed. "I didn't work with them, I just met with them and shook hands in front of the camera. You know what they call that now? A photo opportunity. And that's all politics is, believe me. One long photo opportunity, chance to get your picture in the papers . . . Well, now it's TV and the internet, but same thing, same thing."

"But still . . ."

"It means nothing, nothing at all, The past is the past. It's the present that counts. Enjoy it while you can. Trust me, you'll never get it back. Take it from an old bastard like me."

"You're not so old."

"But I am a bastard, right?"

Marc-André tried to cover the faux-pas with an embarrassed smile but Lafontaine just patted him on the arm.

"Come on in, come on in. Don't get too many visitors out here. Not since my wife died."

"Yes, I heard about that. I'm sorry for your loss."

A brief shake of the head was the only reply as they entered the salon, a pleasant room with a library, a fireplace, and several winged chairs, but they didn't sit down. They walked straight across the room, through French doors to a glass solarium that overlooked the pond. Here was a handsome set of patio furniture, a round table, and four chairs, surrounded by a mass of healthy-looking green plants.

On the table was a sleek laptop computer, several hard copy files, a digital agenda and a hands-free phone, all the accoutrements of a modern home office. Despite his relaxed attitude and gentle bonhomie, this was obviously a man who could never totally let go.

"Still busy working, I see," said Marc-André as they sat down.

"Try to keep in touch," replied Lafontaine, dismissing it all with a casual wave of his hand. "Now, what can I do for you?"

"Well, as I mentioned on the phone, I'd like to go over your deposition, if you don't mind. Just a few final questions, a few things we need to clear up."

"Okay, I think we can handle that."

Marc-André opened up the worn black satchel he'd carried in and pulled out a thick file. It contained the relevant papers for the major corruption case that would soon be going to trial, a case involving the awarding of construction contracts that had kept him fully occupied recently. The crown prosecutors were calling on Pierre-Paul Lafontaine as an expert witness to testify to the court about administration protocols: what procedures would be normal in bidding, what wouldn't, and how the judgment would be made. It was a complex affair and the amount of detail was astounding.

Unfortunately, as Louise had already discovered, the corruption didn't appear to have spread as far as the deal to gentrify Pointe St-Charles, the location of Doyle O'Shaughnessy's stable. On her insistence, Marc-André had searched, but he'd not been able to find any connection. However unsavory it might be from a human point-of-view, legally, it appeared to be totally above board.

There was one thing Marc-André promised to do, though, and he decided to broach it now, before they got into the principal case. "Before we start, there's, well, there's another small matter I'd like to talk to you about, if you're willing. Something you can maybe help me with."

Lafontaine glanced at his watch, a matter of habit, then sat back in his chair, as if realizing that time meant nothing anymore. "If I can," he said amiably.

"It's not a big deal, really. I almost don't like to trouble you with it."

"Young man, I think it might be quicker just to ask me than to keep apologizing."

Marc-André nodded at the wisdom of that. After another moment's hesitation, he asked, "Do you know a councilor, name of Quintal?"

"Georges Quintal? Sure, I know him. What's the old fart up to now?"

"Interesting you call him that. He's trying to shut down a stable because of the smell."

"A stable?"

"A *calèche* stable, run by an old Irishman."

"Oh, sure, I know that place. Down at the Pointe. Been there a long time."

"Can he do that? Just shut it down like that?"

"Not officially, no. A stable permit's awarded by the city."

"Well, in this case, there's a construction project . . ."

"Yeah, I know about that."

"Anyways, Quintal's using it as an excuse to close the place."

"Is he now?" Lafontaine sat back in his chair. "And if I may ask, what's your interest in all this, Sergeant? Is there a crime somewhere in there?"

"That's what I'm trying to find out."

"Fine, but first I have to know why you're trying so hard. Don't have enough work to do, you have to go looking for more?"

Marc-André smiled at how easily his motives were being picked apart and decided to come clean on this one. "It's a personal favor."

"To the Irishman?"

"No . . . not exactly." Marc-André looked at the man, wondering whether to confess. Then, he thought, to hell with it, all or nothing. "To my girlfriend, actually. She kind of takes care of the old man."

"Ah, now, a favor for the girlfriend. That's different."

"I'm sorry to waste your time . . ."

"No, no, I admire your guts. Takes a lot to admit something like that. Says a lot about a man's character. You know, favors are what keeps that whole damn city going, believe me." Lafontaine leaned forward and reduced his tone to that of a stage whisper. "Especially favors for girlfriends." Then he laughed, pleased with his own sagacity.

Marc-André just felt awkward. "If you prefer not to answer, that's fine, I understand ..."

Lafontaine interrupted him. "All right, listen to me. The two things are different. He can shut the stable for redevelopment but he can't remove the permit. And if he's shutting it, he has to pay fair and reasonable compensation."

"Does that mean the real value or the city's value?"

"What it means is 'fair and reasonable' compensation. That's what the statute says."

"So the old man could just buy a new place if he wants?"

"In theory. But I wouldn't stay in that borough if I were him. Not if he's not welcome."

"And you're sure he's still got the permit?"

"Sure? What do you mean, sure? I just told you, didn't I?"

"Sorry, I just meant ..."

"Look, once and for all. They can't take a permit away unless the city votes a special ordinance and there's nothing like that on the agenda as far as I can see." At that, Lafontaine switched moods, something he did very easily, like shifting gears in a race car. "Laws ..." he said more philosophically. "Too much aggravation, too much disturbance. You make too many enemies trying to pass laws, then you can't run anything. That's why favors are so important, understand?"

"I believe so."

"Good, good. Maybe you'll run for office one day. Young man like you. Bright, honest, gutsy. I'd change the outfit though, buy a good suit."

"Thanks."

"Thanks, but no thanks, right? Okay, let's move on."

"There's just one more small point ..."

Lafontaine gave out with a sigh. "All right, come on, let's have it. May as well get it out of your system. I'll need your full attention on the big stuff."

"Well, it's just that ... I heard it's hard to move a stable to another district. Nobody's going to want it."

"Who told you that?"

"Somebody my girlfriend spoke to."

"Nonsense. There's heritage money comes with a stable. Shop it around. Somebody'll want to stick his snout in that trough, I guarantee it."

"So why doesn't Quintal want it?"

"Quintal ..." replied Lafontaine with some distaste. "Making too much from the construction deal to worry about any damn heritage fund. That's off the record, by the way. If you ask me later, I never said it."

Off the record or not, Marc-André was still a detective and that was still an accusation. He couldn't pretend he hadn't heard, especially when he'd already scanned that particular file himself. "Do you think I should be ..."

Lafontaine didn't even let him finish. "I doubt you could prove anything against Quintal. I've been trying for years, never got anywhere. My advice? Don't get distracted. Stick with the main case, better use of your manpower."

"And the stable?"

"The stable? If it's that important, just find a new district. Try Verdun, they're always looking for handouts. Or Lachine maybe ... although that may be a bit far for the horses to travel. At any rate, do the research. Someplace where there's lots of old warehouse space and not too many residents.

"But like I said, shop it around, get the best deal. It's the perfect solution. The Irishman gets a new building, the Pointe gets developed, Georges Quintal can afford his retirement, and I get to say good riddance to the old prick. Everybody's happy ... which, by the way, in case you're ever interested, is the best way to succeed in politics. See? You come visit me, you get free lessons, very valuable. Now, can we move on, or does your girlfriend need any more favors? What's wrong, not giving her enough?"

"None of your damn business."

"Well said. Okay, next topic."

Twenty-three

L ouise could hardly believe the news. She was excited about telling Doyle and even before leaving the apartment, she was online, finding out about real estate agents, about how there were two different kinds, commercial and residential, and that it was the former they'd be needing. She'd need a plan too.

A step-by-step approach to moving the stable, so she didn't miss anything along the way: how to "shop it around" the districts, as Marc-André had told her. How to make sure the borough came up with the settlement in time.

Perhaps, even more importantly, how to recruit the stable's four drivers into the project so they'd be a help, not a hindrance. She even wanted to get Mowbray involved. The kid was turning out to be someone she could count on and that was a real surprise.

All this went through her mind as she showered and dressed. She knew Doyle would be awake early, as he always was, even now at the hospital, and she was anxious to get there, start the discussion before he became too tired. She grabbed a quick bite with Marc-André and gave him a special kiss before leaving: a long, sensual kiss that she hoped would tell him how she felt. It was amazing what he'd managed to do.

Yesterday's wild gusts had brought in several layers of clouds this morning, shades of gray on gray, and they were even predicting the first few flakes of winter, so she pulled on a warmer jacket, the red one with the hood. Too late, she noticed there was a slight tear on the pocket from last fall, something she'd intended to fix, but she couldn't worry about that now. She just wanted to be on her way. A quick check of her purse to see that all was in order and she was out the door.

The bus journey across the city, south down Parc, then the transfer west along Pine, was especially slow this morning, taking a half-hour longer than normal, but she used the time to continue her thoughts, staring through the window at the dull morning. The city was going about its normal business but, inside, she was bursting with the idea of telling Doyle.

Eventually, she saw the familiar hospital, its ugly, redbrick structure dominating the landscape on this side of the mountain, and she waited impatiently for the other passengers to disembark. Some were outpatients and had to take their time.

Once inside the lobby, she held the elevator doors open for a pair of male orderlies as they wheeled in a gurney, then sidled up against the wall to give them enough room. They were going to the same floor. She thought nothing of it until the doors opened and she saw the same young duty nurse who'd been present at the webcam link-up. But the nurse's face was no longer fresh and smiley. It was frowning and serious, and the young woman immediately set about supervising the orderlies, leading them along the corridor.

Louise sensed immediately what was going on. "Doyle?" she asked, and saw the nurse turn at the sound of the word, her expression grave. In that one instant, Louise knew the worst. Her hand went to her mouth, her legs almost gave way and the young nurse had to reach forward in case she fell.

"I'm sorry," said the nurse softly. "There was nothing we could do. It happened quickly. One minute he was awake, asking for his coffee, the next . . ."

Louise couldn't respond, couldn't even think. She just stood there shaking, all color having drained from her face, until the nurse guided her by the arms down onto a bench. She tried to pull herself together, but she couldn't fight the feeling inside her stomach and the instant reddening around the eyes as the emotion gathered its strength and then gushed out like a loose hydrant. She was unable to prevent it.

"How? When?" she managed to say. "You didn't call me."

"Let me ask the doctor to come see you."

"I was . . . I was on the bus. It was slow this morning. The weather . . ." She was saying the words as if she were at fault for not having gotten there sooner. If she'd arrived sooner, she could have told him the good news, about the permit, about the horses, about Groucho, but now he'd never know. "Can I see him? I need to see him." She had to tell him, and she made to get up but the nurse put a hand on her arm.

"I'm sorry," the nurse said again. "Please, just wait here, if you would."

"I need to see him."

The young woman looked at Louise with gentle eyes. She hadn't been working long enough to take on the veneer of hard-bitten professionalism that some of the more senior nurses adopted.

"I'll see what I can do," she said quietly. "Please . . . just wait here for now." Then she hurried off, a petite figure on flat shoes, her body kept lean by the constant pressure.

Louise watched her go through blurred vision, the streams cascading down her face, dripping from her nose and chin. She tried to clutch tissues from her purse, fumbling with the tiny packet, but they were soon soaked and she didn't have any more, so she just held her hands to her face as she rocked back and forth, distraught, lost in her own world of disbelief.

It was a few minutes before the nurse returned, this time accompanied by a middle-aged man with receding hair and a furrowed brow, wearing an over-starched white coat which hung open. In the top pocket were his eyeglasses and around his neck hung an old stethoscope like it was his badge of office. He looked like he'd been working all night.

"I'm Dr. Coombs," he said in English. "Are you the next of kin?"

Louise looked at him, not really knowing how to answer. Then she recalled what she'd said before, on another occasion. "I'm the closest he's got."

"I see. Well, I'm afraid he had a relapse." The doctor's voice was clipped and abrupt, as if he wasn't used to speaking in layman's terms. "It was extremely sudden."

"But yesterday . . ."

"A brain injury like that can be unpredictable. I'm very sorry."

"Can I see him?"

The man thought about it, glanced at the nurse, then gave a brief nod. "The nurse will take you. Do you have any questions?"

Louise looked up at him as best she could, at the fatigued, lined face which seemed old before its time. What questions could she possibly have? She knew nothing about the internal functioning of the brain. "I just want to see him," she said.

The doctor nodded once more, then left to attend to other matters as the young nurse helped Louise to her feet. Together, they walked slowly along to the same ward, but Louise had to pause at the doorway before going in, just to prepare herself. Nearby were the two orderlies with their gurney, just hanging around, waiting for further instructions. Encouraged by the nurse, Louise stepped inside the room and saw him lying there in the bed, head back on the pillow, eyes shut, no expression.

He was still wearing bandages around his head, but the machines had all been detached. She didn't want to touch him in case he felt cold. She didn't want that, so she just gazed at him, trying to convince herself that he was now at peace. But in the back of her mind, she couldn't help wishing she'd got here at least a few minutes earlier so that she could have told him the news.

She didn't even know how long she stood there as the recollections invaded her, one after the other. Doyle in the church after her mother had died, attempting to speak but saying nothing. Doyle with the horse in the stable, stroking the animal's nose. Doyle upstairs in his ramshackle apartment, handing her a blanket the night she left her husband. And Doyle just a couple days ago, his face bright with surprise and joy at seeing Groucho live on the screen . . .

Then the nurse spoke to her, disturbing the flow. "Your name is Louise Vallières?"

When Louise nodded, the nurse opened the narrow drawer in the bedside table, lifted out a long white envelope and handed it to her. It had her name on it, but it was in script, not Doyle's usual block capitals.

"It's my writing," said the nurse. "He asked me to write it for him when I came on duty. He was awake at six, waiting for me. I didn't know if I was supposed to do something like that. I didn't tell anybody about it ..." Her voice trailed off as Louise opened up the envelope.

"I shouldn't really say it," said the young nurse, "but I think he knew. What I mean is, he seemed fine when I was doing it but now when I think about it . . . He said, if something happens, I should give this to you."

Louise just looked at her for several seconds, trying to understand. Then she opened the envelope with her nail and unfolded the sheet of lined paper which she found inside. It was in the form of a letter, written out neatly and carefully along the lines, as if in a school exercise book. Before she could even begin reading, the tears welled up again, flooding her eyes, and she had to wipe them away before she could continue.

My dear Louise,

I asked the nurse to write this for me in case something happens. You are my best friend, and I would like you to have what I leave behind. The stable and everything else, too, but I don't have much money. I am sorry it's not more money. I would also like you to have Groucho.

I know you didn't want him when your mom died, but I hope you will take him now. Please be nice to him and take care of him, even if he makes trouble. He is just being a horse. He is also my friend, like you. I don't know how it can work with you and him, but you are clever. I know you will think of how to do it.

Thank you for letting me see him again on the computer. Anyway, my dear Louise, if something happens, please don't be sad. I have been very lucky and very happy to look after the horses my whole life, and I hope you will be happy too.

Yours sincerely, Doyle.

After this, there was a one-line space before his awkward, formal signature. *P. D. O'Shaughnessy.* Then came a kind of post-script, also in the nurse's hand.

If there's enough money please help Mowbray with the fare to Jamaica where he wants to go. Also, about Groucho, your mother gave him sugar, but I think apples are better.

At the end, Louise had to reach over to steal the tissue from the box that was still on the table. Then she went back to the top and began again, just so she could hear Doyle's voice in her head. She could easily imagine him speaking these words, trying to sound correct as the nurse wrote it all down.

"I copied it just the way he said it," the young woman told her. "But I don't know . . . What I mean is, nobody's ever asked me to do that before . . ."

"It's okay," replied Louise. She wanted to say thanks for doing it, that it meant a lot, but those words didn't come. She was too full. It was all too much for her to take in, so she just said again, "It's okay."

"We're here to remember a very special person," Louise said to the congregation. She was anxious that she shouldn't tear up again, not now, not here, and she paused to clear her throat. "Doyle O'Shaughnessy was my friend," she continued as she gazed around at the faces in front of her.

"He was there when I needed him. He let me stay in his stable one night and, yes, in a way it made me feel like, well, you know, Joseph and Mary when they couldn't find any other place to go." She gave a quick half-smile to the intense young priest, who was obviously hoping she wouldn't offer a repeat of last time.

"Yeah, I know that in some ways, he found it hard to cope with the modern world. He didn't understand technology, and he didn't care much about money. But he had a big heart, my friend, Doyle. The biggest in the world. Now I talked about Joseph and Mary, but maybe, I don't know, maybe Doyle was more like St. Francis, with his love of the horses." Another glance at the priest. "He wrote me a letter the day before he died to say that he was very lucky and very happy to be with horses his whole life.

"Very lucky and very happy . . . those were the words he wrote. How many people here can say that? He lived a wonderful life, Doyle. He did exactly what he wanted, and he asked for nothing more. He loved the horses, all of them . . . but the horse he loved most was Groucho, who was my mother's horse. When she died, Doyle and Groucho kind of looked after each other. And I think that if Groucho could speak, I'm sure he'd say the same thing as me. He'd say . . . Doyle was my friend."

When Louise finished, there was total silence. She waited a moment, a little unnerved, then she just walked slowly back to take her seat next to Marc-André, the footsteps from her good shoes echoing on the stone floor. And still, the silence held. One after the other, each of the drivers went up and said a few words, with Bertrand even getting a laugh or two with some of his comments, but it was Louise's words which had touched everyone the most.

After the service, they emerged to find the first winter storm of the year, the flakes descending thick and heavy from a dense sky. The early accumulation had already turned the gray asphalt of Verdun to an eerie white, which only brought a sacrilegious curse from Marc-André, because he hadn't yet put snow tires on his car.

In response, she elbowed him in the ribs, not because she'd suddenly discovered any great sense of spirituality, but out of simple respect. For her, the eulogy she gave was like a redemption of sorts, if only from the worst aspects of her own behavior, and she didn't want to disturb that feeling. Reality would impose itself soon enough but not just yet, she hoped, not today.

Twenty-four

Even with climate change, winter in the city could still mean months of sub-zero temperatures. Eventually, inevitably, the time comes when the flurries are fewer, the streets are slushier and, in Pointe St-Charles, the first green weeds of spring begin to show through the unkempt lots.

One morning in late March, when the sun's rays had managed to penetrate a gap in the clouds like an image from an illustrated Bible, an unmarked police car pulled up outside the narrow, row house that the Groves family occupied, Elliott, Katrien, and their son, Mowbray.

More often than not, the presence of this type of vehicle proved ominous for the district's inhabitants but on this occasion, it was exactly the opposite. As the vehicle came to a stop, Marc-André gave two quick blasts on the horn to announce that he and Louise had arrived.

A minute later, Mowbray appeared, dressed up against the cold with a small rucksack over his shoulder. He didn't say what the bag was for, he just sidled into the back of the car, ready to go.

Once the door was slammed shut, Marc-André put the car in gear but didn't put his foot down as he usually did. Instead, at Louise's request, he just crawled along the street past the stable. All she wanted to do, she said, was take one final look. The old place was completely empty, with the metal gates of the compound chained shut and the big wooden doors padlocked, and all she could do was sigh. Not so long ago, it was filled with life, five muscular quadrupeds and one scrawny biped, all living together under the same roof. But now it had reverted to what it once was: a dilapidated building in a derelict part of town. There was nothing left to see, and she didn't even want to get out of the car.

"Okay, enough," she said, "let's go."

She felt the surge of acceleration as they sped away, around the corner and out in the direction of the Champlain Bridge. She didn't want to feel sad, not today, and made a deliberate attempt to snap out of it by swiveling in her seat and talking to Mowbray. "So," she said to him, "when do you leave?" As with Doyle, she automatically switched to English when she spoke.

In response, a smile appeared on Mowbray's face at the very thought of escaping to the island of Jamaica, where the skies were clear and the temperature was always warm.

"Tuesday," he replied. "Couple more days then I'm gone. Outa here. *Au revoir. Arrivederci.*" The last was a word he'd learned from a movie and he just liked the sound of it, so he said it again, stretching it out as far as it would go. "Arree . . . vee . . . der . . . chee."

"You sound pretty happy."

"Hey, three months on a beach."

"Yeah, but you'll be working."

"Workin' on a beach? That ain't workin', that's livin'!"

One of his father's cousins had a small hotel near Half-Moon Bay on the south coast. Nothing fancy, but it was close to the shore, and they were willing to take Mowbray on for the remainder of the high season. The only payment was room and board, but after living so long with his parents, he'd managed to save a little, so he didn't mind. Plus, at Doyle's request, Louise had furnished the young man with enough funds for a return air ticket, so the major expense was already paid.

"Any horses there?" Louise asked him.

"Nah, ain't that kinda place. But they got a rap band in a club nearby, so I'm figurin' I can maybe hang out wi' them dudes."

"Rap?" said Marc-André, joining in from the driver's seat. "I thought it was all reggae down there."

"Hey, where you been, man? That's like ancient history."

"Bob Marley? Gregory Isaacs?"

"Yeah, they gods an' all, but they old gods."

"You know, you're even starting to sound like a rapper."

"Gotta get into it, man. Gotta get writin' some lyrics."

"Is that what you're gonna do?"

"Gonna try. Man, sittin' on the beach writin' lyrics. That's livin'."

"Better than shoveling shit?"

Mowbray knew Marc-André was just teasing him but he chose to answer the question anyway. "Wasn't so bad," he said. "Never had a problem wi' shovelin' the shit. I mean, I know I complained to the old man an' all, but it was okay. Last few months, I wasn't even doin' that. Lanky was doin' it. Me, I was, like, takin' care o' things."

"And you did a great job," said Louise, just to make him feel good. In fact there'd actually been a few mistakes, including a minor fire alarm one time just before Christmas, but no real harm was done, and when the drivers finally moved their horses out to other stables, the animals were still in excellent condition.

Mowbray was pleased with her compliment and sat back to watch the scenery as they crossed the broad expanse of the river. The ice had broken up and the surface below was like a giant's jig-saw puzzle of silver and charcoal. Louise turned on the radio, and although the music that emanated from the speakers was more pop than rap, the insistent rhythms soon had all three of them tapping and bopping along.

After an hour of highway driving, they saw the exit to Bromont and turned off past a line of fast food outlets and gas stations. All around were high rolling hills, with a remainder of snow that looked like cake frosting, all except where the manicured ski trails ran down. There the texture appeared more like whipped cream.

"This is cool, man," said Mowbray, who'd never been out this way before. It was a general comment addressed to nobody in particular, and he continued to gaze out in fascination as they drove on through the rural landscape. "Hey, horses," he said at one point, indicating a couple of chestnut thoroughbreds on the other side of a broad pad-dock, grazing contentedly on the thick, tufty grass that was starting to push through everywhere.

"Yeah, horse country all around here," Louise said, turning in her seat to face him. "When I was a kid, they had the Olympics, you know about that?"

"Here?" Mowbray looked around but could see nothing but fields and hills.

"Well, not here, back in the village where we just passed through. They built a special place just for the horse events and stuff."

"So everybody had to drive out here every day, with the horses an' all?"

"No, no, they were based here. The horses, the riders . . . they set up a whole thing."

"Equestrian," corrected Marc-André.

"What's that?" she asked.

"They don't call it horse events, they call it equestrian."

"Ee . . . quest . . . ree . . . yan," repeated Mowbray, for nobody's benefit but his own. Another word to add to his collection.

Another few minutes and they were at the estate of Pierre-Paul Lafontaine, the ex-city manager. When they climbed out of the car, they discovered it was several degrees colder out here than in the city, and Louise shivered a little. Mowbray, on the other hand, just grinned and couldn't resist saying very slowly, "Ja . . . may . . . ka," just to taunt her.

This time, it wasn't the Portuguese housekeeper who opened the door but Lafontaine himself, shaking hands with each of them. He helped Louise off with her parka, leaving the other two to handle the disrobing themselves: jackets, scarves, boots, and in Mowbray's case, the rucksack too. "So you're the famous Louise," said the older man. "Pleased to finally meet you."

"Famous?" she replied.

"I know all your secrets," he confided.

"You do?"

"Everything."

Marc-André offered a smirk. "He's just trying to get me into trouble."

"I'm sure you don't need my help," Lafontaine replied.

"And this is our good friend, Mowbray Groves," said Marc-André, switching to English.

"Ah, right, right," Lafontaine replied in the same language. "You're the horse expert I've heard so much about."

"Hey, not me, man," answered Mowbray. "I think you got me mixed up."

"No, I don't think so. As it happens, I know a lot about you, too, young man."

"Yeah?"

"In fact, I was wondering if you need a job."

"A job? You serious?"

"Sure I'm serious."

"What kinda job?"

"Mathematician," said Lafontaine with a straight face.

"Excuse me?"

"I'm joking, I'm joking. Don't you know a joke when you hear it? I want you to come take care of the horses."

"But you got somebody already."

"I do, but he gave me notice. Soon as I can find somebody else, he's heading out to Alberta. God knows why."

"'Cause that's where all the money is," said Marc-André."

"I suppose. Oil and horses. Damn place is turning into Texas. Still, what can you do? Way of the world. So, what do you say, young man?"

Mowbray looked at each of them in turn, a little embarrassed. "Well, that's nice of you an' all," he said to Lafontaine, "but I'm goin' to Jamaica."

"Vacation?"

"No, man, to work."

"How long?"

"Three months, maybe."

"Maybe?"

"Yeah."

"Okay, tell you what. If I can persuade my guy to stick around through spring and you tell me you're definitely coming back in three months, I'll keep the job open for you. How about that?" Mowbray didn't know what else to say and looked at Louise for guidance.

"Your life," she said simply. It was the same thing she had once told Doyle.

"Okay, okay," added Lafontaine. "Too much pressure, I know. Tell you what, you don't need to decide today." Then, after a slight pause, he smirked and said, "I'll give you until tomorrow. Call me back before lunch, it's yours. If not, I'll find somebody else. Deal?"

Mowbray just grinned, partly at the novelty of making a deal and partly because he actually liked the man's style: straight, direct, and no nonsense. It was rare. "Okay, man, I tell you tomorrow."

"Excellent," said Lafontaine, as he led them away, back through to his favorite room, the solarium.

"Now what can I offer you?" he asked. "Coffee? Tea? Scotch?" He turned to Mowbray. "Jamaican rum?" This brought on another grin. To Mowbray, the guy was a riot.

Since it was still morning, none of them wanted anything alcoholic, which was just as well because when they arrived, they found that the housekeeper was already setting the table for coffee, an overly formal arrangement with fine china, silver and napkins.

Beyond the glass walls of the solarium, the pond was still frozen and they all gazed out at the broad landscape, taking in the full expanse of its harsh beauty. For a few long seconds, the only sound was the soft, steady *tick-tick* of a grandfather clock, until Lafontaine invited them to take their seats and took up the conversational slack.

"What's happening with the stable?" he asked nobody in particular.

It was Louise who replied. "Nothing," she said simply.

"Any word yet on compensation?"

"You mean the money? They sent me a letter before Christmas, but nothing since."

"What did it say, the letter?"

"Not much. Just that they were reviewing the file, whatever the hell that means."

"You want me to make a couple of calls?" he suggested.

"Could you? That'd be great."

Lafontaine nodded. "Know what you're going to do with the money when you get it?" he asked her.

"No . . . not really."

This was a difficult issue for Louise. The amount coming to her as Doyle's designated heir was for the stable building. But since the drivers had all moved out and Mowbray was leaving, there was really no need to buy another building, and this meant the funds had nowhere to go except into her own bank account. Yet she felt awkward about it, as if she were somehow taking money that didn't really belong to her.

"You want my advice?" Lafontaine told her. "Buy yourselves a house, the two of you."

It was a surprising thing to say, and she wasn't expecting it. "I don't know . . . I mean, I don't know if it's such a good idea, you know, a house . . . whether it's right."

Lafontaine wasn't too interested in her moral conscience. "You pregnant yet?" he asked her bluntly.

Throughout his career, he'd always enjoyed shocking people like that, just to sit back and watch their reaction.

"What's that to you?" asked Marc-André, jumping immediately to her defense.

This time, it was Louise who was more circumspect. Not so long ago, she would have been the one to over-react. "We're kind of working on it," she replied.

"Work harder," said Lafontaine, as if issuing an order. "Nothing like kids for boosting the tax base." He let out a quiet chuckle, then made an apology of sorts. "Don't mind me," he told them. "That's what retirement does. Too much time alone."

"What retirement?" asked Marc-André. "You sit out here on your own, but you're still pulling all the damn strings back there."

Lafontaine's chuckle became an open laugh, one of his big, resounding, baritone laughs, but he was saved from answering by the arrival of the housekeeper with her tray. On it were three cups of coffee, a small round pot of tea for Louise, and a plate of home-baked shortbread.

He invited the elderly lady to stay and join them, but she just shook her head, very shy and very correct, and went off back to her kitchen. She was an old-fashioned woman who liked to keep things the way they should be. She'd lost her family and found a home here with a very important man, and she wasn't about to abuse that privilege by becoming too familiar.

In the meantime, Louise happened to notice that Mowbray had been completely left out of the conversation, so she obligingly switched back to English. "So . . ." she said to Lafontaine, "how's our hero today?" Everybody knew what she was talking about. It was one of the reasons they'd come all this way.

"Soon as we're done here, we'll go see."

They trooped back along the hallway, pulled on their winter layers, and stepped through the door. The chill was immediate and Mowbray made a noise with his teeth that sounded like he was about to succumb to instant frostbite.

The three guests followed Pierre-Paul Lafontaine along a plowed walkway around the side of the house, away from the pond and toward the collection of outbuildings. One of the barns had been fully renovated and converted into an efficient stable. Unlike Doyle's old place in the city, this was large and light and airy, almost pristine in appearance, with climate control, good insulation, and efficient plumbing.

It was suitable for several horses but at present there were only three: an impressive double team of gray-black Percherons, which had won numerous awards at the Brome County Fair, plus a stiff old sorrel with a flaxen mane who was half a hand higher than either of his neighbors.

"Hey, Groucho!" called Mowbray, as soon as he spied him in the stall. "Hey, man, what gives? How you doin'?"

Groucho's ears twitched at the sound of the voice, before bobbing that mighty head in welcome.

Mowbray reached into the rucksack he was still carrying and pulled out a bag of bright red apples, a sweet California variety that he'd bought at the Atwater Market especially for today. As soon as he took one out, Groucho reached forward and snuffled it gladly with the same soft-eyed pleasure he'd always shown. As he chewed on it, enjoying the juices, Mowbray rubbed his muzzle.

"Yeah, that's the way. Man, you can sure put away them apples. You know how to do that, all right. So how's it goin'? You enjoyin' life out in the boonies? Great place you got here, like a deluxe hotel. Dee . . . luxx! Hey, if you're nice, maybe the boss man here gonna buy you a wide-screen TV to watch, how about that?"

"If you take the job, maybe I'll think about it," Lafontaine answered from behind them.

It had been Marc-André's notion to send Groucho to Pierre-Paul Lafontaine, suggesting it the evening of Doyle's funeral service at the church. He and Louise had gone out for Lebanese food and it was over a giant platter of lamb and couscous that he'd mentioned it. For the briefest moment, she'd sat there looking at him, unable to believe how obvious the idea was and how perfect it would be and how Marc-André just seemed to have a knack for finding such solutions.

From that time on, it was just a matter of arranging it: making the request, setting the date, and finally, organizing the move, which was no minor operation. In the end, it was Lafontaine's experienced stableman, Gilles, the one who was about to leave, who'd driven all the way to Pointe St-Charles with the trailer.

Yet, once there, it took two full days trying to get Groucho to step inside. Doyle would have perhaps been horrified at the amount of apple and sugar bribery it took, but eventually the two young men working together managed to entice the horse up the ramp and bolt the trailer gate safely behind him.

That had been the hardest part. By the time Groucho arrived out here in the country, he was so glad to escape the confines that he reversed out all on his own and strolled calmly into the warmth of the stable, exhausted by his own fretting. After that experience, it took a month of careful acclimatization before Groucho finally began to feel at home.

Did he miss Doyle? Or Mowbray? Did he still miss Jacqueline? Or his old home? Or the city and its streets? It was difficult to determine, even for someone as knowledgeable as Gilles.

The simple answer would be that horses don't miss anything or anyone. They just feel loss. They operate on instinct, and they sense, rather than know, when something's not right. After a while, the instinct adjusts to a new reality and they adapt.

However, that's not to say they don't remember afterward and the love affair now happening between Groucho and Mowbray was clear evidence of that.

They were still focused on the horse, making a fuss of him, when Gilles arrived to strap on Groucho's halter and lead him outside. They all followed. This time there was no tantrum, no stomping from Groucho. On the contrary, he seemed eager to go, looking forward to getting out there.

Not far away was the main exercise paddock, a gently undulating area several acres in size that was bordered on one side by the pond and around the rest of the circumference by a solid fence, built old-style in rough-hewn wood. While Pierre-Paul Lafontaine and his guests leaned on the fence, Gilles led Groucho through the gate, closed it behind him, then unfastened the halter and removed it completely.

For a second or two, Groucho just stood there, even when he was free to go, turning his head slightly to gaze at the humans behind him. Then, slowly, he paced forward, soon accelerating into a trot, then a canter. Then with a loud whinny, he stretched his neck and pushed into a great gallop, not sleek and rippling like a racehorse, but firm and muscular like a draft horse, his heavy hooves pounding into the grass and kicking up the snow.

And that's when Louise realized exactly what she was seeing. That's when it occurred to her. "Living his dream," she said quietly, almost to herself. She was recalling Doyle's words, and here it was, actually happening. The work horse who'd never run on grass, never galloped, was out here living his dream. Next to her, Mowbray was conscious of it, too, his face wide open with that big grin.

Meanwhile, Groucho was still going, and when he reached the other side of the field he just swerved, changed direction, and continued, his great strength restored, his thick limbs full of renewed vigor.

Back in the center of the paddock, he finally stopped, lowered his head, then raised it up, high and proud, tasting the clean air, and was immediately away again, mane and tail flowing, rejoicing in the sheer escape, free from the harness, liberated from the traffic lanes.

Louise linked arms with Marc-André and just watched, unable to keep the smile from her face. Then she whispered, "Wanna get it?"

Marc-André understood and gave a slight answering nod, before walking off, back toward the car. A couple of minutes later, he returned with a small cardboard box which he held open for Louise. Then, as the others looked on, she tentatively lifted out the container with both hands, a precious object that had to be treated with the utmost care. For a while, she just stood there, as if reconsidering the whole notion of what she was about to do, but the fact was that everyone had approved; thought it was a great idea.

This was what he would have wanted, they all assured her. If given the choice, where would he prefer to be? In a disused stable that was about to be demolished? Or out here, sharing the open pasture with Groucho? It had been no contest.

At last, Louise made up her mind once and for all and she moved forward slowly, still holding the container in both hands. Gilles held the gate ajar so she could pass through into the vast paddock. From here, she took her own good time to walk across toward the center, her eyes partly on the ground in front of her, so she wouldn't stumble, and partly on Groucho, who had slowed and was more than a little curious about what was going on. He trotted up to her and came to a standstill a short distance away.

She looked at the big animal as he looked back at her, two figures under an arching sky. For a moment, she hesitated and took a breath. Then she removed the lid and gently turned the container upside down so that the ashes flew out, scattering on the breeze before they floated to earth—the heart and soul of Patrick Doyle O'Shaughnessy, here with his good friend, Groucho, in death as in life.

It was late when Louise and Marc-André got back to the apartment. They'd offered their thanks to Pierre-Paul Lafontaine for his hospitality and his help in everything. Also to his stableman, Gilles, for being so patient with Groucho. And when they got back to the city, they'd wished Mowbray good luck and bon voyage before dropping him off at his parents' home. Now, at the end of a long day, they were more than ready for sleep.

Marc-André's eyes were already closed, but before Louise sank down next to him, there was one last thing she wanted to do. Padding her way barefoot into the living room, she turned on the small reading lamp and stood in front of the new pine bookcase they'd bought in one of those big-box furniture stores.

On one of the shelves, space had been cleared to allow for a display, almost a shrine of sorts. Here were the framed newspaper articles: the first, written by Prudence Carmichael of *The Gazette* with the portrait of Doyle and Groucho; and the second, the piece from *La Presse,* which spoke eloquently about the end of an era.

Here, too, was the silly flat cap that Doyle had worn only once for Walter Sullivan over at the gardening center. Lastly, there was the mug with the Groucho brand logo printed on the side, the design portraying Groucho's likeness inside a horseshoe. From the day Doyle received it, he never drank his coffee from anything else, except when he went into the hospital, the place from which he never emerged.

Louise lifted the mug and gazed at it. Cheap as it was, it somehow symbolized the spirit of both of them: an iconic old man and an eccentric old horse. Each had a mind of his own but each in his own way needed the other. Then, with an air of finality, she put the mug back in its place, said her silent goodbye and turned out the light.

Afterword

I describe this novel as having been inspired by a true story—but it's perhaps more apt to say that it was inspired by many.

First, the horse protagonist is remarkably similar to Catari, a magnificent mare now sadly deceased. Like Groucho in the book, Catari was a big draft horse with the same coloring and the same independent, eccentric character. Unlike in the novel, however, Catari lived her entire life comfortably pampered on a country property in Quebec's Eastern Townships, exactly the kind of place in which Groucho was finally put out to pasture.

There was also, in the heart of Montreal's old industrial neigohrhood, an Irish-run stable known as the Horse Palace. It was not unlike the one I describe, serving as a home for several of the city's calèche horses, which today still haul tourists around the historic streets of Old Montreal.

For many years, the stable was threatened by developers until just recently when the traditional owners finally sold out and the old place succumbed to time and progress. As I write, there's a heritage effort underway to preserve its memory.

In another strange case of life imitating art, an incident occurred not long ago in which a calèche horse escaped the aging driver's control and bolted along the city street, just the way Groucho does in the book. In this real life episode, an American passenger was very slightly injured but in a fine, forgiving gesture, she came along later to meet and pet the horse, declaring for the news cameras: "No harm done. He was just being a horse!"

To create the story, I put all these facts together, added real locations and institutions, threw in a cast of characters based on people I've met, and ultimately emerged with this novel. It was a heartwarming tale to write and I'm grateful to the many people who helped me in my research.

This included Catari's owner, my good friend Bill Demers, who was a fund of knowledge about the care of horses, as well as all the calèche drivers, police, lawyers, clerks and others around the city who answered my endless questions with patience and friendliness.

Leon Berger & Catari

About the Author

Leon Berger

For me, writing is a passion. I wake early in the morning, usually around 4am, and if I can put in 3 hours before breakfast, I'm happy the rest of the day.

I first began writing when I returned from overseas 15 years ago and I now have 6 novels published, plus my recent work of non-fiction.

In my day job, I'm a consultant specializing in the field of marketing, branding and communications, having worked and traveled extensively across 5 continents. At various times I've been based in London, New York, Singapore and Beijing, but these days I prefer to spend as much time as possible back in Canada.

My home is in Montreal where I got to know Charlotte, the venerable subject of my book *Lunch with Charlotte*. I'm also fortunate to have a country property where I spend my weekends, and it was here that I met the unique animal which inspired my novel *Horse*.

Connect with Leon

Email
lberger@videotron.ca

CPSIA information can be obtained
at www.ICGtesting.com
Printed in the USA
LVHW092151081219
639856LV00005B/30/P

9 781938 821011